MAKING HER HIS

A SINGULAR OBSESSION BOOK ONE

LUCY LEROUX

PUBLISHED BY: Lucy Leroux

http://www.authorlucyleroux.com
ISBN: 978-1-942336-00-6

First Edition.

❀ Created with Vellum

TITLES BY LUCY LEROUX

The Singular Obsession Series
Making Her His
Confiscating Charlie, A Singular Obsession Novelette
Calen's Captive
Stolen Angel
The Roman's Woman
Save Me, A Singular Obsession Novella
Take Me, A Singular Obsession Prequel Novella
Trick's Trap
Peyton's Price

The Spellbound Regency Series
The Hex, A Free Spellbound Regency Short
Cursed
Black Widow
Haunted

The Rogues and Rescuers Series
Codename Romeo
The Mercenary Next Door

Knight Takes Queen
The Millionaire's Mechanic
Burned Deep - Coming Soon

Writing As L.B. Gilbert
The Elementals Saga
Discordia, A Free Elementals Story
Fire
Air
Water
Earth

A Shifter's Claim
Kin Selection
Eat You Up
Tooth and Nail
The When Witch and the Wolf

Charmed Legacy Cursed Angel Watchtowers
Forsaken

CREDITS

Cover Design: Robin Harper
http://www.wickedbydesigncovers.com

Editor: Rebecca Hamilton
http://qualitybookworks.wordpress.com

Readers:
Thank you to all of my guinea pigs! Thanks to Priti, Leslie, Kenya, Evelyn, and anyone else I might have forgotten! Special thanks to Jennifer Bergans for her editorial notes. Extra special thanks to my husband for all of his support even though he won't read my sex scenes!

PROLOGUE

A horn blared to his right, letting Alex know he'd gotten too close to a neighboring car. "Fuck," he muttered, gripping the steering wheel to adjust, accelerating through a narrow gap between two trucks.

The wind whipped across his face through a crack in the open window. He really shouldn't drive so fast when he was in this bad a mood, but he couldn't help it. Brunch with his father's new family was more than enough to set off his temper, but on top of that, he was running late. He'd procrastinated at home so long that he barely left himself enough time to get there before they sat down to eat.

Gritting his teeth, he gunned the engine of his vintage Shelby Mustang, whipping through the lanes as fast as the heavy traffic allowed. His father's estate outside of London wasn't much farther, but he was still going to be late. Which meant he was going to get another lecture from his father on trying harder to accept his new stepmother. It made his skin crawl just thinking about it.

He didn't need this right now. He was planning a big business deal with a new Chinese partner, and this was a distraction. Not that he didn't want to see his father. But the additional presence of Mary and her kid was going to drive him crazy. Attending his father's wedding to the American gold-digger had been bad enough. Now he had to waste an entire Sunday afternoon on them: the new wife and her nonentity of a daughter, a chubby and quiet teen he'd only seen once shortly after Costas had announced his engagement.

He glanced at his watch as he pulled the car into the long drive of his father's house. Only ten minutes late. He ran into the large mansion, taking the steps two at a time, and stopped in the foyer to make sure his mother's watercolor painting was still hanging on the wall. They'd lost his mother, Elena, when he was eleven after a long illness. At the time, his family had been living in New York, after relocating from Greece so she could have the best medical care available. In the end, it hadn't made a difference, and she'd died. Needing a change, his father had moved them to the UK a few months after she passed.

He had honestly believed his father would remain a widower for the rest of his life. Costas probably had, too. For so long, it had just been the two of them. But that changed when Costas met Mary.

Sighing, Alex conceded that, since his remarriage, his father seemed far more youthful and energetic. The change was so obvious that Alex hadn't had a choice—he had stopped fighting him over the marriage. At least until they had started arguing over the prenup.

Alex had insisted Mary sign one, but Costas hadn't seen a need. The series of arguments that followed ended only when Mary, an attractive brunette in her mid-forties, intervened and told Costas she would sign anything his son wanted because they weren't going to get divorced. Just like that, the fight was over.

Satisfied that the painting hadn't gone anywhere, his mood was somewhat improved when he was shown to the terrace, where he joined the two people already at the table partaking of a light and elegant brunch. He greeted them hastily and sat down in the seat opposite his father at the head of the table.

The clicking of heels alerted him to Mary's approach. She stopped short of the table and raised her hand in a brief and awkward wave.

"Hello Alex," she said with her habitually friendly smile, hovering close to his chair.

His father cleared his throat, "Wouldn't you rather sit next to me, Alexandros?"

"Why?" Alex asked absently as he reached for a glass of freshly squeezed orange juice. Picking it up, he noticed a smudge of lipstick on the rim. "Oh, sorry," he said, but rather than change seats, he simply switched glasses as all the other flatware appeared untouched.

"It's okay," Mary said hastily, changing seats to sit on his right.

Costas caught her eye and they exchanged a pointed glance as she sat down. Alex was annoyed. Was it some sort of power play? Did the woman have to have the hostess seat opposite his father? Was she sending a message about her position in the family?

The moment passed as Mary made polite enquiries about Alex's business dealings with a knowledgeable air. He paused with his fork halfway to his mouth before he remembered that she was a trained corporate accountant, a new employee of Hanas Industries when she'd met his father. Costas had married her only eight months after their first meeting.

Though his father was still nominally involved in the business, Alex was now in charge of the day to day running of the company. It was his ruthlessness and slavish devotion to the company that had made Hanas Industries a billion-dollar operation in the last decade. As a result, he had little time for anyone other than his father and a handful of university friends he still kept in touch with. Which was why he was finally swallowing his pride and attending brunch with the new family. He would do whatever was necessary to make Costas happy…within reason.

"Do you not like Chanterelles?" a clear melodic voice asked.

Surprised, Alex turned to the daughter, Ellie something. He found himself staring into a pair of eyes with the most arresting color combination. They were a deep green and grey, like moss on a stone. The girl continued speaking, but he didn't hear her. He was too busy noticing the details he'd gotten wrong. She wasn't fat after all. Her small, heart-shaped face was dwarfed by the large plastic rims of her glasses. And her form was as petite as her mother's. It was just that she was wearing the most ridiculously oversized sweat-shirt and a loose pair of pants that probably hung off her when she walked.

"It's okay to eat them. They're perfectly safe," she repeated.

Confused, he focused on his fork and the pasta dish he'd been enjoying, a light angel hair liberally tossed with pieces of golden Chanterelle mushrooms.

He ate the forkful he'd been holding and answered. "I like them fine. Why wouldn't they be safe?"

Mary cleared her throat. "Elynn collected the Chanterelles herself yesterday. She's an avid mushroom hunter and a budding mycologist."

"A budding mycologist?" he asked dumbly, feeling a little thrown off course.

"Mycology is the study of fungi," Elynn informed him animatedly, a little glow lighting up her face. "Cook took me out to her favorite woods last month to show me some good hunting grounds, and I've been going on my own since. Well, with Andrea," she corrected, gesturing to a female bodyguard patrolling on the lawn.

Frowning, Alex's eyes followed the woman's retreating figure. Since when did his father employ female bodyguards? And why did they appear so visible? Guards were a necessary part of their world, but when they were at home, they were usually discreet and blended into the background. With a frown, he recalled that there appeared to be more of them in recent months.

Elynn studied his face and squirmed in her chair. "You don't have to worry. I know how to tell a Chanterelle from a Gomphus. To be absolutely sure, I had the pharmacist confirm my findings," she explained earnestly.

"I'm not worried," Alex assured her, although he wasn't exactly sure now. "What's a Gomphus?"

"*Gomphus floccocus* is the false Chanterelle. It's poisonous but isn't really that similar. Not if you know what you're looking for. But it's always important to check with a local expert when you move so far away from your normal hunting ground. Things that appear to be an edible you're familiar with might be something entirely different. It's very nice that pharmacists can identify mushrooms for you here. I wish they did that back home. It might prevent several unnecessary deaths," the girl finished uncertainly, looking as if she wished she hadn't started speaking.

"Deaths?"

Alex was completely thrown now. He stared at his dish stiffly, imagining that the bits of mushroom had started to glow a radioactive green.

"Don't worry," Costas cut in. "The mushrooms are the same Cook uses all the time."

"Yes! I don't mean these at all. It's just that in the U.S., there are a number of mushrooms that get confused for edibles from other countries and there are an unfortunate number of poisonings," Elynn continued in a rush, as though to reassure him.

"Like what?" he asked, picking up his fork with a bravado he wasn't sure he felt.

Once Alex resumed eating, Elynn continued. "Well, for example, there's a mushroom called *Amanita phalloides*, the death cap mushroom, that bears a strong resemblance to the Paddy Straw mushroom common in Asia. New immigrants, with history of mushroom hunting in their cultures, go out and find the death cap thinking it's the edible and...well, after you eat it, only a liver transplant can save you," she finished in a chagrined tone.

Alex nodded at her and ate the dish in silence, refusing to admit he was worried about being poisoned. Costas made a concerted effort to ease Alex's tension with a steady stream of business-related small talk. Mary also added to the conversation, but Elynn remained relatively silent. She seemed anxious that she'd upset him over the mushrooms and kept giving him worried little smiles whenever he managed to catch her eye again.

Despite his intentions to remain cold and aloof with his father's new stepdaughter, he couldn't stop himself from trying to put her at ease. He knew she was enrolled at an exclusive girls' school nearby.

"What are you studying?" he asked between bites.

Elynn blushed. "Oh, everything. This semester, mostly Organic Chemistry and Physics as well as Biotechnology. That last one's the funnest of the three. In addition to that, there's the normal stuff... English, Calculus, and History," she said ducking her head shyly and avoiding eye contact.

Alex raised a brow. It was a demanding course load heavy on the science. He asked a few more polite questions, and she responded with her eyes mostly on her plate. She was seventeen, although in her loose clothing she looked fourteen.

"And your extracurriculars?" he asked when she remained quiet, her plate untouched.

She shrugged and played with her fork. "Science club, chess club, astronomy club, and Mathletes."

Wow. And he thought he'd been a nerd in high school. Elynn didn't seem to have any of the hobbies or interests a girl her age should have. Not that he was entirely sure what those were. However, her pursuits were definitely of an unfashionable geeky bent. She wouldn't be popular at school, he thought, and then wondered why he cared.

Brunch ended with Alex in a quiet and contemplative mood. He'd come here fuming, with every intention of giving his father's new family the deep freeze. But he hadn't been able to pull it off with those anxious green-gray eyes on him. He departed with a cordial enough farewell and drove back to London, noting at least two additional bodyguards on the property as he drove away.

Elynn collapsed on her bed, shoving her head under a pillow to muffle her groan. Alexandros probably thought she was a basket case. Or worse, a poisoner.

She had been psyching herself up for this brunch for over a week, ever since Costas had confirmed that his son had finally agreed to come. Vowing to do anything to make it go well for her mom's sake, Elynn had prepared dozens of talking points. She had written them out on note cards and quizzed herself in an effort to avoid becoming tongue-tied in front of her intimidating new stepbrother. It was the exact same strategy she used before doing any presentations in front of her class at school. Her notecards helped her cope with the stress of being in front of an audience.

But all of her careful preparation had turned to dust the second Alexandros had stepped onto the terrace. He was just too much. Too big, too handsome, too powerful. He exuded confidence and aggression, even when he was being polite, like today. It really hadn't been as bad as the last time she'd seen him. The wedding didn't count—he'd sat in the back and had left just after the *I do's*.

No, the last time she'd really seen him was when he'd come over to talk his father out of marrying her mother unless she signed a prenup. There had been a huge argument between father and son. And an angry Alexandros Hanas was a sight that was hard to forget. Thus, all of her work to come up with dozens of ideas for conversation.

Elynn figured that she would be able to avoid becoming mute in his presence if she was prepared. Now she wished she'd been unable to speak. Instead of using her prepared topics, she'd stupidly rambled on about mushrooms. *Poisonous* ones.

The door opened and she heard her mother sigh and walk across the room. She sat on the bed, causing it to shift slightly under her weight.

"He thinks I tried to kill him," she moaned from beneath the pillow.

Mary laughed. "I doubt that."

"You saw his face. He turned *green*."

"No, he didn't. His complexion is naturally that olive color." She laughed again.

Her mom was certainly a lot calmer now that brunch was over. Especially if she was capable of laughing. It was probably a manifestation of her relief. Elynn knew her mother had also been stressed out all week about seeing Alexandros too.

Mary tried to shift the pillow off her head, but Elynn held it tight. She did, however, move it enough to be understood. "I'm sorry I'm acting like this. He just makes me so nervous. All I wanted was for it to go well," she said, her voice still partially muffled by the pillow.

"It *did* go well. As well as could be expected under the circumstances. And don't worry if Alex seemed a little...put out at first. He's a thrill-seeker. Thrill-eating shouldn't be too much for him to handle —not that there was ever any question about your identification of the mushrooms," she added with a reassuring pat.

That was enough to make Elynn pop her head out from under the pillow. Her mother was right. Alexandros jumped out of airplanes for fun. He also went deep sea diving and spelunking. There were pictures scattered around the house of him doing all sorts of crazy things. Alexandros probably ate dangerous things all the time, like *Fugu* sushi—the kind that could poison you if it wasn't prepared perfectly by a highly trained chef. He seemed that type of man.

"We don't have to do that again anytime soon, do we?" she asked hopefully.

Mary smiled bracingly, expelling her breath in a rush. "We will if Costas can convince Alex to make the time. He wants us to be a close family, but I don't think we have to worry anymore. The worst is over."

Elynn didn't know who she was trying to convince. "Well, that's great," she said, trying to sound as if she meant it.

The thought of seeing Alexandros on a regular basis was enough to make her want to dive back under the pillow.

Alex had just gotten back to his place when he got a call.

"How did it go?" Calen asked without preamble.

Calen McLachlan, along with Sergei Damov and Gio Morgese, were his best friends. After they graduated from university, it had gotten a lot harder for them to get together, especially since Sergei had moved to New York and Calen had gone back to Boston. Alex had seen a lot more of Gio, who was based in Rome, up until his dear friend got married. But it had always been Calen who called the most often. Which was good on days like today.

"Better than I thought it would," Alex admitted as he threw his keys on the side table.

"So you didn't slip up and call Mary a gold-digger to her face? No leaping across the table or sudden emergency messages calling you away?"

Alex rolled his eyes as he tossed away his sport coat. "Nothing happened. Things were tense at first, but I didn't want to make a scene. The kid was nervous enough."

"The fat girl? The moody one?"

"Elynn," he acknowledged, turning the simple but unusual name around in his head. "Except she's not fat or moody. She's just shy and wears really baggy clothes. She's actually kind of sweet."

"Is that so? That's a major change of heart," Calen observed drily.

"Yeah, well, maybe I've been a dick about this whole thing," Alex admitted grudgingly.

His widowed father remarrying wasn't the end of the world. His family situation was nowhere near as complicated as Calen's or Sergei's. He should be grateful.

"That's what I've been trying to tell you," Calen said. And he had been. His friend was very fond of Costas, probably because of his more complicated relationship with his own father. "Granted, a certain amount of suspicion was justified in the beginning," he added. "But the prenup was signed and your father is happy. Costas deserves a little bit of companionship, even if it means you're saddled with a new little sister."

Sitting down, Alex frowned. "She's *not* my sister. And I won't be saddled with her. Elynn's a nice kid, but I doubt I'll see her very much at all."

CHAPTER 1

The doorman's message that his father was on his way upstairs caught Alex off guard. He rushed his current paramour, a well-known model, out of his penthouse with a haste that deeply insulted her.

"Don't expect me to be waiting by the phone when you call me again. I won't forget this," she seethed as he hustled her out.

When he didn't fall at her feet to apologize, she stalked out the front door, slamming it for good measure. Alex sighed and poured himself a drink. It was Sunday evening, and he'd just gotten back into town late last night after a long and grueling business trip. It had seemed like a good idea to call Mela and blow off some steam, but outside of the bedroom, he had little interest in what she did or said. And though she clearly enjoyed her time in his bed, he was already finding the sex a little stale. If she broke up with him now, it would only save him the trouble of doing it himself.

Costas was probably here to give him an earful about missing brunch earlier today. Since that first summons a few months ago, his father had been quite insistent that Alex join in the new Sunday tradition whenever he was in town. Only travel was an acceptable excuse, though Costas was accommodating enough to cart everyone to exclusive restaurants near his penthouse to make it easier when Alex's schedule was heavy.

Watching Elynn in those restaurants was one of the few pleasures Alex had in life. Tasting new gourmet dishes had inspired an interest in gastronomy. She dissected dishes like a super-taster and often requested to speak to the chef to question him about his methods. Her knowledge of culinary technique and exotic ingredients always impressed the chef, but few others outside the family.

The few times Costas made the mistake of inviting friends with young daughters Elynn's age to join them, the snobs treated her condescendingly while simultaneously trying to flirt with him. The last one, Anastasia, had been a really spiteful little cat. She subtly put down all of Elynn's friendly inquiries and comments while attempting to engage with Alex like a seasoned socialite trying to pique his sexual interest. And she had sneered at Elynn while speaking to him in a manner that implied they were sharing in a private joke at her expense. After that, Alex had put his foot down and told his father to stop inviting others outside the family to brunch.

He felt guilty for missing it today, but he shrugged off the feeling when his father came in with his 'I'm about to give you a lecture' face.

"Don't start Dad. I just got back into town yesterday and I was too tired to drive all the way out to the house for brunch," he said before offering Costas a drink with a motion to the bar.

"Too tired, huh? But not too tired for models," his father chided. "At least that's what the young lady who I saw leaving in such a huff appeared to be. Unless she's another starlet. Not that it matters," he added dismissively as he accepted the whiskey Alex offered. "I just came by to deliver this invitation for Mary's birthday dinner and to offer to drive the girls into town for brunch next week," he said holding up an envelope and putting it on the table.

Alex shook his head. "Dragging them to town isn't a good idea when Elynn has a test, and she has one next Monday," he said with a frown as he poured his own drink.

Costas raised his eyebrows. "I'm surprised you know that much about Elynn's schoolwork."

"Just trying to be a good big brother," Alex countered with a touch of sarcasm.

"I'm not buying that," Costas said drily. "Besides, Elynn's test next Monday is calculus, and she's going to ace it. Not everyone has to struggle with it," he added with a teasing smile.

"I didn't struggle," Alex said, annoyed, as he sat down on his soft leather couch with the Scotch he'd poured himself.

He'd had some problems initially, but he conquered it like a Viking and ended up with the highest marks in the class.

"You did at first. But don't worry about Elynn. She has an innate grasp for all things mathematical. She could be a professor if she wanted," his father added proudly.

"I'm sure she could," Alex replied with a hint of a grin, but there was a distinct lack of edge to his words.

If his father had made such a statement a few months ago, Alex would have probably resented it and the girl in question. But Elynn was just so harmless and sweet that he didn't begrudge her a bit of parental pride.

"You didn't come all the way out here just to deliver this?" Alex asked as he reached for the envelope.

Costas shook his head. "Mary and I are meeting some friends for dinner in town. In fact, I need to get going, or I'm going to be late. I just wanted to remind you of my offer to work around your schedule regarding brunch and about the party. I hardly see you now that I don't go to the office every day," he said, rising to leave.

There was a tiny hint of a plaintive note in his father's voice. Now that Costas was almost officially retired, they really didn't spend as much time with each other as they used to. It was quite a change after working side by side for so many years.

Feeling guilty, Alex nodded. "I'll make it to brunch next time," he promised.

"And the party?" his father asked hopefully.

"*If* I'm in town," Alex promised reluctantly before walking him out.

RAIN POURED down in sheets the Wednesday before Mary's birthday. Alex had to leave for a business trip the next day and was going to miss the big event. Though he wouldn't have thought twice about missing his stepmother's party, the handmade invitation in Elynn's handwriting his father had delivered made him feel bad enough to agree to drive out to the house for dinner before he left.

Costas was pleased he was making an effort to spend more time with the family and had asked him to come over early, so Alex wrapped up his last meeting at two. He had his driver take him out to the estate soon after. He usually preferred to drive himself but always used a chauffeur driven car on the days he went into the office so he could work and make calls.

When he arrived, the house was quiet and dark. He checked Costas' office and the library, his father's usual haunts, and found both empty. Wondering if Costas was in the master suite, he headed for the stairs and ran into Mrs. Braden, the head housekeeper, coming out of the kitchen with a dishtowel in her hands.

"Have you seen my father?" he asked. "He asked me to get here early but he's not downstairs."

"I'm sorry Master Alex, your father was called away to a last minute meeting in town, but he promised to be home in time for dinner," the cheerful matronly woman said. "Only Miss Elynn is home. She's watching television in the family room."

Annoyed, Alex swore in Greek, only to be swatted with the dishtowel. Mrs. Braden clucked her tongue at him, so he gave her his most charming smile before backing up a step. The housekeeper had been with the family for ages, long enough to have picked up enough Greek to know when Alex was swearing. And as a child, she hadn't been the least bit intimidated by his spoiled rich brat attitude. More than once, she had cheerfully washed out his mouth with soap. But her discipline had always been well-deserved and was normally overshadowed by her warmth. Alex adored her.

"Will you be wanting to set up in your father's office?" she asked him.

Alex considered that. "No, I'll look over my paperwork in the family room with Elynn," he said.

He ignored Mrs. Braden's surprise as he walked to the family room. One of the new female bodyguards passed in front of the door and continued down the hall. He tried not to frown as she nodded at him before continuing a circuit of the ground floor. Making a mental note to talk to Costas about it, he went inside.

The room was empty. Elynn must have stepped out. A TV tray held the remnants of a sandwich and a half-empty bottle of iced tea. Movie credits scrolled across the huge flat screen television. He waited a minute, but she didn't return. He went to the French doors and was surprised to see his stepsister standing outside in the pouring rain. She was staring at a pink cell phone as if it had grown eight legs and tentacles. Confused, he watched her suddenly pull back an arm and throw the phone as far as she could. It landed in the nearby swimming pool.

Alex didn't hesitate. He opened the doors and stepped out into the rain. "Elynn? What's wrong?"

She jumped and spun around. Her face was as white as a sheet.

He put his hands on her shoulders. "Who was that?"

Elynn shook her head. "No one," she said, her face suspiciously blank.

Alex frowned. He didn't really know Elynn, but he could tell she was lying. "Come on," he said, taking her hand and pulling her inside out of the rain.

He went to the couch and pulled a blanket off it and threw it over her shoulders. His suit jacket was a little wet, but she was soaked through. And she was trembling, her hands shaking.

"Who was on the phone?" he asked quietly as he pulled off his jacket.

Elynn shook her head again and grimaced. "It was no one. Literally. Just someone breathing. I think—I couldn't tell for sure. There was no reply when I asked who was there. It was probably a wrong number. I just got weirded out. It was stupid to throw the phone away," she said with a little self-recriminating wince.

Alex made a noncommittal noise while studying Elynn. Something was wrong. The kid was scared of something. Or someone. Maybe she'd been getting prank calls.

"Well...it was very pink," he said finally. It had even sparkled. Costas had probably bought it. It was the sort of thing an older man would buy for a young girl when they didn't know any better. "I don't really blame you for getting rid of it."

Elynn snorted slightly, and her shoulders eased. But she still looked a little too pale for his taste.

"Go change and come back down," he suggested softly. "We can watch TV or something."

Her expression changed. "You're staying?" She sounded relieved. He nodded in what he hoped was a reassuring manner. "Costas said you were coming for dinner, but you're a few hours early," she added.

"He asked me to come as soon as I was free, but apparently he got called away to a meeting," Alex said carefully.

"Yeah, I was still at school." Elynn nodded vaguely before looking down at her wet clothing.

She was still wearing her school uniform, a plaid skirt with a button down shirt. It was by no means anything like the outfit Britney Spears made famous, but for the first time, he could see that Elynn had an incredible figure. It was hard to miss given the way her wet clothes were plastered to her skin. She usually went to great lengths to hide her body. Even when they went out to the most fashionable restaurants, she wore large sweatshirts or sweaters. He was starting to wonder if there was a reason for it beyond normal teenage shyness.

"Go change," he ordered when she continued to stand there distracted and confused.

She looked up and smiled with a little rueful nod. Picking up the edges of the blanket so they wouldn't trail on the floor, she left the room.

Alex sat down on the couch with a thump. What the hell was going on? Either Elynn was a particularly paranoid teenager or she was hiding something.

It's not paranoia. Whatever was going on, Costas knew about it.

There had been an undeniable air of tension in his father's household lately. He wanted to question Elynn further, but she had seemed so fragile standing out in the rain with those huge eyes trained on nothing. He didn't want to upset her any more than she already was.

While she was away, he snooped on her tablet, but there were no threatening emails on the screen. She was reading a forum thread about ghosts. He was tempted to switch to the mail app and spy, but he restrained himself. They weren't close enough for him to violate her privacy that way. Or so he told himself, but he was still holding the tablet when she finally came back in.

"What is this?" he asked gesturing with the tablet, trying to cover up the fact he'd been debating whether or not to read her private correspondence.

"It's the creepiest thread on Reddit," she said with a blush. "I shouldn't have been looking at it. It got me all worked up," she added almost apologetically while running a hand through her wet hair.

"Why? What's it about?" he asked, feigning ignorance.

"It's a collection of posts on the creepiest thing you've ever heard a small child say," she said.

"What can little kids possibly say to scare you?" he asked with a twist of his lips.

"Oh, the most awful things. Like the devil is behind you. Or they point to an empty space and ask who is that?" Elynn said with a little shiver, glossing over the thing with the phone in favor of something genuinely scary. "There are these examples where small children simply *knew* that someone had died or if they were pregnant. But the most compelling ones are when a little kid mentions details of previous lives out of the blue. There are multiple posts of similar stories in this thread."

Alex made a face. "Do you actually believe all that?" he asked skeptically, wondering now if Elynn had an overactive imagination.

Perhaps she'd thrown the phone away for nothing. Maybe she had simply overreacted to a wrong number or one of her schoolmates was pranking her. She was a pretty girl. Maybe she had caught some boy's eye, he thought before remembering she went to an all-girls school.

"I don't know," Elynn said with a shrug before lowering her voice to a conspiratorial tone. "But sometimes, when it's dark, I'm afraid of ghosts. I've never seen one," she added quickly. "But I imagine one is around the corner, and I get a little thrill up my spine. The idea of them just creeps me out." She ducked her head shyly. "That probably sounds stupid."

Alex snorted and shook his head. "I don't like zombies," he said honestly, getting up to grab a drink from the bar. "And they're *everywhere* right now. I'll still watch the movies, but not by choice."

"Really?" Elynn asked. Her eyes lit up. "Hey, do you think Jesus was the first zombie?"

Alex nearly choked on his whiskey. "No. I think that was Lazarus."

Elynn blushed. "Sorry. I didn't mean to offend you."

"I'm not offended," Alex frowned, confused.

"But you go to church," she pointed out. "I shouldn't joke about that kind of stuff."

Alex shrugged. He went through the motions of the Greek Orthodox Church on occasion because it pleased his father.

"I do that for Costas, don't worry about it," he said lightly, but he honestly couldn't remember when he had last had such an intense conversation with anyone, let alone a member of the opposite sex.

"Why don't we watch a movie?" he suggested, rather than letting the conversation get heavier.

He was supposed to be distracting her, not the other way around. Alex didn't even talk to his friends about his beliefs. Not even during all of those drunken arguments Calen and Sergei had had about existentialism and the meaning of life. He was more like Gio, less thoughtful when it came to all things spiritual.

"Okay," Elynn readily agreed, getting up to go over to the DVD cabinet. "Costas got the latest releases from one of his movie industry contacts. Which one do you want to see?" she asked, holding up three Blue Ray discs.

"Not that one," Alex said, pointing to the latest romantic comedy in theaters.

She glanced at the cover and laughed a little, "Oh, right. That's one of your exes isn't it?"

Busted. "And how would you know that?" he drawled, secretly relieved she seemed back to her normal, lighthearted self.

"Costas can't stop himself from buying the tabloids you're in," Elynn said with a teasing smile. "He leaves them all over the place."

She was right, but Alex wasn't about to admit it. He chose a blockbuster sci-fi movie that had just hit the theaters, and they settled down to watch it while he waited for Costas to come home. But the movie was slower than he'd expected, and halfway through, Elynn dropped off to sleep, her head and shoulder twisted awkwardly over a throw pillow.

She was going to wake up with a bad crick in her neck. Getting up, he shifted Elynn's body onto a pillow and reached down to put her legs up on the couch. He lingered with his hand on her ankle, thinking before he straightened, managing not to start in surprise when he saw his father standing in the doorway, a terrible frown on his face.

He started to say something, but Alex cut him off with a nod to the sleeping girl. Costas gestured impatiently towards the door. Picking up his case, Alex followed him out, but not before stopping to put a cashmere blanket over Elynn. For some reason, Costas froze, but Alex didn't want to stop and ask what was wrong in case they woke her up. He led the way out of the room, and Costas gestured in the direction of his office. On the way Alex noted two additional bodyguards on patrol in the mansion.

After stepping inside the office, he sat in one of the leather armchairs across the desk from his father's chair. "All right. What is going on? Why are there so many bodyguards? And what emergency meeting did you have that I wasn't aware of?"

His father no longer scheduled meetings without his knowledge. If the meeting had been business-related, Alex would have known.

But Costas wasn't about to be derailed. "What exactly were you doing with Elynn?"

"We were watching a movie, and she fell asleep. She was all twisted up, so I helped her stretch out." Alex shrugged. "I thought you were pleased that we're getting on so well."

Costas put his hands on his hips. "I don't like the way you were looking at her just now," he said with a dark glance. "It was fine when you were being brotherly, but this is different."

Genuinely affronted, he stared at his father. "You've got to be kidding. You are kidding right?"

Costas shook his head wearily. "You just have to be careful around Elynn, son."

"If she develops a crush—" he began.

"No, that won't happen," his father said, shaking his head and waving away his concern. For a second, Alex was almost insulted, but his father's next words cut off the sentiment. "You have to be careful. She's been through a lot. Too much…"

Costas turned away, and Alex finally noticed how tired and haggard he appeared. It was weird. For the first time, his father looked old.

"Dad, why do you have so many bodyguards?" he asked again quietly.

Costas looked at him and sighed heavily before taking out his keys. He opened a locked desk drawer and pulled out a file. His eyes were troubled as he reluctantly put a photo in front of Alex. It was of a young man, eighteen or so, with blond hair and blue eyes. The kid was in a football uniform and he was smiling.

"Is this a former boyfriend of Elynn's?" Alex asked, wondering why he found the idea distasteful.

"No. Her mother and all the witness reports are quite clear on that subject. Elynn doesn't have any interest in boys. Not yet anyway. But some boys have a hard time being ignored."

There was pointed silence.

"Tell me everything."

His name was Stephen Wainwright, and he was a son of privilege in the small town where Mary raised Elynn. His uncle was the mayor, and his grandfather was lieutenant governor of the state. He was successful and popular and had his pick of girls. But some guys only wanted what they couldn't have.

According to her neighbors, Elynn tripped through town unaware that boys even existed, except as friends. She collected insects and lizards in addition to mushrooms in those days. Most people considered her a nerd, but Elynn didn't seem to care what people thought of her. And then she hit puberty, and the people who had called her names stopped and stared at her instead. Not that she noticed. Mentally, she was a late bloomer who was unaware of the way others saw her.

When she was just fifteen, Wainwright took to cornering Elynn in the hallway to flirt with her, efforts that were completely misunderstood by her. She was friendly but did not flirt back. She didn't know how. Eventually, he asked her on a date, but she told him she wasn't allowed. Undeterred, the boy asked Mary if Elynn could date him.

Concerned by the boy's intense manner, Mary told him that Elynn could only go on supervised or group dates. She didn't want her daughter to miss out on any seminal high school experiences, but she wasn't prepared for a full-blown romance yet. Except Elynn wasn't interested in any of those things.

When Wainwright cornered her again, Elynn begrudgingly agreed to a group outing, not realizing it was a date. She took a bunch of classmates with them mushroom hunting. According to the testimony of her friend Michael, Wainwright grew furious when Elynn disappeared for half an hour. He was already annoyed with her for virtually ignoring him. At the end of the outing, Michael warned Elynn not to spend any time alone with Wainwright.

She refused the boy's subsequent requests for more dates, and according to everyone, Wainwright just lost it. He started following Elynn home, frightening her and her mother. Things were found broken in their yard, clay pots and garden tools. Then things escalated and dead birds and squirrels were found. The women were living in a state of constant fear and anxiety when things started disappearing from inside their house.

"What kind of things?" Alex asked, dread pooling in his chest.

"Hair things at first. You know those barrette things and hair ties. Knick-knacks. And then some...underthings," Costas said, his mouth twisting.

Alex saw red. He was suddenly angrier than he had ever been in his life. Bile rose in his throat, and he wanted to punch something. "For Christ's sake, she was just a kid. She still is. Did Mary call the police?"

"Yes, but it didn't do much good. His family denied he had done anything wrong. He hadn't been seen breaking into their home. The police claimed there were no prints, but I seriously doubt that. The police would have been on the boy's side. It was a small town, and the Wainwrights were the most influential family in it. Mary decided they had to move away, but before she could find another job, Wainwright broke into their home when she was at work and Elynn was alone."

Alex didn't know how he managed to keep his voice steady. "Did he rape her?"

"No...No...but only because she fought back. Harder than he expected, I'm sure. Soon it was about more than rape. She fought for her life," Costas said with tears in his voice, fingering another photograph in the file.

"Let me see it," he told him, but the older man shook his head sadly.

Alex stood up and took the folder from his father's unresisting fingers. And then he wished he hadn't. There were multiple photographs of Elynn taken at the hospital. Her face was bruised so badly he barely recognized her. She was hooked up to tubes. Others of her hands showed defensive wounds, torn nails, and scrapes. There were a lot of bruises on her body and even a faint bite mark on her shoulder.

"You're sure he didn't..." Alex couldn't finish the question.

"The rape kit was negative. He didn't get to finish what he started. Mary and a friend of hers came home while he was still there. They heard him tearing out of the back door, but they didn't see him. Elynn was in a coma for two days."

"Oh God. That poor kid," Alex mumbled.

He was sick to his stomach. How could anyone hurt Elynn? She was such a sweet person and so damn innocent that it was crazy to think someone could target her that way.

If I ever see that kid I'm going to kill him.

"We were so relieved when she actually spoke to you and seemed to like you," Costas said after a long moment. "She hasn't reacted well to men in general. Especially the blond ones. When you sat next to her that first time at brunch, we were nervous. Sometimes she has panic attacks, although they're becoming less frequent now."

That explained the supposed power play at that first brunch, he thought, reflecting on his father's and Mary's odd behavior when he took the seat next to Elynn instead of the one opposite.

"Don't let on you know," his father instructed. "It upsets her when people find out. Even if it's just a bodyguard that needs to be informed."

He nodded. "The female guards," he said, putting two and two together. "I thought that was weird. And your meeting today—I take it there's been some development," he continued.

"Stephen Wainwright entered the country two days ago on his own passport."

"How is that possible?" he asked furiously, sitting up in his chair.

"Despite overwhelming public sentiment against him, Wainwright managed to buy his way out of a prison sentence," Costas said with a disgusted shake of his head. "A lot of money must have changed hands. Not that Mary waited. As soon as she got the all clear from the doctor she packed up Elynn and left town. They lived in Connecticut briefly before she got the job working for us. Mary confided in me after I proposed. She wanted to explain why Elynn was so skittish and withdrawn. She's a lot better now, but not as comfortable with other members of the opposite sex as she is with you. The irony of it is I think she finds it comforting that you're only ever interested in supermodels and actresses. She feels safe with you. Don't disturb her peace."

Alex ignored the warning. He wasn't a threat to Elynn—and she knew that or she wouldn't have wanted him around this afternoon.

"Someone called her," he said suddenly. With all of the revelations, it had almost slipped his mind. "Someone who didn't speak. Just breathing. It scared her, and she threw the phone in the pool."

Costas tensed, his face growing dark. "Do you think it's a coincidence?"

Alex shrugged. "Does it matter? Don't take any chances," he said, half-wondering if they should add more bodyguards. Costas nodded, and Alex rubbed his temple. "Is she getting therapy?"

"She has a counselor she likes now. She went through a few of them in the first few months. But the last one clicked."

"That's good," Alex murmured absently.

Costas still looked very upset. Alex knew he should have said something else to comfort him, but he was trying to digest all the news. And it was hard thinking clearly when he was so angry.

ALEX WAS in China in between meetings when he called Elynn on the phone directly for the first time. He had delayed his business trip as long as possible in case his family needed him, but eventually he'd been unable to put it off, and he'd left.

Except for the one mysterious phone call, which they hadn't been able to trace, there had been no signs that Wainwright was trying to get in touch with Elynn. None that they could detect anyway. Costas had decided the call was a simple wrong number, but Alex wasn't convinced. He insisted on getting regular reports from the security staff and had chosen Elynn's replacement phone himself. He picked one in her favorite color, navy blue, and had demanded that it have the kind of security encryption normally reserved for CEOs and politicians.

Eventually, Costas told him that Wainwright had left the UK without incident. But Alex had wanted to hear from Elynn herself, to check and see if she was okay, even if she hadn't been aware that Wainwright had been in the country.

She was very surprised to hear from him. He asked her if she wanted him to try and find some Paddy Straw mushrooms.

"No, but maybe if you have time you can ask one of your people to go to a Chinese herbalist and get an assortment of medicinal mushrooms. They use a lot of different things there that we can't even imagine. I'd enjoy seeing some of that stuff," she said wistfully.

"Done," Alex said and then made enough small talk to make even his most experienced PA turn to him in surprise.

Alex was notoriously short with everyone when he was working on a big deal. Phone calls home never lasted more than a minute or two. Even calls to his father.

After that, calls to Elynn became a regular occurrence. His duties with Hanas Industries took him all over the world, and it was nice to have someone normal to talk with. Someone who never made any demands on his time or for his money. He kept a breakneck pace that would have wrecked a normal man. The turnover on his personal staff was high; in fact, they frequently quit in exhaustion. Those that remained were loyal and worked hard to meet his exacting standards, but he never confided in them or asked them about their lives. Elynn was different.

A crisis in the Chinese stock market called Alex away the week of Elynn's eighteenth birthday. He'd wanted to be there but had been mollified to learn that all he was going to miss was a quiet family dinner because Elynn didn't want a big celebration. He was pissed off when his father told him Mary had talked her daughter into inviting a few school friends over for dinner and cake.

It was Elynn's first birthday party in their family and he wasn't going to be there. Well, screw that. He proceeded to attack the business at hand with a brutal efficiency that startled his seasoned staff. There was no way he was missing that party.

Despite his exhaustion, Alex practically ran up the stairs of the house on the evening of Elynn's birthday celebration. He had just flown twenty hours to get there, and he was even later because he'd had to stop at his penthouse to get his gift. He'd stumbled on it in Prague a few weeks earlier and had known the moment he saw it that he had to get it for her.

He swept into the dining room, shocking everyone, especially his father. But it was worth it to see Elynn's shy smile and the quick furtive hug she gave him when she opened her gift. It was an artisan's sculpture of a forest of delicate hand-blown glass mushrooms with a little fairy peeping out from behind one. The fairy had black hair, just like Elynn.

She was still marveling over the wonderful gift when Alex edged away from the flock of chattering girls surrounding her. Several were giggling and giving him flirtatious looks. Hurriedly, he went to pour himself a drink from the sideboard only to make eye contact with his father. Costas was frowning slightly and staring at him with a grave expression.

"I want to speak with you before you leave," Costas said before he joined the festivities again.

An hour later, Alex left the house feeling raw and angry, hanging onto his temper by a thread. He threw himself into the Shelby and tossed his coat aside onto the passenger seat, before putting a Tupperware on top of it with more care. Elynn had surprised him with an extra piece of birthday cake on his way out.

His father's words rang in his ears. As much as it galled him, Alex knew Costas was right. However, patience was not one of his strongest virtues.

At least the argument had served one purpose. He was no longer tired, which was good. It was a long drive back to the airport and an even longer flight back to China.

CHAPTER 2

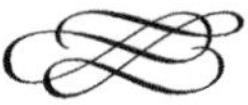

ALMOST FOUR YEARS LATER

"Elynn, where did you put those samples?" Eric, the lab manager, asked her.

At twenty-five, he was four years older than her and young for his position. He was also gay, and he and his partner Fred were probably Elynn's closest friends in town.

"They're in the freezer," she mumbled, concentrating on the field under her dissecting scope.

"Hey, did you see the latest tabloid spread on your big brother?" he asked, leaning in conspiratorially.

"Stepbrother, and no," Elynn said, looking up and laughing.

Regular appearances of the great Alexandros Hanas used to be a regular thing in the gossip rags. But in the last few years, they'd dropped off considerably. His father's lectures had probably sunk in at some point. Costas frequently murmured to her mother Mary that Alex was finally learning to respect women, citing their happy marriage as a source of inspiration for him.

"Was it a supermodel or an actress this time?" she asked, smiling as she turned back to the scope.

"It's the new *it* girl, that actress Sonia Steele. They were seen entering one of those VIP lounges in a club last night," Eric said, leaning against the lab bench.

"Is that all they got?" she asked.

Stories from the early days of their parent's marriage were far more salacious.

"It's more than anything they've gotten in a while," Eric pointed out. "He's zealous about his privacy these days, isn't he?"

"Well, Costas says he's matured. Maybe Sonia Steele is a real girlfriend, although her name is so fake."

"So are these tits." Eric waved the tabloid photo, which only clearly featured Miss Steele. Alex had his back turned. "She's a diva through and through, but so talented. There's Oscar buzz this year for the one movie she did."

Eric was ecstatic. He was a huge fan and had dragged Elynn to the stupid romantic comedy a few weeks earlier.

"I doubt I'll meet her. Alex doesn't ever bring anyone to brunch," Elynn said, getting another sample and turning her attention back to the scope.

Eric was sorely disappointed to hear that. He wheedled and whined for a long sought-after invitation to brunch, and Elynn regretfully turned him down, reminding him about Alex's family-only rule again.

She left work early and walked into her flat in Oxford just before the landline rang. Grabbing the phone, she went over to feed Jaws Three, her beta fish. Jaws One and Two had gone to the great big fishbowl in the sky. All three had been gifts from Alex. So was the cute little box turtle munching on lettuce in the corner. She was allergic to cats, and her landlord didn't allow dogs, so Alex had settled for the fish and turtle. She loved them both, of course.

"What are you up to?" Alex's drawl seemed to reach out from the receiver.

"Feeding Jaws Three and Alex Junior," she teased.

"I can't believe you freely admit to naming that beast after me. Try to remember who you're talking to on occasion. I know that's difficult for you," he said in a resigned and put upon tone.

"I know exactly who I am talking to. Alexandros the Great. He walks on water, and when he's done, he turns it into wine. Hey, thanks for that case you sent by the way." Alex had sent her an assortment of wine from California during his last business trip, knowing which mellow vintages and dessert wines she was partial to. "I don't know how you expect me to finish it all by myself."

Elynn didn't entertain or socialize much. She was too focused on her studies. Since she had missed a big chunk of high school because of her long hospital stay when she was sixteen, she had entered Oxford University a semester after other students her age. Her intense work ethic had paid some serious dividends, however. She had caught up and was graduating on time alongside her class. Her final project was a molecular analysis of various fungi used in ancient Chinese medicine.

"Those bottles are for when I come by for dinner. You can't get anything decent in your local grocery, and I have particular tastes," Alex said.

"When is this dinner supposed to happen?" Elynn asked in disbelief as she kicked off her shoes.

Alex was always threatening to come to dinner, but his busy schedule kept him in London or out of the country. He hadn't ever made it out to her apartment for a personal visit. He did manage brunch every once in a while when Mary and Costas came down to visit, but their cherished Sunday tradition was by necessity less frequent now that she lived in Oxford.

"Soon. Are you coming up for the holiday?" he asked.

"I should be there by Friday night."

"Good, brunch is at my place this time. Don't be late," he commanded before asking her about work.

While they chatted a bit longer, Elynn moved around, watering her inoculum. She didn't keep plants. Instead, she cultivated mushrooms. Scattered in the dark corners of her apartment were various mushroom-growing kits—some she had bought, and some that she made herself for button mushrooms, portabella, oyster, and shiitake. Elynn was still trying to get her own home-made chanterelle kit to grow, but they needed a symbiotic association with certain trees to grow properly, and the saplings always died on her. She was hopeless with plants. No matter what she did, within a few weeks, they withered and died. Alex had stopped giving her bonsai trees and exotic orchids some time ago. He said it made him too sad to send all those innocent lives to their doom.

Elynn hung up the phone with a smile. Alex couldn't help ordering everyone around. But he was unfailingly kind to her, despite his ingrained bossiness. And protective. Over the years, he'd become her best friend, although she would never have admitted that to him. One did not impose such feelings or titles on Alexandros Hanas.

Despite the gruff warmness Alex reserved for her and his father, he generally kept everyone at a distance. Even after all these years, he was still a bit formal with her mother, although he was always polite. He did have a group of college friends he kept in touch with, but Elynn had never met any of them.

Elynn knew she was closer to Alex than most other people, but she also knew exactly where the boundaries to their relationship were. She had her own boundaries as well, and he respected them. For that she was grateful. There were just some things she did not want to discuss with her stepbrother.

Not that she had a lot to tell him. After they had moved to the UK, she had settled into a happy studious life with few disruptions. While she was still in high school, there had been the occasional silent untraceable phone call. Those had completely unnerved her, and whenever she got one, she had lived looking over her shoulder for months. But over the years, the mysterious calls tapered off. There might have been one or two last year, but whoever it was hung up quickly, so she'd decided it was probably a wrong number. Elynn put them out of her mind and continued her life, secure in the protection of her family.

Early the following Sunday, she made her way to Alex's penthouse in the city. The night she had spoken to him on the phone, he had takeout delivered to her from one of her favorite sushi places. Alex often did that sort of thing when she was very busy at school. Elynn wanted to thank him and give him his birthday surprise.

She had found a 1936 Jaguar SS100 in Oxford and, after several failed attempts, had talked its reluctant owner into selling it. The car was in terrible shape, and she had spent all of her savings to buy it, but it was worth it. Alex had mentioned several times that he wanted to add that model to his collection, but he hadn't yet found one that suited him. He was constantly scouring ads looking for one, saying he would rather find and restore one than buy one from a specialty dealer.

Alex had probably never intended to buy one that was nearly a junk heap, but Elynn knew that at least this way he could have it restored to his exacting specifications. She was just sorry that he hadn't been around for his own birthday last month or she would have given it to him then. Instead, she'd mailed him an assortment of homemade cookies that she'd spent an entire evening baking. He'd probably taken them to the office for his staff, but she didn't mind since he always pretended he ate everything himself.

Elynn was shown into Alex's luxurious penthouse suite and directed to the terrace balcony. It overlooked the Thames and had a fantastic view of the city. Excited, she pulled a ribboned box out of her bag and set it on the table in front of his chair. It contained a picture of the car she had stored in a garage in Oxford. She was sitting down again when a woman's annoyed voice came from the second story balcony, which was connected to the one where she was sitting by a wrought iron staircase.

"What the hell do you mean?" the woman said.

Elynn didn't hear anything else clearly as a door above slammed shut. After a minute, it opened again and a voluptuous blonde stalked down the stairs to the terrace. She was wearing a slinky dress and three inch heels. Had she spent the night?

"Hello," Elynn said brightly.

I guess I spoke too soon, she thought as she remembered telling Eric that Alex never invited women to brunch. It was indeed Sonia

Steele in the flesh. *I guess I was right. He does have a girlfriend.* She wondered why she felt a little queasy at that realization.

"Who the hell are you?" the over-endowed blonde demanded.

"I'm Elynn. It's nice to meet you," she said, taken aback but standing and raising her hand to shake.

The woman looked at Elynn like she was something that had just crawled out of the gutter. Self-consciously, Elynn looked down at her jeans and white button down shirt. The shirt *did* have a small soil stain on it. She'd been out looking for mushrooms earlier that morning and had transferred some dirt when she'd changed clothes. Self-consciously, she wiped at the mark with her free hand.

Elynn's face flushed red when she realized that the woman wasn't going to shake her hand. Slowly she withdrew it and sat down. The woman continued to stare daggers at her until the door above opened a second time and Alex looked down from the balcony to see both women staring at each other.

Alex, scowling, rushed down the stairs and took Sonia by the arm above the elbow. He pulled her aside and hissed something in her ear.

Eyebrows raised, she finally pasted a smile on her face and addressed Elynn stiffly.

"It's a pleasure to meet you. I've heard absolutely nothing about you," Sonia said, smoothing out the front of her dress with her hand in a move that accentuated her cleavage.

Despite the smoothness of the actress' voice, Elynn could detect the disdain in it.

"Are you staying for brunch?" she asked, trying to smile despite her instant dislike of the woman.

"Miss Steele has to go. She has an important meeting," Alex finished in a stern voice.

"Okay. I really enjoyed your last movie," she called out politely as Alex hustled the woman out.

He came back quickly, frowning and running a hand through his hair.

"Don't worry, I won't tell Costas about your latest conquest," she teased. "I know you'll do anything to avoid another lecture from him."

She poured them both cups of coffee, feeling slightly more generous with him now that she knew he hadn't invited that woman to join them.

"I'm sorry she was so rude," he apologized as he sat down next to her.

"The big-chested ones always are," Elynn sighed reflectively as he lifted the cup to his lips, causing Alex to choke on his first sip of coffee. "They are," she insisted, as if his choking was a denial. "Do you remember that horrible Anastasia? She used to plop that rack of hers right in your face like it was a gun and then proceed to win the 'I'm the biggest bitch' contest."

Alex burst into laughter. "I know several kind, well-endowed women," he said cautiously.

"Do you now?" Elynn's voice was wry.

"And so do you. Mrs. Braden is one," he pointed out before taking another sip of coffee.

"Yeah, cause that's who you were talking about," Elynn said with a slight roll of her eyes.

"Why are you so early?" he asked, changing the subject.

"To give you this before Mom and Costas get here," she said, nudging the box he hadn't noticed in front of him.

Alex tore open the box and broke out into a huge grin. "Where did you find it?"

"I was at a rummage sale when I saw it all dusty and in pieces in the back of the garage. The owner didn't want to sell, but I went back three times until he finally caved," she boasted.

"I should put you in my sales department," he teased her, pretending to be impressed.

"Yeah, right. You would have had that car for a tenth of what I paid," Elynn said, sipping her coffee. "No, I take that back. That old man would have just given it to you along with his firstborn once you were done negotiating," she added in total seriousness.

"Thank you for this. It's great," Alex said, studying her for a long moment.

He started to say something else but cut himself off when their parents arrived. Distracted, Elynn forgot to ask him what he was going to say when Costas and Mary announced an extensive tour of Italy at the start of summer. They would depart soon after Elynn's commencement exercises, and they wanted her to go with them.

"I can't for longer than a week," she protested. "I have to work."

"You missed our tour of the Greek Isles last summer because you were working. You work too much. You can't spend the entire summer toiling away in the lab," Mary argued.

Costas was quick to agree. "You can afford more than a week. A month off is better."

"I can't," Elynn said, feeling pressured. She loved her mother, but she didn't want to commit to spending all of her time off with her and her doting husband. "I've already made my plans to get a jump-start on my Ph.D. project. And I'll be assisting with an ongoing project, which means I get my name on another paper," she added, having explained many times how important it was for a scientist to publish as often as they could.

"Elynn can join you for a week, but a young woman her age needs some independence and freedom," Alex said, and she shot him a grateful smile.

With Alex on her side, she couldn't lose this argument.

Costas and Mary tried to insist, but in the end, Mary reluctantly agreed to a short visit during their time in Venice, one of her favorite cities. Afterward, Costas and Alex exchanged a few odd serious glances, but soon Costas backed down as well. He and Mary left for their town house slightly preoccupied—no doubt figuring out new arguments to convince her to go with them. But Elynn lingered, happy to have Alex to herself for a little while.

Brunch the following week was at London's newest and most exclusive restaurant. Elynn was waiting outside for her parents and Alex when a familiar face greeted her.

"Eric! What are you doing in town? We're both due back in the lab tomorrow."

"Well, Fred and I decided to come to town for some shopping and to see a show," Eric said while looking over her shoulder before pivoting to check out the crowd behind him.

"What did I tell you about the family only rule, Eric?" she asked, crossing her arms over her chest.

"Why, whatever do you mean, Miss Scallett?" he asked in faux outrage.

"I mean you are looking for Alex right now you bad, bad boy," Elynn said, widening her eyes for emphasis. "He's really very stern about the only-family-at-brunch thing."

Eric's face was the picture of innocence. "I'm not waiting for anyone except Fred, I swear. But since you mention it, isn't big brother running late?"

"Alex is always ten minutes late, which gives you exactly four minutes to run along. He won't be impressed if you crash brunch. You're going to meet him at graduation anyway, so you should go now. I promise I'll give you all the details on Monday."

She wondered if she should mention meeting the illustrious Ms. Steele, but decided the better of it. He would never leave if she started telling him about what a cow she had been.

Eric sighed dramatically, "Okay, drill sergeant. But I expect a detailed report tomorrow."

He went to hug her and ended up sweeping her into a Hollywood style dip. He kissed her cheek, and with an, "Until tomorrow Miss Scallett," Eric set her back on her feet.

Laughing to herself, she watched as he practically sashayed away down the street.

ALEX WAS GETTING out of his town car across the street when he spotted Elynn standing outside the restaurant. He smiled to himself. He could always count on her to be on time. She was paranoid about being late. Locking his car, he was starting across the street when he saw a young lanky man with red hair go up to her. She smiled warmly at him, and Alex froze. When the young man grabbed her and swept her into a dramatic kiss, his gut clenched. It felt like someone had punched him in the stomach.

Alex stood there like an idiot before a sudden rush of anger came over him. He felt like tearing someone apart. And he planned on starting with the redheaded toothpick waving goodbye to Elynn. He reached her the same moment Costas and Mary arrived. Chuckling about something Elynn had said, Costas ushered them into the restaurant.

The older couple was full of plans. "We've decided to throw a party just before we leave for our tour of Italy, to celebrate our fifth wedding anniversary," Mary announced with a huge smile.

"Oh, that's a great idea," Elynn said, and the three of them fell into a discussion about the party and travel plans.

Alex felt the jovial mood lap around him like warm water at the beach, but he was untouched by it. He was having a difficult time being civil and was giving monosyllabic answers to every question. It wasn't reasonable to be angry with Elynn…but he was.

Wordlessly, he stared at her while she engaged in an animated conversation with her mother. No, he was just angry with himself. He obviously hadn't been watching her closely enough. It was clear to him now that he had been overly cautious. Waiting around for Elynn to be ready for a relationship had simply allowed some other man to sneak into her life. Well, that was over with now.

No more waiting.

CHAPTER 3

Elynn studied Alex apprehensively as their parents left. He was still sitting quietly, as though lost in thought. When he had first joined them, he had resembled a bomb ready to go off, but as the meal went on, he seemed to have slowly warmed up to the company around him. Which was good, because he'd been behaving the way he had before their parents were married. Although he hadn't seemed angry with them. Maybe he'd had a fight with Sonia.

Maybe the actress means more to him than I realized, Elynn thought with a sinking heart.

"Are you okay?" she asked. When he didn't answer, she leaned forward to reach for his hand, "Did you quarrel with Sonia?"

"Sonia?" Alex sounded surprised. "No, we're not seeing each other anymore."

"So that's not what's upsetting you? Do you miss her?" Elynn asked with mixed feelings.

"No, it's not that. It's nothing," he said, leaning back into his chair.

"Alex, I can tell that something is wrong. You know you can tell me anything," she reassured him, giving his hand a squeeze for good measure.

He stared at her hand on his for a long moment before gripping it tightly in return. He held it when she tried to retrieve it and looked into her eyes. "Something has just come to my attention…something important."

"I hope everything's okay," she said, her stomach sinking with sudden suspicion.

"It's nothing serious," Alex assured her hastily. "I just realized that I missed something important."

"Like a business thing?"

"Sort of," he said, looking at her pensively. "There's a project I need to get started on. Something I have apparently put off for too long."

"Oh…okay. Well, I'm sure you'll make up for lost time and achieve yet another remarkable success," she said in a calmer voice, taking a last sip of her coffee before saying goodbye.

She left him with a reassuring smile.

ELYNN WAS GETTING ready to go home after a long day in the lab when her phone rang.

"I'm in town," Alex announced without as much as a hello.

He always plunged straight into conversation without any of the formalities.

"You are? What's brought you down?" she asked, surprised.

"The car of course," Alex said.

"The Jaguar? I thought you'd just make arrangements to have it sent up to you instead," Elynn replied.

Alex had dozens of minions to take care of his every need, something she teased him about mercilessly. She'd told him more than once that she was surprised he bothered to tie his own shoes.

"Why when I can do it myself and take the opportunity to have dinner with you?" he answered with a laugh.

"Really?" she answered, pleasantly surprised.

"It's too late to prepare a meal at your place, so why don't I pick you up and we get dinner out somewhere?" he suggested.

"Oh, I'm not at home right now. I can meet you—"

"No need. I'm standing outside your lab," he said.

Elynn hurried outside to find Alex leaning on his car. He greeted her with his usual restrained warmth. Though a stranger would have found his behavior with her reserved, she understood he was simply accommodating her insecurities. He knew that maintaining a little physical distance made her more comfortable. He drove them to a little restaurant near her place that she'd had no idea even existed.

The restaurant was romantic and elegant. "This would be a great place to take a date," Elynn suggested as she looked around the dimly lit interior.

Alex smiled slightly, but didn't reply. They ordered and received a delicious meal while they caught up. Happy to have more time with him, Elynn asked Alex about his work and his friends. He told stories about them all the time, and even took calls from them during brunch, something she rarely got away with, but he had never introduced her to any of them.

"Why have I never met your friends?" she asked, after a few glasses of wine. "Sergei, Calen, and Gio all seem like legends, larger than life figures, more than real men after all the stories you've told. But you've never introduced them to me. And I know they've been here to visit. Wasn't Sergei just in town?"

"Only for the weekend, and you were down here at school. And I mostly visit the guys when I go to New York or Rome for business," he said. "Besides, Sergei is the last guy I would introduce you to. Him and Calen both. Hell, I wouldn't even trust Gio within a mile of you. These are *my* friends we're talking about, after all."

Elynn blushed. "I thought you said Gio was married."

Alex sobered and leaned back in his chair. "He's getting divorced now, thank god."

"Why do you say that? Didn't you like his wife?" she asked, wrinkling her nose.

"Hell no. I'm glad he's rid of her. She was a piece of work."

Elynn frowned. "Alex, are you sure this isn't a little misplaced misogamy?"

He looked indignant. "*No.* Just because I didn't like this particular woman, it doesn't mean I dislike all women. Believe me, she gave me good reason to hate her."

Elynn laughed. "I said misogamy, not misogyny. Misogamy is the hatred of marriage."

"*Oh*. Well, no. Besides, I don't hate marriage," he protested, refilling her wine glass.

She raised a skeptical eyebrow. "Who are you and what have you done with Alex?" she asked, laughing before taking a sip of her wine.

"People change," he said, looking at her intensely, unsmiling.

The air seemed to swirl with unspoken meaning. She blinked and changed the subject. "How are you going to get the car up to London? Did you rent a trailer or something?"

"No, I rented a house," he announced with a big smile.

"*What?*"

Elynn turned beet red. She had practically yelled that. Twisting to look around them, she quickly scanned for irate diners. Luckily they were in a relatively private corner of the restaurant in a cozy little booth. There were no witnesses to her outburst.

"I decided to do the work on the car myself. And I decided to do it here. So I rented a house outside of town. I'm going to come down on the weekends to work on it," Alex said, leaning more deeply back into his chair as their dessert arrived.

"Can you even fix a car?" she asked in genuine surprise.

"I assure you, I am more than capable," he said, shooting her an indignant scowl.

"Sorry. I didn't know being a grease monkey was on your long list of accomplishments," she teased, aware she was one of the few people who could get away with talking to him like this.

"Well, it can…sort of. I decided not to take the car to London until I can drive it there myself. And it's not going to be in any shape to do that anytime soon. So I took a place here."

Despite the opulence of the house Costas had used as a primary residence since Alex was a boy, she just couldn't picture him anywhere else but the bachelor pad he called home.

"That's some plan. I just can't picture you down here. Or living in a house," she said.

"I grew up in a house."

"I know," she said, "but now I can't see you ever having lived there."

His mouth quirked up on one side as he leveled his gaze right into hers. "I think I'm going to surprise you."

ELYNN WAS TERRIBLY FLUSTERED. She had less than an hour to get ready. After spending all morning cleaning, she had gotten a late start on preparing dinner. Luckily for her, the deep-dish pizzas were ready early, and so were the assorted hors d'oeuvres. She rushed to set the table for eight people, and then ran to take a shower. She had just finished when the doorbell rang. Wrapping a towel around herself, she checked to see who had arrived so early. Peering through the peephole, she swore under her breath. Alex was standing there in her hallway in his shirtsleeves and a pair of casual slacks.

"You're early. I'm not ready yet," she called through the door.

"Let me in. I've got ice cream, and it's going to melt."

Elynn felt a thrill of panic course through her. Swallowing her apprehension, she shrugged off her momentary discomfort. It was just Alex. She opened the door and backed away to her bedroom quickly.

Alex swept into the room holding a bag with a foil lining. He stopped short, his attention fixed on her towel. Her very small towel. His mouth fell open slightly.

Elynn blushed and continued to back away. "Go ahead and put the ice cream away. The freezer is just through there," she said, pointing to the kitchen.

She ran to her bedroom and shut the door, catching a glimpse of him as she did so. He had closed his mouth, but his chiseled cheekbones sported a slight blush of his own.

Oh God.

Elynn was more than embarrassed now. She and Alex weren't

close enough for the type of display she'd just made. She had obviously shocked him—and herself—a bit.

Why didn't I ask him to wait outside?

Catching sight of her red face in the mirror, she forced herself to relax. Taking several deep breaths, she did one of the relaxation exercises her therapist had taught her long ago. After a few minutes, her racing heart had calmed enough for her to get dressed.

"Who is the Dude and why does he abide?" Alex asked when she joined him in the kitchen.

She glanced down at the first clean t-shirt she'd found and put on. "Have you not seen *The Big Lebowski?"* she asked, grabbing at the conversational opening as if it was a life raft.

She proceeded to give him a complete synopsis of the movie followed by an admonishment to watch it.

"Why do I need to? You just told me everything that happens. You didn't even say spoiler alert," he said, laughing and shaking his head.

"That's no reason not to watch it! It's a cult classic," she replied, taking the pitcher of iced tea and lemonade she had made earlier from the fridge.

She puttered around, making small talk and getting everything ready while he leaned on the kitchen counter, watching her every move. Feeling unreasonably hot, she went to the windows and threw them wide open to let in the night air. I might need to turn on the AC, Elynn thought, willing her embarrassed flush to fade away.

"What kind of ice cream did you bring?" she asked when there was a lull in the small talk.

Alex went to the freezer to dig out the tubs. He displayed the exotic flavors with a flourish and assured her it was the best artisanal ice cream available in the area. She smiled in genuine amusement. Alex had to have the best of everything.

Elynn was suddenly seized by anxiety. Her friends weren't anywhere close to the sophisticated and rarified social circles Alex was used to. She herself usually avoided any social functions that forced her to mix with high society. Large groups made her uncomfortable, although after four years of being in the Hanas family circle, she had learned to cope with the odd party or business function.

"I can tell you're disappointed," Alex said, breaking her reverie. "I know what you really want."

Smiling, he pulled out a half pint of her favorite ice cream, Strawberries and Cream Haagen-Dazs. She let out a squeal as she took it and thanked him profusely. She put it back in the freezer to avoid temptation and asked him for the tenth time if he was sure he wanted to eat with all her friends.

"Stop repeating yourself. I told you I want to meet them, and that is that."

Chastened, Elynn twisted the dish towel she was holding. "It's just they're all lab grunts. In different labs, of course, but you know they're not…fancy. And neither is the food I made, just so you know," she finished with a warning finger.

"You're no grunt *paidi mou,*" he replied, crossing his arms and looking even more forbidding.

"Don't cross your arms like that. You're going to terrify my friends," she chided as the doorbell rang.

Relieved to escape for a few minutes, she went to open the door for Eric. "Fred is going to be late," he told her breathlessly while shrugging out of his coat.

Elynn laughed as she took in his appearance. Eric was dressed to the nines in a sleek new suit and tailored shirt. Even his shoes shone from a fresh coat of polish.

"Trying to impress someone?" she asked with a raised brow.

"Who me?" he asked, doing a little twirl for her before joining in the laughter.

Alex walked in while they were still laughing. She rushed to introduce the two of them and then went back to the door to let in her other friends. Everything is going to be fine, she thought as she turned to Alex with a smile.

A scant half hour later, she was praying for death.

ELYNN DIDN'T KNOW what had gone wrong. All of a sudden, Alexandros was doing his best impression of an iceberg. He was talking in single syllables and wouldn't crack a smile, despite the collective efforts of her friends to entertain him. She wanted to throw her pizza pan at his head.

The stilted conversation limped along painfully. Furious, she shot him a heated glance at odds with the frozen smile fixed on her face. Eric, who seemed to be getting the worst of the deep freeze, jumped up as if he was on fire when the doorbell rang.

"That must be Fred," he said, nearly running out of the room.

Elynn leaned over to Alex. "What is wrong with you?" she hissed.

"Nothing. Your friends are…charming."

His stiffness and taut features contradicted his words. Elynn opened her mouth to say something scathing when Eric walked in with Fred. Fred was the more flamboyant partner in their relationship and didn't sit down until he had done his rounds of air kissing everyone he knew. He bravely introduced himself to Alex and sat next to Eric after giving his partner a meaningful look and a reassuring squeeze of his hand.

Sometimes you need a gay guy to rescue a dying party. When Fred arrived, Elynn had already resolved to either ignore Alex's grim and inexcusable behavior or take him out back and shoot him. But with Fred's brash and amusing conversation, the evening took a turn for the better. Soon Alex was joking and telling witty anecdotes that had everyone laughing out loud. Elynn gave Fred a grateful smile as she sipped a Pinot Noir from the case Alex had sent her.

Lingering over dessert after the others had left, Eric and Fred peppered Alex with questions about Sonia Steele and the other famous women he'd been associated with over the years. Sipping a French Armagnac he'd brought with him, Alex skillfully evaded their questions without becoming angry, much to Elynn's relief. She finally had to rush the pair out before he had a change of heart and lost his temper. Alex had been very mercurial lately, and he'd indulged her friends far longer than she would have dreamed. She closed the door behind them with a sigh of relief.

"They're a nice couple," Alex said from behind her.

"Yeah, they're great. They have a lot of fun dinner parties at their place. They love to entertain. They're a lot better at it than I am," she said, collapsing against the door.

"I think the evening was a decided success. I even liked the pizza. Never had deep dish before," he said.

"Yes, well, *eventually* it was a success," she replied pointedly.

Alex flashed her a guilty glance. "You're right. I want to apologize for earlier," he said uncomfortably. He shoved his hands into his pockets and stared at her as if he was trying to decide what to say. "I was suffering from a misapprehension about something. It…upset me," he said finally.

"About what?" she asked with a frown as she began to clear the dishes.

"It's not important now."

Elynn studied Alex's tall, tense figure and the way he avoided making eye contact. He seemed genuinely upset. She didn't know why he was being so evasive. Her stepbrother was unfailingly direct about most things, even to the point of bluntness. She felt her annoyance melt into concern.

"You know you can tell me anything," she said, watching him with wide eyes.

"And I will someday…soon. Why don't you give me a tour of your flat," he said. "You didn't get the chance earlier."

"Well, there's not much to see," she said, deciding not to pry for now.

She led him through the small series of rooms. He asked about the different mushroom cultures in the corners and smiled as he walked toward her with his hands in his pockets.

"And the bedroom?" he asked.

"Err...it's right here." Elynn took him to the door of her room. "Also not much to see."

Alex looked over her bedroom with interest. Glad she had made an effort to pick up her dirty laundry, she watched him examine her bed, which was large for her but probably seemed pretty small to him. Her laptop was on an adjoining table, and her closet stood open on her simple wardrobe of mainly dark colors.

"Nothing frilly or feminine in sight," Alex observed as he ran his hand over her mostly bare dresser. "How different you are," he murmured.

Elynn frowned. "Different from who?"

"Hmm? Oh, no one, I was just talking aloud," he said before turning around to face her. "It's a little spartan," he said, gesturing to the bare walls. "No paintings or pictures. Not even a mushroom poster."

"I'm not much for decorating," she said with a shrug.

The gifts he'd given her over the years were prominently displayed in her cozy living room. But there weren't many decorations in her bedroom. She did have a few framed photos on the bedside table behind her laptop, but they were only visible from the bed when she closed the laptop—which she did every night at bedtime. There was one of her with their parents and another picture of her and Alex on her last birthday. He went over to pick up the photo of the two of them with a smile.

"I never seem to have the time or the energy to hang stuff up," she explained as he put the photo down next to the laptop, where it would always be visible.

Feeling unreasonably anxious, Elynn made herself cross the threshold so she would be with Alex inside the room. She wanted to show him her collection of postcards, which she kept under the bed. Whenever Alex travelled on business to a city she had never visited, he sent her a postcard. She had tons of them and had organized them into an album of sorts using a binder with transparent dividers, so the message on the back would still be readable.

The postcards, combined with Alex's stories, had inspired a deep desire to travel, but so far she had only done so with Costas and Mary. She hadn't worked up the courage to travel alone, and going with the one or two girlfriends she was close with didn't seem safe enough.

Feeling silly for being nervous, Elynn took a deep breath and went over to pull out the binder from underneath the bed. She sat and opened it to display her collection.

"I saved all of your postcards," she said, handing him the binder.

Alex took the album with a widening of his eyes. "I didn't expect you to keep these," he said with a soft smile as he flipped through the pages. "This is like our whole history." Embarrassed, Elynn didn't say anything until he finished and handed the binder back to her. "I should let you get ready for bed," he said. "I'm going to break in my own at the new house tonight. It's my first night there. Tomorrow I tackle the SS100."

Elynn put the folder back under the bed and followed him out of the room. He paused at the front door and pulled her in for a hug. Startled, she hugged him back. It was different from the quick and polite hugs they exchanged on birthdays.

Alex had pulled her body in so close that it was pressed completely against his. She was so much shorter than he was that the top of her head only reached his shoulder. Her legs were touching his and she could feel his heartbeat under her temple. It felt very fast, but she wasn't entirely sure because her own blood was rushing in her ears.

Feeling very hot and awkward, Elynn took a deep breath to calm herself. Instead, she inadvertently inhaled Alex's scent, drawing it deep into her lungs. It was heady stuff, vaguely spicy with hints of vanilla, traces from his soap. Her chest tightened and she took another deep breath. The tips of her breasts were incredibly sensitive as they made contact with the top of his hard abs. And then she felt something else.

Alex seemed...aroused. Startled, she tensed, and in the next heartbeat, he released her.

"Good night," he said, lifting her face to his with a hand on her chin.

He studied her face before kissing her softly on the forehead. Then he left. Confused, Elynn stared at the closed door for a long moment.

That was weird.

Fucking idiot. Alex got into his car and sat there for a long while, willing away an uncomfortable erection. Rolling down the window, he breathed in the cool night air until the heat in his veins began to fade.

Laughing to himself, he shifted his erection to give it more room. He had never felt so hard and hot, and all he had done was hug Elynn. Which may have been too much for her, he realized, slamming his hands on the steering wheel in frustration.

Everything had been fine for a few precious moments. Elynn had been confused, but she had been soft and compliant in his arms. And then he had grown hard. He hadn't been able to help it. He'd let go right away but she must have noticed—it was probably why her whole body had stiffened.

Alex laughed bitterly about his stupid assumption about the redhead, Eric. He'd been pushed straight into a caveman rage by an over-affectionate and demonstrative gay man. One with a little crush on him, if he'd been reading the vibes correctly. And now he'd gone and scared Elynn. For years, he'd kept his distance, respecting her unspoken boundaries, even if it had been hell on him.

She had felt so right in his arms. *Jesus*. His heart was still pumping too fast. One simple hug had opened the floodgates of desire in him. There was no going back for him now.

But would Elynn want him in that way? Or would her fears always lie between them? Or worse, what if she did want someone in her life someday, but not him? Not as anything more than an unofficial brother? Should he keep waiting?

Alex stifled a curse. He couldn't, not anymore. It would drive him fucking insane. Crazier than he already was. And really, Elynn would be happier once they were together. They would take things as slow as she wanted. Once she knew she was his, everything would fall into place. For both of them.

CHAPTER 4

Elynn stared at the message on her phone, trying to decide how she felt. Alex had texted her on and off for the past few weeks. He had been unable to spend the last few weekends in Oxford working on the car because he'd had to go to New York for a series of meetings. And Elynn was relieved. She'd managed to convince herself that the hug was nothing. It couldn't have possibly meant anything to him. He'd only forgotten whom he was with for a minute.

Her preoccupation with the hug was starting to drive her nuts. She needed to get her mind off it. But Alex had been texting a lot more than usual, keeping him fresh in her mind. At most, he used to call her once a week—twice if they hadn't seen each other at brunch recently. And his calls had always been short, friendly inquiries about her life and her work.

Now he was expecting her for brunch at his new rental on Sunday. In typical Alexandros Hanas fashion, he hadn't asked her to join him. He had simply texted her the time and address and said he was expecting her. Their parents were tied up with a charity event that day so they wouldn't be there.

Except for the dinner party at her place, she couldn't remember a time when she had been completely alone with her stepbrother for longer than a few minutes.

Just go and stop worrying about it. Alex was her friend, and he wouldn't hold her silly behavior against her.

WHEN ELYNN finally arrived at Alex's 'rental,' she slammed on the brakes of her VW Beetle. In front of her was a pair of imposing wrought iron gates. Apparently there were hidden video cameras monitoring the entrance, because when she leaned out to press the intercom button, a voice greeted her by name and buzzed her in.

Shaking her head, she drove up an impossibly long driveway that ended at an equally massive and elegant Georgian mansion. She let out a bark of laughter. Did Alex ever do anything low-key? This place was like something out of the movies, an estate that eclipsed his father's more modest country home.

The interior of the house matched the exterior in its imposing elegance. The foyer led to a huge central staircase and a long gallery was located on the ground floor. Elynn would not have been surprised if there were a ballroom as well.

She was directed by an unfamiliar maid out onto a terrace with a gorgeous view of green hills leading to an extensive wooded area to the right and a small lake to the left.

Alex was waiting for her at a table shaded by a big umbrella. He smiled at her and brushed his lips over her cheek in greeting, another change. Feeling warm, she sat down in the chair he offered her on his right.

"Well, you sure know how to downplay your real estate choices. Is this really a rental?" she asked.

"Yes, with the option to buy," he said, helping himself to the freshly baked croissants and preserves.

"You can't possibly be thinking of buying this place," Elynn said with a frown as she laid her napkin on her lap.

"Why wouldn't I? It's a superb estate. I like the views. It has a full gym, spa, and a movie theatre. If I put in a helipad, it would be perfect," he said as he poured her a glass of orange juice. "I find it relaxing. I may buy it."

Elynn laughed. "You can't be serious. You won't be happy living so far from London. You once said you'd rather watch all of Gossip Girl than spend more than a week in the country."

"Things change," he said before proceeding to distract her from his strange and sudden desire for domesticity with a steady stream of conversation.

"How goes the dissertation writing?" he asked near the end of the meal.

"It's not bad, actually. I'm a little ahead of schedule," she admitted as she sat back and closed her eyes.

The sun felt good on her face. With a contented sigh, she curled up in the oversized wicker chair and basked in the warmth.

"Well, it's good that you're ahead," Alex said. "That means that you don't have to rush home. You can help me check out the grounds."

"Yeah, why not?" she said, smiling lazily as she opened her eyes. "How is the car progressing?"

"Slow, actually. Finding certain replacement parts is proving to be a challenge. But not one I mind," he assured her.

"I'm still not sure why you aren't having the car restored for you. You have so many other demands on your time," she said sympathetically.

Alex worked like a dog. He lived by the 'work hard, play hard' mantra, but she didn't think he took enough time to relax and decompress.

"There are some things a man wants to do with his own two hands," he replied with a strangely arresting look.

Elynn felt another blush creep up her face. His gaze had barely deviated from her throughout the entire meal, and she was beginning to feel strange under his focused single-minded attention. Her chest felt tight, and she wondered if she resembled a tomato.

"Do you want to check out the woods now?" he asked.

"Yes," she said, a tad too eagerly.

A little time away from his intense gaze was just what she needed.

"Good, let's go," he said, getting up and slipping on a pair of sunglasses.

Startled, she looked at him blankly. "Oh, you don't have more calls to make?"

"No, I'm all yours. Come on," he said, holding out his hand.

She was a little slow to get up and take it, and he put it down as he patiently waited for her to get up and stretch. He led her down the stairs to the edge of the woods. They walked in companionable silence under the canopy of leaves for a few minutes before he spoke again.

"I was assured by the estate agent that these mixed woods would be productive for a variety of mushrooms. If I choose to stay here, you should take advantage of the new hunting grounds," he said offhand as they picked their way through a litter of dead leaves.

"You're not going to stay here," Elynn said with a laugh. "You'll run screaming back to the jet-set life in London before—"

"Before what?" he asked, making her jump when his voice came from directly behind her. She hadn't realized he was standing so close to her. "Sorry," he said, steadying her with a large hand before stepping to her side.

Elynn swallowed and kept walking. "Before the leaves turn," she finally said.

"Maybe I'll surprise you," he replied. "Would you care to wager on it?"

This time her laugh was distinctly nervous. "What do I get if I win?"

"Whatever you want."

"And if you win?"

"Whatever I want," he said.

"That sounds ominous."

"It is," he assured her.

Elynn stopped short and looked up at Alex's chiseled face with its sculpted cheekbones and strong, straight nose.

He doesn't know how suggestive that sounds.

"Okay, deal," she agreed, putting out her hand to shake on it.

Alex glanced down and took her hand in his with a small secretive smile on his face. Elynn left shortly after that, but not before being told that she was returning for brunch in two weeks' time.

ALEX WAS in Rome between back-to-back meetings, and he was in a bad mood. His father had called to cheerfully inform him that he and Mary would be able to meet for brunch at his Oxford home the following Sunday.

He had thanked his father in a slightly flat tone. Costas was obviously suspicious. The move to Oxford had been too out of character. Clearly he had tipped his hand with the recent move to the country. And now Costas was going to interfere with his plans. But as much as he loved his father, that wasn't going to stop him. Once he committed to a course of action, there was no going back.

On impulse, Alex decided to sell his penthouse apartment in the city. It wasn't right, Elynn visiting that place where he had entertained other women he hadn't particularly liked or respected. But he hadn't been able to live like a monk while he waited for Elynn to grow up. He still needed a place in the city, close to the office, but he would look for a house instead.

Frustrated, Alex raked a hand through his hair. He had honestly believed it would take years before Elynn would be ready for a relationship. Just last year, she'd been rattled by an uncomfortable situation with a male guest at one of their parent's dinner parties. Her reaction to the handsome, but decidedly pushy blond young man, Samuel somebody, had convinced him she wasn't near where he wanted her to be.

It had been obvious during the meal that young Samuel admired Elynn. The little shit didn't try to hide it, but he wasn't the first dinner party guest to get ideas, so Alex shrugged it off. He did, however, keep a close eye on the guy. He always did whenever his parent's guests included young men...or any men actually.

In the case of Samuel, though, Alex's overprotectiveness had been justified. After dinner, Samuel cornered Elynn in the alcove off the dining room. She refused Samuel's dinner invitation, but the guy was persistent. Too persistent. Elynn was obviously agitated by the time Alex had interrupted them.

Alex had told her to return to the dining room. Tellingly, she hadn't looked back at him or Samuel. If she had, she would have seen him throwing their guest against the wall and threatening to rearrange his face. The younger man had practically run out of the room and was off the estate in a matter of minutes. He left in such a hurry that Alex had to make up a fake emergency for him when he got back to the dining room because he hadn't stopped to tell his parents goodbye.

That was a while ago, Alex reassured himself. And he wasn't some jackass off the streets. Elynn trusted him, and for good reason. Pushing his misgivings away, he refocused on his work. But later that night, after a dinner meeting, Alex's patience took another hit. He was leaving the restaurant when a scantily clad Sonia Steele sidled up to him.

Ugh, not now, he thought as she took his arm and gave him a peck on the cheek.

"Darling. How are you?" Sonia said in an affected sultry tone.

Out of the corner of his eye, a flashbulb went off. *Oh, perfect.*

Alex swiftly extracted himself. "Hello Sonia," he said with a hint of annoyance as he took out a handkerchief to wipe away her lipstick.

"Join us for a drink," she invited, pursing her pouty full lips.

Angling her cleavage in a pose that was probably supposed to be seductive, she tried to take his arm again. Waiting a few feet away was an extremely pissed-off-looking man in a suit. Sonia hadn't waited long to find his replacement, but Alex didn't care.

"Sorry, I have another meeting. Have a good evening," he said politely before escaping.

Slipping into the car, he pulled out his cell to call his publishing contact. If there was a way to stop the publication of that photo, his man would find it. But knowing Sonia, it was already too late. That photo had probably hit TMZ or Gawker seconds after it had been taken.

Brunch the following weekend was uneventful. Elynn was distracted by her dissertation, and Costas watched him like a hawk. There had been no opportunity to be alone with Elynn. Resigned, he let the moment pass and decided to pick her up for dinner on Saturday night instead.

Maybe I should ask her first.

No. Giving her the chance to say no was not the way to do this.

Because she might actually say no?

Alex crushed that thought. It was time to start working on his car. At brunch Elynn asked how far he'd gotten on the restoration again, and before he could stop himself, he'd lied.

"Oh, it's looking good," he mimicked himself.

What had possessed him to say such a thing? He had never lied to a woman before. There had never been a need, but now he was trying to show off to impress Elynn. And he hadn't touched the Jag once since he'd moved it to the Oxford estate.

Alex studied the wreck of a car in his garage. Despite his boast to Elynn, he didn't know the first thing about car repair. He knew makes and models and what kind of engines he preferred. But he was a connoisseur of fine cars, not a mechanic.

For a minute, Alex seriously contemplated having a specialty mechanic come in to work in stages. He could easily bluff Elynn into believing that he was doing the work himself. Then he pictured her, those big green-gray eyes on him, while he demonstrated his progress.

No, he better make the effort himself. He had never taken credit for another's work in his life, and there was no way he was going to start now.

Maybe the For Dummies series has something on restoring classic cars.

With a self-mocking roll of the eyes, he decided to start by removing the seats. At least he wouldn't need a how-to manual for that.

ELYNN WAS WORKING LATE in the lab when Alex texted her that he was waiting outside to take her to dinner. She called him back immediately.

"Hi, I didn't know you were in town this weekend. I'm afraid I can't go to dinner just now. I have to passage some cultures."

"I'll be right up," he replied and cut the call before she could say anything else.

Elynn stared at her phone. "Okay then," she murmured to herself before going downstairs to let him in.

Alex was still waiting outside, not having realized he needed an electronic pass to enter the building. Even though he was casually dressed in a black sweater and designer slacks, he was out of place among the passersby in the street.

He looks incredible. Oh, hell. Where did that thought come from?

Worried, she opened the door and let him in. He swept past her, all six foot three inches of him dwarfing the people around them. He was even taller than his bodyguard.

He stopped in front of her, frowning. "What's wrong?"

"Nothing, I just can't get away right now," she said apologetically. "Thanks for stopping by, though."

Alex's lips twisted as his gaze lingered on her face. "You still need to eat. You haven't had anything yet. I can tell. Go finish up, and I'll call for something to be brought around."

Elynn flushed. "You don't have to do that. I have a microwave meal in the lab fridge, and I'm sure you have more important things to do. It's Saturday night. Don't you have a date or something?"

"Microwave meals aren't good for you. Why don't you do whatever you need to do, and I'll wait."

"Okay. If you're sure," Elynn said, nervously tucking her hair behind her ears.

She led him up into the lab and directed him to her desk—at least to the part of it that was visible. It was covered in piles of scientific papers, as well as her laptop and some racks of test tubes growing fuzzy bits of fungi inside. She slipped on a lab coat and took the racks before walking over to the laminar flow hood a few feet away.

"One of the other students is on vacation, and she asked me to propagate her cultures," she said, switching on the hood and turning on the interior light.

"Sounds...suggestive."

Elynn snorted. "All I mean by propagation is taking a small bit of this culture and placing it into fresh slants so the cultures will keep growing. These particular samples grow very slowly, so this only has to be done once a month at most."

She explained how the slants were made by pouring a hot sterilized mix of nutrients and agarose into the tubes as she worked, using a Bunsen burner to sterilize her tools between sample transfers by dipping them into a little flask of ethanol and lighting them on fire. "You lean them to one side while the agarose is still hot to make a slant. For more surface area," she said, before lapsing into a slightly awkward silence as she tried to concentrate on making the transfers.

She was very conscious of Alex's dark eyes following her every move. She dipped her inoculation loop into the ethanol and then into the flame while keeping one eye on Alex.

"Damn," she muttered as a stray drop of burning alcohol landed in her flask of ethanol, setting it on fire.

"What's wrong?" he asked from his seat at her desk.

"Nothing," she hastily assured him as she smothered the nearly invisible flame with a thick piece of foil, singeing her gloves in the process.

Elynn swallowed hard. Having Alex there was distracting. Shoving his too-imposing presence to the back of her mind she refocused on her task, trying her hardest to avoid setting anything else on fire.

CHAPTER 5

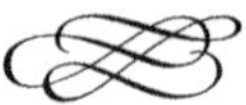

Alex didn't mind waiting for Elynn to finish up. He had never actually seen her at work before. She was so focused on her transfers that it gave him the opportunity to study her without her awareness.

Under the open lab coat she wore, her clothes were fashionable but simple. Mary had clearly bought the outfit, a pair of pants and simple cuffed shirt. Elynn wouldn't have bought something that fitted her body so well. She didn't hide behind oversized sweatshirts anymore, but she still instinctively bought loose clothing that didn't show off her figure. And her glasses suited her small face now.

Elynn had stopped explaining what she was doing and was completely focused on her task.

"What kind of fungus is that?" Alex asked. She didn't answer. "Elynn?"

She remained completely fixated on her work. Annoyed, Alex silently asked himself if another woman would forget his presence to the extent that Elynn had. It had never happened before.

Well, that's why you want her isn't it? She's not like anyone else you know.

Irked, he swallowed his impatience and decided to take Elynn home with him. Images of dramatically sweeping her up and carrying her to his car filled his head, making him smile. He was still smiling when she turned back around to him.

"I'm all done now. I just need to put these away." She put the test tubes in a nearby incubator and turned back to him. "I need the laptop," she said gesturing to the one in front of him.

The sleek little computer was secured to the desk with a cable lock. She took out the keys and was about to hand them to him when he pushed the chair back and gestured for her to unlock it herself.

Smiling awkwardly, she moved in front of him, the backs of her legs brushing his knees because he hadn't moved back far enough. She quickly packed her computer and they walked down through the darkened building. One of his men was waiting at the entrance with several takeout containers in hand.

"This way," he said when she turned in the direction of her apartment.

He put a hand on the small of her back and guided her to his town car. Pavlos, his driver, greeted Elynn warmly as he opened the door. Happy to see him, she chatted for a few minutes before Alex managed to get her in the car.

Elynn's sweet and considerate manner ensured she was a great favorite with his staff, but if he let her, she would spend an hour talking to his driver. Suppressing a smile, Alex, speaking in rapid Greek, instructed Pavlos to take them to his estate.

Elynn stared out the window for a few minutes, then turned suddenly back to Alex. "Hey, aren't we going to eat at my place?"

"I think you should spend the night in one of my guest rooms. It's already late, and you'll save yourself the long drive tomorrow."

"Seriously? It's only a thirty-minute drive. Besides, I don't have any clothes for tomorrow."

"It's closer to forty minutes. Everything you need will be provided for you. You already have your most important necessity," he said, gesturing to the bag with her laptop. "Think of it as a mini-holiday. My staff will meet your every need, and tomorrow I'll drive you back."

Elynn frowned, saying nothing.

"I stocked up on your favorite ice cream," Alex continued, "and I can get a masseuse to come in tomorrow morning. Nothing in your lab is ergonomic. You could probably use a massage."

Her expression changed. "Ooh. I could use a good massage. My neck is killing me from looking down into the scope all day."

This time he did smile. "I knew you could be persuaded."

For dinner, he'd ordered chicken cannelloni for Elynn, which was topped with a sundried tomato and cream sauce. As he predicted, she loved it, and he was satisfied with the osso buco he'd chosen for himself. For dessert, he had ordered her favorite Italian dessert, a panna cotta with a mixed berry coulis.

They ate in the recently renovated kitchen, sitting on barstools off the central island with most of the lights off. It was the most domestic meal he'd ever shared with a woman. He polished off his dessert, leaned back and relaxed, hooking an arm over the back of his chair while he watched Elynn finish.

"This kitchen is a chef's dream," she murmured looking around.

There were two large stoves and three sinks. Specialty appliances littered the marble countertops, and a huge Sub-Zero fridge and freezer dominated one side of the room.

"It was remodeled by the previous owner, but I counted it as a major factor in my decision to rent this place."

"But you don't even cook."

Alex gave her a mock scowl. "My chef does," he protested, making her laugh.

ELYNN FINISHED her panna cotta and hopped off the barstool to stretch like a cat. The large meal was making her sleepy, and she couldn't stifle a yawn. Alex smiled at her while he cleared away the takeout containers and threw them into the bin.

"That was delicious." She sighed as he led her out of the kitchen to the back stairs.

"You always say that about chicken cannelloni," he countered.

She laughed softly. "Because it's true. But tonight was the best."

He beamed at her as though he had cooked it himself, which only made her grin grow wider. But Alex always gave credit where it was due.

"Yes, that restaurant does it well. Come on, I'll show you to your suite. It's the one next to mine. The staff put your laptop there earlier."

"Okay," Elynn said, yawning again.

Her legs felt so heavy that she was having a difficult time clearing the top of the stairs. Alex laughed and backtracked a few stairs to get behind her so he could push her up the last few steps. Giggling, she let him guide her to a door that opened to reveal a lovely room done in navy blue with white accents.

The bedroom was so large that the huge four-poster bed didn't dwarf it in any way. Mahogany bedside tables complemented an antique vanity table and matching dresser. It was the perfect bedroom, furnished exactly as she would have done if it had been hers. Well, exactly like she would have told an interior designer to anyway.

"My room is through there if you need anything." Alex pointed to an adjoining door to the right. "What time shall I have the masseuse arrive?"

"Hmm... Ten?"

"Ten it is. Goodnight," he said, casually pulling her to him with one arm and kissing the top of her head.

Instead of going through the hallway, he walked through the adjoining door, giving her a brief glimpse of the darkened interior behind it.

She stared at the closed door for a few seconds, feeling unsettled. She briefly considered locking the door, but it felt odd locking it against Alex. Shrugging off her disquiet, she proceeded to undress. Giving her the bedroom meant for the mistress of the house was a compliment on his part. It was very sweet of him.

ELYNN WOKE LATE the next morning. She had slept soundly all night. The bed was a massive cloud that swallowed her up. She would have to ask Alex about the mattress. She wanted one right away for her own bed.

A knock on her door signaled the arrival of the masseuse, a wonderfully trained German woman in her forties who specialized in the deep tissue technique. Though it was at times a little bit painful, when it was over, all the tension in her back was gone. Feeling wonderfully relaxed, she decided to finish off by soaking in the enormous tub before going downstairs for brunch. In the bathroom, she found an array of bath salts, scented soaps, and bubble bath. All the scents were feminine.

Hmm. Clearly Alex has brought women here before, she thought while soaking in the tub.

Afterwards, she slipped into an oversized terry cloth robe she had found in the closet and returned to the bedroom. The robe was new, with the tags still attached to the sleeve. She was looking for her clothes from yesterday when there was a knock at the door.

"Hello dear. Are you in there?" Mrs. Braden called out.

"Mrs. Braden! What are you doing here?" she asked as she let the older woman inside.

"Young Master Alex made me a better offer. And a chance to make this grand place my home was just too good to pass up," Mrs. Braden said with a twinkle in her eye.

Elynn giggled, "Master Alex isn't that young anymore. How did Costas react to you jumping ship for Alex's job offer?"

"Oh, he and your mother travel so much these days that he was just fine," the housekeeper said, bustling in with several parcels and bags with exclusive brand names on them. "Master Alex had these things bought for you," she said laying out the bags.

She pulled out several designer outfits, all of them dresses or feminine skirts.

Elynn looked at the selection with trepidation. "There aren't any pants?"

"It doesn't appear so," Mrs. Braden said, checking through the other bags. "Oh, these are lovely," she said pulling out some strappy sandals with a low heel. "These would look terrific with this," she said, pointing to a dark green silk dress. "It would bring out the color of your eyes."

"It's a nice shade. I guess that one is fine." Elynn shrugged.

Mrs. Braden left so she could change. After slipping off the robe, she reached for the dress. It had a wrap top and a skirt short enough to show off her legs. She was suddenly glad she had shaved them on impulse while in the tub. Dressing quickly, she put her hair up in a casual pile on the top of her head.

Worried that she was late for brunch, she hurried down the grand central staircase only to be informed by an unfamiliar servant waiting for her that Alex was on a conference call.

Alex has a lot more staff now. She didn't even recognize most of the servants here. Of course, the house was much bigger than his penthouse, so it had probably been necessary to take on more people. Still there were so many new faces and they were so unobtrusive, completely unlike the motherly Mrs. Braden.

Elynn smiled as another unnaturally quiet servant passed by, doing his best to blend into the surroundings. *I'm surprised Alex doesn't make them wear livery.*

With the sumptuousness of the house and its regal grounds, it really wouldn't have been out of place. She felt like she had stepped into a period drama on television. The classic house didn't seem like Alex. She had always associated him with a modern streamlined look, like the decor of his penthouse, but it sort of worked. He was definitely a fitting lord of the manor.

The cool breeze on the terrace was welcome after her warm bath. On impulse, she decided to walk down to the nearby lake while she waited.

"I won't take anything until Alex wraps up his call," she told the hovering waiter before walking down to the water's edge.

It really is a beautiful place, Elynn reflected as the breeze ruffled her hair. Alex had mentioned that the lake was stocked for sport fishing, another activity she couldn't picture him doing. But this place was so amazing, she just might lose the bet she'd made with him.

Noting the mud at the edge of the lake, she took off her new shoes and wandered along the shore, lost in thought. A few minutes later, she heard her name being called. Alex was waving from the terrace. He still had a cell phone in hand, and he appeared to be talking to someone.

He was gesturing with his hands in that way she'd come to associate with Greek men. Costas made similar gestures while speaking. Smiling at the likeness, she began walking across the grass, carrying her shoes in her hand.

She hadn't gotten far when a pain in her foot made her gasp. Looking down she saw a wasp on her leg. Before she could move it stung her again and a sharp pain shot up her leg. She cried out and crumpled to the ground, unable to put weight on her foot. Another sting quickly followed and she gasped in pain.

"Elynn!"

Through a haze of tears, she could see Alex running toward her. He was shouting in Greek and more men were running behind him. But Alex reached her first.

"I'm okay," she said in a thready voice as he scooped her up into his arms, his face frantic.

"What is it? What's wrong?"

Alex shouted his questions as he broke into a run back to the house. His panic was infectious and suddenly she was terrified.

"Wasp," Elynn said with gritted teeth as her leg was jostled.

The pain burned, and every movement of her leg made it throb.

"Are you allergic?"

"I...I don't...know. But my...leg hurts...so much."

The words came out in broken breaths, the effort to say them too much. She closed her eyes against the pain and barely registered Alex's lips and face against her own. More jostling indicated she was being taken up the stairs. Elynn opened her eyes long enough to see that she was back in the guest room. Alex shoved the new purchases off the bed and laid her down gently in their place.

"You're going to be okay. A doctor is being picked up by the helicopter now," he said urgently.

She started to tell him that he was overreacting, but her heart was racing and she was struggling to breathe. Maybe a doctor was a good idea. Her head throbbed and her vision started to blacken at the edges. Alex was talking to her, but it seemed like his voice was far away, and she couldn't catch her breath long enough to reply.

He reached for her hand and gripped it tightly. She tried to hold onto him, but her hand stayed limp and weak in his. Then the light faded, and she slipped into unconsciousness.

CHAPTER 6

Elynn drifted awake slowly. The room was dark. Someone had drawn the curtains, but there was a chink of bright sunlight in the gap between them. Struggling to sit up, she felt something drag along her chin and chest. There was something plastic over her nose and mouth. An oxygen mask?

What happened?

There was a murmur of conversation nearby. She took off the mask and called out. "Alex?"

Her blurry vision focused on him as he rushed towards her from the hallway.

"Put the mask back on," he ordered with a scowl.

When she didn't move, he did it himself. Another person moved into view, a friendly looking older man with whiskers and a bald spot that was obvious even from her reclined position on the bed.

"You gave us all quite a scare, young lady," the stranger said.

"What happened?" her voice was muffled under the oxygen mask.

"I think it's fine if you take that off now," he said.

"No," Alex said. "Absolutely not."

"Really, it's fine," the doctor reassured him, and Elynn pulled off the mask gratefully. "I'm Doctor Sterns," he told her before whipping out a penlight to check her pupils.

"I'm okay," she told Alex with a pat of her hand. Experimentally, she tried to shift her leg. The pain was gone, but it felt numb. "Why can't I feel my leg?"

"I gave you something for the pain. There may be some numbness, and you should stay off the leg for a bit. At least until the feeling comes back," the doctor continued as he checked her pulse.

"I got stung by a wasp. Did I have an allergic reaction?" she asked.

"We'll need to get the test results back to be sure, but I suspect a number of factors led to this little episode. You were stung multiple times. There was actually more than one wasp; they were attracted to a discarded piece of fruit. One of the stings directly hit a nerve. Wasps have poison similar to rattlesnakes, so their stings can be painful. Your shortness of breath seems to have been exacerbated by a bit of undiagnosed asthma. Do you have problems in the spring? Any breathing issues of any kind?"

Elynn thought about it and shrugged. "I sometimes get these coughing fits, but I don't wheeze or anything."

Alex was starting to look less panicked and more angry now. He folded his arms and stared down at her with a frown on his face.

"Sometimes people with asthma don't wheeze as much as you see in attacks on TV. It can be subtler. The coughing was your most obvious symptom. The shortness of breath combined with your panic made you faint. It may not have been an allergic reaction to the wasp at all. I'm going to prescribe an inhaler for the spring months. Monitor your symptoms more carefully from now on. And we should do a full battery of allergy tests. Treatment these days is easier than in the past. No more injections. Just a few medicinal drops under the tongue every day. Completely painless. You should be right as rain by tomorrow. But take it easy if you don't feel well," Dr. Sterns said.

"I've arranged for her to have the day off tomorrow. You can come back to conduct the tests then," Alex ordered.

It was Elynn's turn to frown. "I have to work tomorrow."

"Your boss is going to have your experiments monitored for you, but you don't have many at this stage. Your task is mainly writing now. With your laptop, you can work from here tomorrow. You need to rest," he said, putting his hands on his hips.

"I'll be fine. I am fine," she assured him as he turned away.

But Alex was already walking the doctor out of the room, engrossed in conversation.

His concern was touching, but his bossiness was not. She called out once more only to have him close the door behind him.

That is going to get old fast.

ELYNN WOKE up with a little start. She didn't know when she'd dozed off, but it was night now. The curtains were open, washing the room with moonlight.

"Are you hungry?"

Startled, she turned to find Alex sitting in a chair next to the bed.

"God! Don't do that," she said, taking a deep breath and putting her hand over her heart.

"Sorry, I didn't mean to startle you. I was just checking up on you. You must be hungry. I'll go get you something to eat," he said, getting up and heading out the door.

Tentatively, she sat up, surprised to find herself still wearing the silk dress. Hopefully she hadn't ruined it. Putting her legs over the side of the bed, she attempted to put her weight on the foot that had been stung. It was still slightly numb, but not painful anymore.

"What are you doing out of bed?" Alex burst out.

Elynn jumped. "*Stop yelling*. It's all right. I feel better," she said as she took a tentative step away from the bed.

Alex gave her a dark glance, his face red, before he walked up and swept her in his arms. For a second he just held her, surprising her into speechlessness. Slowly he laid her on the bed and took her hand.

"Uh." She didn't know what to say. Alex was very close. Close enough for her to smell his skin and feel the heat radiating from him. Feeling warm, she tried to put some distance between them. "My leg is fine now. It's just a little numb," she said, before trying to climb out of bed again from the other side.

"*Na pari i eychi!* Why don't you ever do what I say?" Alex rasped, reaching out to put his hands on her upper arms.

He dragged her across the bed to him and bent his head to take her lips in a hard kiss.

It felt like the world had stopped. Elynn could feel her heart beating in her ears. Even her fingertips seemed to be pounding as her hands gripped Alex's shoulders for support as he pulled away and stared at her face. She watched him with wide eyes, completely transfixed. There wasn't a single coherent thought in her head. Slowly Alex moved his mouth back down to hers. The movement was almost glacial. She realized he was giving her every opportunity to stop him. But she didn't—she couldn't.

He stopped short, a mere fraction of an inch away from her. She hesitated for a moment, but then she closed the distance between them. Their lips met softly and he pulled her closer, his upper body pressed tightly against hers. Her head was spinning and she almost jumped when he bit her lower lip.

Reflexively she opened her mouth and Alex slipped his tongue inside. It stroked hers aggressively, demanding that she respond.

Elynn couldn't catch her breath, but she was unwilling to tear her mouth from his. Tentatively she touched her tongue to his. That small little sign of acquiescence on her part seemed to set him on fire. He inhaled deeply, the sound harsh in the quiet of the room before he climbed over her to cover her body with his.

Alex's mouth devoured hers as he pushed his knee up to nudge her legs apart. He slipped between them and rubbed against her in a rhythmic rocking motion, a perfect storm of heat and sensation. It was amazing, until she became aware of a growing hardness against her leg. Her eyes flew open and she stiffened in surprise.

What the hell was she doing? What was he doing?

Alex looked down at her face and swore a blue streak. At least she thought he was swearing—she couldn't understand him because he was speaking in Greek. He leapt up from the bed as if it were on fire.

"I'm sorry," he said hoarsely.

The door slammed, and he was gone. Frozen, she stared at the closed door for several minutes. A knock finally startled her into awareness, but it was only Mrs. Braden with a tray of food for her.

Elynn ate her sandwich. It was a roast beef on a croissant with mayonnaise and tomato, her favorite. Had she told Alex it was her favorite?

She wasn't sure, but he always seemed to know what she liked. It was as if he had some sort of sixth sense. He knew her tastes exactly. He had never failed to give her a gift that wasn't precious to her in some way.

This is crazy.

She tried to make herself go find Alex, but she didn't know what to say to him. He'd kissed her. Passionately. And not just then, but before when he carried her into the house. He'd kissed her then, too. She'd buried that detail when she woke up. It hadn't seemed real. Did Alex want her in that way? Was he genuinely attracted to her or was it some misplaced lust?

In a million years, she wouldn't have guessed that any of those things could ever be true. Alex was out of her league, astronomically so. Any suggestion to the contrary was outright lunacy.

Wasn't it?

He had always been good to her, but from a distance. But lately he was spending more time with her. And he had started touching her. A brush of his fingers here, a caress there, the way he would put his hand on the small of her back to guide her somewhere...

Don't forget about the hug at your apartment.

She'd tried to convince herself that he hadn't been aroused, that she'd imagined the whole thing. But she'd felt him against her just now, and that hard-on had not been imaginary.

A shiver ran down her spine. Was she excited or scared? Both?

Yeah, definitely both.

The thought of her and Alex together in that way made her dizzy...and hot.

What had brought on this change in him? A few months ago, he would never have laid so much as a finger on her. For years, he'd respected that invisible 'No Touching' sign she radiated in the company of all men, even his father.

Thoughts spinning crazily, she pulled her legs in close while she waited for Alex to come back so they could talk.

AN HOUR PASSED, and Elynn was still alone. She ate and showered in an effort to occupy her mind, but as the night got later and later, she grew more unsettled. According to the bedside clock, it was close to midnight.

Why hadn't Alex come back?

Maybe she was stupid to assume he would. It was time to find him. They needed to discuss what happened. Riffling through the bags for something to change into, Elynn felt a little dizzy when the only thing she could find to sleep in was a short silk nightgown in the same green as the dress she had worn that day.

Did Alex want to see her in this? The nightie had a square bodice trimmed in a soft lace that felt wonderful against her skin. Impulsively she took off her bathrobe and pulled the slip of silk over her head.

Catching sight of herself in the mirror, she took a surprised breath. The woman in the mirror was almost a stranger.

Elynn had never worn anything so revealing to bed, or anywhere else for that matter. The square bodice surrounded her cleavage like a picture frame, and the short skirt barely concealed her panties. She couldn't go looking for Alex wearing only this.

She searched in vain for a matching robe, but there wasn't one. With a sigh of frustration, she pulled the terrycloth robe over the nightgown. Heart racing, she went to the adjoining door that led to Alex's room and knocked tentatively. There was no answer.

You can do this.

Willing her heart to slow, she turned the knob and went inside. A small bedside lamp illuminated the empty bed and the room beyond.

It was a slightly more masculine version of hers—also navy blue and white with slightly heavier versions of the mahogany furniture that was next door.

Maybe the previous owner liked the same colors as me, she thought as she began a room-to-room search for Alex.

It took a while, but eventually the sheer number of rooms defeated her. She was in the kitchen, about to give up and go back upstairs, when she noticed a light under the door leading to the attached garage.

He was underneath the old Jag. It was still in pretty bad shape. In fact, it might actually look worse than when she bought it.

"Alex?"

Her voice was little more than a whisper, but he still heard her.

He pulled himself out from underneath the car in a quick graceless scramble. He was still wearing the white shirt and dark slacks from earlier, only now they were stained with engine grease.

"Why aren't you in bed?"

"Why do you think? We need to talk, and we would have been doing it a lot sooner, but I got lost. This place is ridiculously large," she said, crossing her arms.

"We don't need to talk," he said, eyeing her crossed arms as if she was about to punch him.

Elynn's mouth dropped open. "You're kidding, right?"

Guilt flashed in his dark eyes before his face settled into a cold expressionless mask. "Elynn, go to bed. We'll talk in the morning."

"Hey!" she said reaching out to touch his taut cheekbones. "Don't do that. Don't shut me out."

Alex expelled a loud breath before covering her hand with his much larger one. "I'm sorry about earlier," he said softly.

"I'm...I'm not sure you should be," she said slowly, her face heating along with every other part of her body.

She waited for a response, but he didn't say anything. Embarrassed, she tried to pull her hand away, but he stopped her. He put his hands on her hips and slowly drew her closer.

"No? Really? You don't have an overwhelming urge to kick me in the nuts?"

"No," she said, laughing, dropping her head to avoid his intense gaze, but the sight of his big hands on her waist did nothing to calm her down. If her heart beat any faster, she was going to pass out.

"Why?"

Why had their relationship changed so suddenly? She had a million questions, but it was hard to find the words when she was feeling so lightheaded.

"Because," was all Alex said before he pulled her up and set her down on the hood of the car.

He took her face in his hands and tilted her chin up so she was forced to look at him. Heart pounding, she studied his face. Suddenly he was unfamiliar, a stranger staring down at her with burning eyes.

He looks like a fallen angel sent to earth to tempt mortal women into giving up their souls. Shaken by the turn her thoughts had taken, she let out a startled laugh. A brief answering smile lit his face, but it was gone the instant his hands parted her bathrobe.

Alex froze when he saw the nightgown she was wearing. His eyes flared with a hunger she had never seen on his face. With a hand that might have been trembling slightly, he caressed the exposed upper half of her breasts, which were displayed like a confection in the low cut square neckline. His fingers ran along the top of the full mounds, which were just a little too large for her frame.

Elynn gasped aloud when he pulled down the bodice of her gown to expose a dusky pink nipple. Transfixed, she watched him slowly lower his head until his breath fanned the rapidly hardening peak.

He paused and stared into her eyes long enough for her to realize he was waiting for her to stop him. When she didn't move, he bent his head and took the stiff swollen tip into his mouth, running his tongue over it before he pulled down the material to give her other breast the same treatment.

Placing shaky hands on the back of Alex's head, she dug her fingers into his thick black hair. Heat was pooling low in her pelvis and a surprising amount of moisture was dampening her panties. Flustered, she tried to squeeze her legs together only to have Alex move his hands down to open them wider instead. He slid between them and pulled her closer, his lips moving up to her neck, licking and kissing his way back up to her mouth. He covered it with his, lips and tongue tangling with hers as he stole the air from her lungs and replaced it with his own.

But he was careful not to press his groin against her, maintaining a small but critical distance between that part of their bodies.

Panting slightly, Elynn stared at him with dazed eyes as he pulled away from her a little. "Alex?" she whispered uncertainly.

"Do you trust me?" he asked, his face flushed.

Tongue-tied, she nodded rapidly and was rewarded by another hot grin before he pushed her higher onto the car. She was splayed with her knees up, her feet resting on the edge of the hood. The hem of her nightgown drifted down and pooled at her waist in a fall of heavy silk.

In a slow deliberate movement, Alex reached out and took hold of her panties. With a wrench, he tore them and tossed the pieces aside.

Heart in her throat, Elynn raised herself onto her elbows to look at him, mouth wide. Alex's smile was tentative, as if he was waiting for her to start screaming at him.

Don't stop.

She wanted to say the words, but they were stuck in her throat. Cautiously, she slid a little closer to him and opened her legs a fraction. His mouth relaxed, the relief in his eyes obvious. Without a moment's hesitation, he buried his head between her legs, aggressively seeking the heart of her.

He ran his tongue along her inner lips, kissing and licking her before taking a gentle bite. Crying out in surprised pleasure, Elynn thrashed, her head falling back on the hood of the car with a dull thud.

"Careful." His voice was muffled as he paused before parting the lips of her sex with his fingers to give himself greater access. "You're so wet. God, you taste so good," he murmured, his breath puffing against her intimate flesh, sending shivers up her spine.

Elynn was a seething mass of sensation. The air was filled with gasps and soft moans that she couldn't seem to stop making. She should have been embarrassed, but it was as if those sounds were coming from another person.

Minutes passed in long moments of almost painful pleasure. She could feel her pussy pulsing and a delicious tightness gathering deep in her core as Alex's fingers rubbed her clit and his tongue moved inside her. It penetrated her over and over again until her body jerked and tightened around him. Crying out, Elynn convulsed as ecstasy pulsed through her and she lost her grip on the here and now.

When awareness finally returned, Alex was leaning over, brushing down the nightgown and closing her bathrobe. "Come on," he said, holding out his hand with a hint of a smile on his face.

Elynn tried to get up, but she couldn't even lift her head up from the hood of the car. "Can't move my arms," she mumbled, her head lolling to the side, too spent and drained to be embarrassed.

With a husky laugh, he picked her up. He cradled her in his arms, completely unfazed by her weight as he carried her inside and up the stairs. Drowsy and sated, Elynn started to drift off as the heat of Alex's body began to lull her to sleep. But she managed to rouse herself when he finally reached the guest suite and laid her down on the bed.

Wide-eyed, she caught his arm and whispered, "What now?"

Alex's expression was guarded as he studied her face. "Now you go to sleep. I'm locking the doors behind me. Both of them. Don't let me in if I try to come back later tonight," he said, flipping the switch on the connecting door before pressing the button on the hall door, locking it behind him as he slipped out.

CHAPTER 7

"Elynn? It's Mom. Are you awake? Sweetheart, why is the door locked?"

She sat bolt upright in bed. With a rush, all of the previous night's activities came flooding back.

Oh God. What the hell got into me? And into Alex? And now her mother was here. And where Mary was so was Costas.

"Be right there," she called out in a tense voice as she jumped out of bed.

Digging frantically, she searched for her own clothes, but they hadn't been returned. With a frustrated growl, she threw on another silk dress from one of the bags lying next to the bed. This one was navy blue with an asymmetrical hemline.

Like the green dress, it didn't look right with her normal shoes. With a sigh she put on the low heels she'd worn the day before. All the other shoes in the bags had been delicate high heels she would never be able to walk in.

"Oh, honey you look lovely," her mother said when she opened the door. "It's so nice to see you in a dress. Did you go shopping?"

Elynn was trying to decide if she should lie, but her mother didn't let her finish.

"When we found out what happened, we had to come and check on you ourselves. I'm so glad you're all right," Mary said warmly, squeezing her arm and kissing her cheek as they went downstairs.

"I'm fine," Elynn said weakly, grateful for her mother's tendency to run off at the mouth.

Downstairs, her mother continued to fuss and bustle around her, chattering away happily. She smiled, marveling at Mary's contentedness. Marriage had done wonders for her. Though Elynn had been very young, she could remember how unhappy her mother had been when her father had died.

At the time, she hadn't understood that her dad wouldn't be coming back. That realization had come much later, after she'd gotten used to it being just the two of them. And then there had been that dark time when they'd first moved out of Windsor, the small town in Massachusetts where she'd grown up. It had been hard on Mary to leave everything she'd had, all the memories of her husband. But now her mother had the life she deserved.

Costas and Alex were deep in conversation at the breakfast table in the sunroom when Elynn and Mary joined them. She tried to act normal, but she knew her face was red. Walking slowly, she made her way closer to the two men. Alex looked amazing as usual, in beige slacks and a black polo shirt.

How did he manage to make something so simple look so good?

Breaking off the conversation, Alex rose and came up to greet Mary with a quick peck on the cheek, surprising her into a blush. It surprised Elynn, too. He was never that physically demonstrative with his stepmother.

As Mary sat down, Elynn whispered to him in a quick aside, "Did you call them?"

"Mrs. Braden called them," he muttered back.

He gave her a quick assessing glance, his face unreadable. "You look much better, completely recovered. But even so, the doctor is coming by in an hour to give you some scratch tests," he informed her as he guided her with a hand on her lower back.

"Scratch tests?" Elynn repeated dumbly, completely disconcerted by the unexpected appearance of their parents and his closed off expression.

"It's a simple allergy test. They just give you a quick prick with a dilution of what you might be allergic to and then the reaction is measured. A drop therapy can then be customized to suit your needs."

"You're quite an expert. Do you have allergies?" Elynn asked, still off balance.

"No. I've been speaking to the doctor. Eat. He'll be here soon," he said as he propelled her to the table and the empty chair next to her mother.

Okay, Elynn thought as she sat and accepted a cup of coffee from Mrs. Braden. She could feel her irritation growing. Alex ordered everyone around. Even Costas sometimes, but he usually managed to keep it to a minimum with her. Like everything else about their relationship, that seemed to be changing, too.

Her mother launched into an entertaining story about a recent charity luncheon, and Elynn's moment of irritation passed. Shortly afterward, the doctor arrived, and her parents left so she could have the tests done.

The allergist laid out an array of bottles on the now empty breakfast table. One by one, each solution was applied to her arm with a sharp metal applicator that was used to scratch her skin, exposing her to the allergen so her histamine reaction could be measured. She had strong reactions to dust mites and grasses, but none to wasps or bees.

Throughout the test, Alex hovered over her with a grim expression. "Stop that," she hissed at him as the doctor grew visibly nervous under his intense scrutiny.

"Stop what?" he asked innocently while the allergist closed the last bottle and put it back in his case.

"Your doom and gloom look is out of place. It's just an allergy test." She gave him another glare, then added, "I think you should wait outside. I would rather speak to the doctor alone."

"No," he said curtly.

Elynn rolled her eyes and decided to ignore him. "Do I have to have shots?" she asked the doctor.

"Only if you like needles. There is a new way to administer treatment. We mix a cocktail of the antigens right for you. Just put a few drops under your tongue for a few minutes a day. Easy peasy."

"Thank you, doctor. Have the cocktail ready later today," Alex ordered.

"Oh," the doctor said. "Sorry, but the cocktail might not be ready today. The lab may take a bit longer than–"

"Today," Alex said firmly. "And some antihistamines as well."

"But—" the doctor sputtered, his expression meek under the weight of Alex's demands.

"Later is fine for the cocktail, doctor," Elynn said with a pointed look at the glowering Greek man. "I wouldn't want the lab to rush and make a mistake."

The doctor shot her a grateful look and rushed to give her several packages of pills and an inhaler before bidding them a hasty goodbye. After the doctor left, Alex stared at her. Her body heat skyrocketed. Hastily, she looked away.

"I should take you home now," he said.

The drive back to her place was quiet. Elynn waited for Alex to say something, but he was completely silent. And restless. His whole body seemed to vibrate with an unfamiliar tension. Their former comfort and ease with each other was completely gone.

Peeking at him from behind her eyelashes, she tried to guess what he was thinking. Everything was different now. Even the way he was driving seemed layered with meaning. He was squeezing the steering wheel too tight. An image of those hands on her naked thighs flashed through her mind, and she shifted in her seat.

Did he regret last night? Why wasn't he saying anything?

Though Alex had always been guarded with her physically, he had been warm and friendly. As warm and friendly as Alex got anyway. But not now. And he was damned intimidating when he wasn't speaking or smiling.

"Aren't you going to talk to me?" she finally asked when he parked in front of her apartment building.

"I...yes. But not now," he said in a gravelly voice.

Slowly, he reached across the seat and tugged her towards him. He took her face in his hands and pressed a brief kiss to her lips. Elynn was relieved, but also unsure what to say.

When she finally opened her mouth to speak, he cut her off. "I have to go out of town tomorrow. Business in New York that I can't reschedule. And after, I have to go to Hong Kong."

"*Oh*. Okay. Will you be back in time for my degree ceremony?" she asked, suddenly afraid that these trips were an excuse to get as far away from her as possible.

Maybe that soft kiss was an apology.

"I wouldn't miss it for the world. I promise I'll be there."

ELYNN SPENT the next few weeks in a daze. She tried to focus on wrapping up her thesis and on her final exams. Fortunately, she only had two of the latter, or she would have failed them. But at least the tests distracted her from the developing situation with Alex.

She wanted to talk to someone about what had happened, but she couldn't tell anyone, especially Eric. Now that he'd met him, he was dying to gossip about her stepbrother. And his choice of topic was starting to wear thin.

"I mean can you just imagine how many supermodels and A-list actresses he's slept with? It must be a who's who of the gorgeous elite," Eric said, playing with a pipette as he leaned next to her desk at work.

"I'd rather not speculate. Alex hates gossip," she said repressively.

"But he's not going to find out about it. And if he did, he wouldn't get mad at you. You're like his kid sister."

"We are *not* related," Elynn said with a force that surprised him.

Eric widened his eyes at her before laughing it off. "Doesn't matter. Me and Fred could tell that he just adores you. We talked all about it. Alex must have regretted not having any siblings. He obviously sees you as the sister he never had."

Elynn was acutely uncomfortable. Clearly that was not the case. And she definitely didn't want to discuss all of Alex's girlfriends. His reputation as a womanizer had faded in recent years, but she herself had seen that pneumatic blonde leaving his bedroom. Just a few weeks ago in fact.

Suddenly that memory hurt. And that was totally unreasonable. But she didn't care if it was reasonable or not when Eric surprised her with another tabloid picture. There was Alex in a business suit with Sonia Steele plastered to his side. She was giving him a kiss on the cheek for the paparazzi. Alex looked stiff and uncomfortable in the picture, but she found little consolation in that.

"When was that taken?" she asked Eric in a low voice.

He inspected the caption more closely. "A few weeks ago in Rome," he sighed. "I've always wanted to go there," he said wistfully.

Rome. Then the picture had been taken before she had stayed over at Alex's house. But not much before. Elynn tamped down a surge of anger. Dropping her head, she tried to hide her reaction from Eric. It happened before our first kiss, she told herself firmly.

What happens next is all that matters.

Truthfully, she had always been secretly amused by Alex's playboy image. Her girlfriends in school had always swooned over him. When they got too persistent about meeting him or gossiping about his girlfriends, she would distance herself, preferring to make friends who were more interested in her than her gorgeous, rich stepbrother.

As for all the women he'd been associated with in the past, she'd rarely thought about them. Since she didn't follow fashion or celebrities, she'd never been that curious about them. And Alex had always been discreet—he'd kept all his girlfriends and liaisons far from the family circle.

In the past, she had wondered how she would feel when Alex got serious about someone. His friendship, such as it was, meant a lot to her. It made her feel special that such an illustrious man had made room in his life for her. Especially with the way he'd reacted to his father's remarriage in the beginning.

According to Mary, Alex had been extremely contemptuous and cold with her when his father first introduced them. He'd been dead set against his father marrying again and had argued against it at every turn.

It wasn't till after the honeymoon that Costas managed to persuade Alex to come to a family brunch. Both she and her mother had been anxious over it. But it had gone better than they had expected. Though he'd been gruff, Alex hadn't gone on the attack.

Not even when he thought you poisoned him, she reflected with a smile.

After that visit, her stepbrother had warmed up little by little. He went from being forbidding and cold to reserved and polite. It took a few months, but he'd eventually welcomed Mary into the family, much to everyone's relief. She had heard her mother tell Costas that Alex's acceptance had little to do with her and everything to do with her daughter. And maybe that was true.

Elynn didn't know how much Costas had told Alex about what had happened to her, but she'd realized long ago that he knew enough. He never brought up the time when she threw her phone away...but he was very careful with her and made a special effort to be kind. For a man used to shouting orders, Alex never raised his voice around her, and he scrupulously avoided sneaking up on her. He protected her, too, never letting strange men near her at their parent's parties. And he had always been careful not to touch her.

Until recently.

Other than Costas and her carefully chosen friends from school, Alex was the only man in her life. And now he was changing the nature of their relationship. She didn't think he would do that lightly. He wouldn't toy with her emotions when he'd spent the past few years looking out for her.

But she wasn't sure what he wanted or what he was thinking. Maybe he wasn't thinking about anything at all. Perhaps he'd done something impulsive because he was horny. Which was extremely stupid under the circumstances. Costas would never approve of a casual relationship between his son and stepdaughter. If he ever found out, he would rain down hell until Alex 'did the right thing'. She honestly couldn't think of a worse development.

In the two weeks leading up to her degree ceremony, Alex didn't call her once. She only got a few innocuous texts updating her on his schedule. He was definitely avoiding speaking with her, but he continued to send her things. More meals were sent to her apartment when she was home as well as flowers and candy. Elynn couldn't decide if he was trying to woo her, or if he thought their encounter was a mistake and was apologizing.

The whole situation had her tied up in knots. On the one hand, she was grateful that things would go back to normal. But a part of her, one she didn't openly acknowledge, was terribly sad.

The day of her degree ceremony was overcast. Urgent business and bad weather had prevented Alex from arriving before the commencement exercises began. He was so late that Elynn doubted he was going to make it at all. She took her place with the other students and accepted her diploma with a smile, unsure if Alex was there to see it.

It wasn't until after the whole thing was over that she saw him standing with their parents. "Congratulations," he said quietly as he bent to kiss her cheek, sending her heart racing, before handing her a huge bouquet of white roses.

White roses were her favorite and there were at least two dozen blooms. The bouquet was so large that when she was carrying it she had a hard time seeing over the silky petals. The day became a blur after that, with their parents hustling her from place to place, several friends joining them for dinner at an exclusive restaurant.

To her relief, Alex stayed for the meal. Elynn was incredibly conscious of every move he made. Her eyes followed every forkful he ate; she couldn't seem to help herself. She desperately wanted to talk to him, but he disappeared shortly after dinner. Upset that she hadn't been able to find a moment alone with him before he went back to London, she was quiet on the car ride back to her apartment.

Her parents dropped her off at her building shortly before midnight. They had spent most of the evening trying to persuade her to join them on their extended tour of Italy.

"Mom, I have a lot to take care of before I can leave," she repeated for the fourth time. Elynn had earned a spot in the University's graduate program. She planned on getting a head start on experiments over the summer with her supervisor's blessing. "I promise to join you in Venice at the end of your trip," she added, kissing them both before she dragged herself up the stairs to her flat, completely exhausted.

She closed the door and leaned against it, her eyes closed, Alex's roses clutched in her hand.

"Elynn."

She opened her eyes with a start. Alex was sitting in her armchair, tablet in hand. He set it aside and stood up. When she didn't move, he rose and took the flowers from her.

"Did the super let you in?" she asked with a little frown.

He didn't answer as he turned to make his way into her kitchen. "It probably won't do much good, but I'll put these in water anyway," he said, examining the wilted blooms before digging around for a vase.

She drifted towards the kitchen after him. "What are you doing here?"

He turned around just enough for her to see his slightly sardonic smile. It was not reassuring.

"I thought we should have some time alone. Did the parents manage to talk you into joining them on the Italian tour?"

"No. I was planning on spending most of the summer here, working. I thought I would do some experiments to get an idea if what I have planned is an appropriate topic for a Ph.D. dissertation."

Alex's head drew back. "You really should take some time off if you don't want to burn out," he said as he walked to the living room and sat down on the couch.

"Yeah, that's what my supervisor said, but I don't have anything better to do," Elynn admitted with a shrug as she hovered, trying to decide if she should sit next to him.

Alex smiled. "Only you would think that toiling the summer away in a lab is a better prospect than an all-expense paid trip to Italy," he said, before pulling her down next to him.

Flushed, Elynn grabbed a pillow to hug in a nervous defensive move. With a predatory grin, he took it from her unresisting hands and tossed it away. He pulled her onto his lap and kissed her hungrily. But all too soon, he backed away to study her features with a serious expression.

The silence stretched into expectation. He was waiting for her to make a move. Elynn's breathing stuttered. Heart pounding, she put her hands on his shoulders and slowly leaned in to kiss his full lower lip.

Having received the permission he'd been seeking, Alex's arms tightened around her. His tongue plunged into her mouth before he withdrew it to nip her lip. She gave a little squeal of surprise, but he didn't let her go.

It was like liquid heat was pouring out of his mouth. It filled her up, melting her from the inside until she was boneless in his arms. He pulled away to study her dazed eyes, laughing softly when she slumped against him, completely enervated by his touch. One hand moved into her hair, gently closing it into a fist. Tugging her head to one side with a little pull, his mouth moved up and down her neck while his fingers made easy work of the buttons on her blouse.

His mouth flamed over her throat as he slowly undid each one. She didn't even notice until he parted the sides of her blouse and his lips moved down to her collarbone. Surprised, she looked down at her chest to see his hands cupping her breasts over her plain cotton bra. His fingers stroked her nipples over the cups until they peaked into hard nubs under the fabric. Reflexively, she grabbed one of his hands. He murmured something she didn't understand, plunging his hands back into her hair to pull her back for another devastating kiss.

Elynn could feel her panties growing wet. She squirmed in his lap, trying to ease the sudden ache between her legs. Alex sucked in a sharp breath.

"Careful, *agape mou*," he said in an undertone and she finally noticed the steel hardness against her thigh.

His kisses had distracted her to the point that she hadn't registered where she ended and he started.

"Oh," she said staring down at his lap.

"*Oh*," he repeated before stealing another kiss.

Soon she was unaware of anything but the heat crawling through her—up until the moment his hand moved up her bare thigh and his fingers trailed up under her skirt. Startled, she looked down and stared as if she could see through the dark fabric. He paused, resting his hand on her mound until she relaxed in his hold and collapsed on his broad chest with a sigh. He kissed the tip of her nose.

"Thank you," he said.

"Why?" she murmured.

"For trusting me."

Alex took her lips again and slid his hand further up, stroking her over her panties. He hissed slightly when he grazed over the moist fabric. His fingers slipped underneath the elastic at her thighs, deftly working over her clit while he pressed his palm against her opening.

Shivering and moaning aloud, Elynn ground her hips against his hand. He continued to stroke the dampened lips of her sex before pushing the tip of his middle finger inside her.

"You're so small and tight around my finger," he whispered, before kissing her earlobe and sucking it into his mouth.

With effort, she reached up to trace Alex's firm jawline. He had one of those sexy five o'clock shadows. She loved the way the stubble felt against her palms. Eyes closed, he turned to kiss her fingers. When he bit one, the sharp ringing of a phone startled her out of her sensual reverie.

Alex withdrew his hand and shifted her off his lap with regret. He stood up and picked up his phone.

"I'll be right down," he said before hanging up. He looked down at her flushed face. "I told them to only give me a half hour after you came in."

"Told who?"

"My driver and bodyguard."

"Why? And you didn't answer me earlier. Did the super let you in?"

He stiffened and stayed quiet. She thought he wasn't going to answer when he finally said, "No. I have a key."

Elynn stood up, "What do you mean, you have a key?"

"I...I have one because as soon as you moved in, I bought the building," he said slowly.

"*What*? You can't have done that. I mean, what would be the point?"

Alex put his hands on his hips. "Look, I wasn't about to let you live someplace I hadn't secured first," he said firmly.

Elynn thought back to the security enhancements that had been made *after* she moved in. The doorman at the reception was new, as were the hallway security cameras. New locks had been placed on all the windows and the lock on her front door had been upgraded to a deadbolt.

A weird thought occurred to her. "Do you have access to the security camera footage?" she asked slowly.

"I haven't been spying on you." His voice had an edge now.

Elynn put her hands on her hips. "So the over-attentive doorman doesn't report to you?"

Alex looked away and her mouth firmed. She was onto something. Mike the doorman was a big friendly man. A former cop, in fact. Elynn shook her head in realization. Of course Alex had hired him to keep an eye on her. It actually seemed like something Costas would do. They probably had a pact to keep an eye on her.

It made you feel safer knowing Mike was retired law enforcement.

She sighed in resignation. "And why do you only have a half hour?"

"So I won't do anything stupid," he said softly, pulling her to him.

He kissed her again before taking her hand and leading her to the door.

"We didn't talk," she said suddenly, tightening the grip on his hand.

"We don't need to. I'll see you at the parent's party. Wear the blue silk gown. The floor length one. I want to see you in it."

"The blue silk?" she asked confused. "Did you choose all of that stuff yourself? All the clothes? It was you and not your staff?"

"I selected and approved everything from pictures," he said as he opened the door.

Elynn blushed. She had assumed his staff had selected things at random. Some of the lingerie had been rather daring. Alex turned back with his hand on the door to run a finger over her hot cheek before he kissed her again. Then he walked out, leaving her alone and still aching.

Without stopping to think about it, she put one hand on the door and moved the other one between her legs. Putting her fingers where his had been, she squeezed and stroked until she brought herself to a mild climax.

Stunned at her own behavior, she took a shower and went to bed. She was asleep as soon as her head hit the pillow.

CHAPTER 8

As a rule, Costas and Mary never invited large numbers of people to their parties, but tonight they made an exception. The house hadn't seen such a crowd since before they married. Even their wedding reception had been small and intimate.

Elynn smiled politely whenever she had to make small talk with her parents' friends while she kept a surreptitious eye out for Alex. Hiding the strain she felt, she moved through the crowd, trying not to get trapped in one place for long. She was no longer uncomfortable in large crowds, but tonight she was getting a lot more male attention than she was used to.

She blamed the dress. It was the most daring thing she'd ever worn in public. The dusky blue silk was fitted at the waist and hips, flattering her figure as if it had been made for her. The square neck was modestly cut by current standards, exposing only a hint of cleavage at the top, but she still felt exposed. She couldn't remember ever showing that much skin.

When she couldn't shake off a socialite's overeager son, she dived back into the group of guests, hoping that he would get bored if she kept moving.

Alex arrived half an hour late to his father's house, swearing under his breath as he went up the steps. When he joined the party, it was in full swing. He swore again, not realizing how many guests his father and Mary had invited.

His gaze found Elynn instantly. She was wearing the dress, but the satisfaction he felt that she'd actually worn it faded the instant he realized how many men were looking at her. Her lovely face and petite curved figure captured every male's attention, despite the relative modesty of her gown. What skin she was showing looked like creamy silk, and her hair gleamed blue-black under the lights.

Damn. The wolves are circling, he thought as he started to make his way through the crowd to where Elynn was smiling politely at a sandy-haired young man. To anyone else, she would have looked normal, but he could see the signs of her discomfort even from where he stood.

He was still a fair distance away when he was stopped by a hand placed on his arm. "Alex, darling, how are you?" purred a young socialite whose name he couldn't remember.

"Fine, fine. And you...Farah?"

"It's Fiona," the socialite said with a little moue of irritation. But the next second she smiled and drew closer, pressing her breasts against his arm. "It's so good that you came. We don't see enough of you," she said in a sultry voice, surely calculated to intrigue him.

"I'm around," he said flatly when Elynn looked up and saw him.

She took one look at the clingy blonde and her polite smile faltered and faded away. Alex didn't waste any more time on the grasping socialite.

"Excuse me," he said before pulling away abruptly.

He tried to get to Elynn, but he was stopped two more times by business acquaintances. Meanwhile, his quarry shifted to another group, her tenacious admirer in tow. By the time he made his way to the other side of the ballroom, he couldn't see her anymore. However, the sandy-haired guy was making his way out to the terrace. Angry now, Alex strode out of the ballroom after him.

"Elynn? Are you out here?" the stranger called out eagerly as Alex followed him out onto the relative privacy of the terrace.

Irritated, Alex looked behind him to make sure they weren't being observed before he put a hand on the kid's shoulder. "She's not waiting for *you,*" he said implacably as he yanked the smaller man by the collar. "Go inside."

"But..." the young man sputtered, struggling a little under his hold.

Alex drew himself up to his full height, which was half a foot taller than his adversary. "I said, go inside," he repeated, giving the guy a shove toward the ballroom doors for good measure.

He didn't bother to look behind him when the kid stumbled back indoors. Sheep usually followed his orders without question. Taking the garden steps two at a time, he started to look for Elynn in the garden.

It took him a while, but he eventually found her moving furtively back to the ballroom doors. She was still hiding; making sure her admirer wasn't in sight before she went back in.

On silent feet, Alex snuck up behind her. He put one hand over her mouth and used his other arm to sweep her off her feet. Elynn struggled, her cry muffled by his hand.

"Shh. It's just me," he whispered before he carried her away, his hand still over her mouth.

He made his way to his favorite greenhouse a little distance away from the main house. Once inside, she made a distinctly frustrated 'Alex!' sound from behind his hand. He laughed, turning her in his arms, pressing her against him as he removed his hand and replaced it with his lips.

After a small hesitation, Elynn parted her lips for his probing tongue. She tasted of the sweet wine they were serving inside. With a groan, he stumbled to the wide, cushioned bench where he used to lie on cloudy winter days, soaking up the warmth of the greenhouse. He laid her down on it and stretched out over her, his hardness seeking her softness. Elynn gave a little gasp, but she didn't sound as if she was afraid. And that was good, because he couldn't stop touching her. He let his hands roam over her chest and waist.

Impatient, he tugged the skirt of the dress up and skimmed her panties down and off as he moved lower down her body. "I want to taste you. I missed your taste," he breathed against the soft skin of her inner thighs.

Elynn gave a little moan as his tongue flicked out to touch her. The scent of her arousal filled his lungs. A little too eagerly, he took hold of her thighs and moved to guide her legs over his shoulders.

"Alex?" she asked uncertainly.

"It's okay, baby, just let me touch you," he said as he bent down and took her with his mouth. Her slightly salty, musky taste exploded on his tongue and he groaned. "God you taste so good," he whispered.

Alex was on a fire. Stark hunger and need pulsed in his veins. He was so hard it almost hurt. And Elynn wasn't freezing up on him. He desperately wanted to be inside her, but he couldn't do that. It was too soon, and this was not the place.

In spite of the mantra he repeated in his head, he crept up Elynn's body to her mouth, stopping to kiss and cup her breasts along the way while his restless hands continued to stroke and caress the rest of her silky skin.

And her hands were on him too, stroking his back and cupping the back of his head as he kissed her.

"Elynn, you have to stop me. Tell me to stop," he ground out.

He hadn't meant for this to happen. If he hadn't seen that kid chasing after her, then his jealousy wouldn't have been sparked, and he wouldn't have carried her off like this.

But Elynn wasn't listening to him. She was too far gone, her little moans and rapid breathing her only answer. Then her hands moved between them and down his body. They both froze when she reached the iron hard shaft straining toward her through the material of his pants.

He held his breath as he watched her small hands trace him over the cloth. Unable to stifle a groan, he held himself still. Her fingers became determined, taking hold of his trouser front and tugging on his zipper.

They had both stopped breathing, making the sound of the far door opening and the burst of conversation that followed extremely loud. A drunken couple had come into the greenhouse, presumably to find a place to do what they were doing. Alex cursed under his breath and stood up. He grabbed Elynn by the hand and dragged her behind him out the back door into the warm summer night.

"Alex, my panties!" she hissed, trying to pull him back so she could go and get them.

He stopped short and turned to look down at her, "It's too late. If I go back for them, they'll see me, and then they'll want to know who I was with."

And it was true. He was a little bit of a celebrity, even in their own circles, and this kind of gossip after years of living in relative quiet would start a feeding frenzy.

"Don't worry," he said, "if they find them they won't have any idea whose they are."

Elynn moaned with embarrassment and covered her eyes with her hand. Alex couldn't stop himself from giving a husky laugh before he proceeded to straighten out her clothes and hair. With the handkerchief he'd had tucked into his breast pocket he wiped traces of her lipgloss off his mouth.

He straightened his coat and tie before propelling her back to the ballroom doors. "Go make nice with the parents," he instructed.

She frowned at him, but she went.

ELYNN FLED to the bathroom to check on Alex's repairs to her coiffure and dress before she rejoined their parents. Her cheeks were burning over the way Alex had basically ordered her inside. Letting him touch her was making him bossier than usual. *Or maybe you're just more sensitive about it now.*

Oh God, what are we doing? she thought with a thrill of panic. She couldn't believe what was happening to her. What Alex was doing to her. What she wanted him to keep doing. That much she could acknowledge. She didn't want him to stop trying to seduce her. But she couldn't imagine that he'd actually thought things through. If their parents ever found out, there would be hell to pay.

Eventually the party began to wind down. When she couldn't find Alex, she went upstairs to her old room. She was spending the night there so that she could have lunch with Costas and Mary before they left for Italy.

She shouldn't have been surprised to find him in her room, but her heart jumped anyway when she saw Alex sitting on her bed.

"You didn't tell me you were spending the night here," he said, raising his brows at her.

"I want to see them off tomorrow. Are you staying?" she asked from just inside the door.

He still had a suite of rooms at the house, but he hadn't used them in years. She glanced down at the bed. It was too small for him, but she couldn't help but picture him in it. His eyes flared, looking her over in a heated appraisal that told her he knew exactly what she was thinking.

"It's your own fault. You shouldn't have told them you were staying here."

His voice was full of reproach.

"I'm not inviting you into my bed," she whispered.

"Yet."

She couldn't deny that, and he knew it. They *would* end up in bed together, and from the way things were going, it would happen soon.

Alex drifted over to her and put his hands on her hips. "I've spoken to your supervisor," he said unexpectedly.

Her head shot up to meet his dark burning gaze.

"Why?" she asked suspiciously.

"I informed him that you wouldn't be working this summer. That you had opted to take the summer off after all to recharge your batteries before you resumed your studies. He approved."

Elynn's jaw dropped, and her temper bubbled to the surface. "How could…" she began in a loud voice, but he swooped in and stopped her mouth with his.

Too soon, he raised his head to look into her eyes. "They'll hear you if you shout like that," he said quietly, his calmness grating on her nerves.

"I can't believe you! Why did you do that?" she hissed at him.

"You're going to be busy," he said softly, tracing her lips with his index finger.

Distracting her from her anger, she mumbled, "Doing what?"

"You're spending the summer with me," he breathed before stealing one more heart-stopping kiss.

ALEX LEFT AS QUICKLY as he could. He didn't trust himself to sleep under the same roof with Elynn while his father and Mary were still around. He was outside, reaching for his keys, when he found her panties in his pocket. He must have shoved them in his pocket after he took them off her and hadn't even noticed.

Laughing aloud, he switched them to his breast pocket, symbolically placing them over his heart. Smiling, he got into his car and drove back to London.

CHAPTER 9

Elynn stayed on at Costas' house long enough to see him and her mother off on their trip. She'd had a restless night, unable to sleep because she had been reliving every time Alex had touched her and was trying to decide what to do.

She was about to throw her bag into her car when a SUV and a limousine arrived, blocking the drive. Elynn straightened up when Alex got out of the limo with a warm greeting. A stocky man who resembled a bouncer came up and took the keys and bag from her unresisting hands. Meanwhile, Alex guided her into the back of the limousine before she regained her composure enough to utter a single word.

"Where are we going?"

"My home. Summer starts now," he said, wrapping her in his arms and pulling her in for a searing kiss.

"I don't think that's a good idea," she began apprehensively as he leaned over to press the lever to raise the privacy partition.

She had come to the decision not to change her plans for the summer. If Alex wanted to spend time with her, then he could do it when he came to Oxford or when she went up to London.

He was bending to kiss her again when she stopped his lips on their descent with her hand. "I've been thinking about it, and I can't go and spend the summer with you as if I were one of your...your women," she said.

It took a lot of effort to keep her voice steady and reasonable now that he was in front of her.

Alex's face grew cold. She waited, but he didn't respond, turning away although he continued to hold her. Frustrated, Elynn wrenched at his shirt collar to make him face her. Her small show of aggression must have amused him, because his reserve cracked a bit, enough to let the glimmer of a smile break through.

"You're not one of my women, you're *my woman*. There's a difference," he said finally.

That little announcement threw her. "What does that mean?" she asked suspiciously.

She hadn't forgotten the sexpot Sonia. Or the fact that he had still been seeing her, even after he said they weren't involved anymore. And now he was telling her that *she* was his woman. She waited for an answer, but Alex was obstinately silent as he held her, choosing to play with her hair instead. He brushed a lock off her face and followed it down to where it fell against her collarbone and breast.

Blushing hotly now, Elynn could feel her completely justified temper slipping away. "I can't spend the summer with you. I have things to take care of," she protested.

"Your apartment will be looked after. I wouldn't want your mushroom kits to dry out. In fact, I'm having them moved to London for you. The turtle and fish are also being taken care of," he said pulling her closer to his side with a satisfied sigh.

After that, he fell silent again, continuing to play with her hair instead of talking, occasionally stealing little nibbling kisses that drove her crazy.

The trip back into the city felt like minutes, but it must have taken the better part of an hour. Eventually they stopped in front of a large, gracious house in Kensington.

She got out of the car and gave the imposing facade of the house a thorough once over. "Where are we?"

"Home. What do you think?" he asked with an expectant air.

"It's beautiful, but what happened to the penthouse?"

"I thought it was time for a change," was all he said as he led her inside.

The interior of the house was beautiful but sparsely furnished. "Did you just move in?"

"Yes, just this week. I wanted the perfect place for us to spend some time together, but I still need a place in town near the office. We can stay here this week and shift down to the Oxford house on weekends when we're not actually on the road. It took a little time to find the perfect house. The decorator hasn't had time to do much, but I didn't want to wait, so I had some essentials put in."

It was almost too much to process. "I still don't know what made you decide you wanted a house now. *Another* one. Aren't you going to miss the penthouse?"

"No. This is what I want now. Why don't you help me decide how to furnish it?" he asked as he led her through the mostly bare rooms.

"What do you mean?" she frowned as she looked around. The spacious interior had an open modern floor plan that didn't match the classic exterior of the house. "You want my decorating advice?"

"Of course," he said, stopping to watch her as she walked through a lovely room with curved walls that opened onto a small sunroom.

She raised her hands. "I don't know anything about decorating a house. You've seen my place, it's pretty...basic."

"That's only because you haven't had a blank canvas before. And I'm not asking you to pick out the end tables and throw pillows. Just give me your impressions. What would you do if this were your place? The decorator will take care of the rest," he said, leaning against the doorframe, his eyes tracking her movement before extending his hand to her.

And with that tantalizing offer, she let him lead her throughout the house. When pressed, she made a few suggestions. He was indulgent with her more non-traditional ideas and encouraged her to speculate wildly on some totally off-the-wall decorating themes.

"I think you should do an Arabian nights thing in here," she said when they circled back to the room with curved walls.

Alex laughed and pulled her close for a scorching hot, but brief, kiss.

"If you're going to laugh at my ideas, I'm going to keep my mouth shut," she said with pursed lips as she gave him a little push.

"I love your ideas. I'm going to implement all of them. Especially the Atlantis themed room and the Arabian Night's room. I'm going to love playing the Sultan. And you're going to love playing my favorite harem girl," he teased as he pulled her back for more kisses.

She gave a distinctly nervous laugh and let him continue his tour in silence. The last room he showed her was the master suite. Her tummy did a little flip when she saw the huge four-poster bed. He didn't stop at the bed however, just continued crossing the room to throw open the bathroom doors. After leading her inside, he showed her the Jacuzzi tub and power shower. When he began to show her how to use the shower's complicated control panel, she stopped short.

"Alex, where am I sleeping?"

He stopped fiddling with the shower controls and led her to the bedroom. He sat her down on a large divan and studied her carefully, keeping a grip on her fingers.

"I would like you to sleep in here with me," he said.

Elynn caught her breath and looked down at their joined hands. He waited for her to speak, apparently unwilling to say another word until she decided.

"Alex, do you really want to do this? With me, I mean?"

"More than anything."

Blood rushed to her cheeks but she still didn't look him in the eyes.

"Why?"

"Because I've waited long enough."

"It's only been a few weeks," she couldn't help saying, still not meeting his eyes.

Though it felt a lot longer, only a little time had actually passed since he had first touched her with more than just brotherly affection.

"It's been a lot longer than that for me," he said.

Elynn's eyes shot up. A thrill raced up her spine...but then she remembered Sonia Steele and her dramatic exit from Alex's bedroom. She withdrew her hand and crossed her arms across her chest. "I find that hard to believe. I know better than to assume you've been interested in me for very long."

"I was no longer sleeping with Sonia when you met her," he said bluntly. Elynn's head drew back to stare at him. "Yeah, you're easy to read," he added with a nod. "But I'm serious. I wasn't sleeping with her anymore."

Surprised and startled that he would break the habit of years and discuss one of his liaisons with her, she stared into his eyes, trying to find the truth in them.

Alex's temper, usually so well contained around her, flared. "I wouldn't lie to you," he said, scowling.

"I know," she murmured, realizing it was true.

Alex didn't lie. But she was still surprised he was explaining. He always refused to discuss any of his relationships with his father. *Well, you can't blame him for not wanting to do that.*

"I hadn't slept with her in months," he continued. "She went off to shoot a movie, and I decided we were done. When she came back, she wanted to pick up where we left off. I agreed to go with her to a club to talk things out because she'd become annoyingly persistent, but I didn't take her home. She was pissed and she came over the next day to..."

"To sleep with you," Elynn answered for him, hiding the jealousy she felt.

"To get back on the front page. That's all she wanted from me. She was finished with me from the second she arrived that day. Everyone I've ever...kept company with knows better than to disturb me on a Sunday when I'm in town."

Okay. What to say to that? She remembered the picture in the tabloids and her weak resolve grew decidedly firmer. "I don't enjoy the idea of being one of a long list," she said, her mouth firming.

He growled in frustration. "You're not. Obviously you're different. Don't play dumb and pretend you don't know that," he said sharply.

"*Hey*. Don't talk to me like that. I don't know what's in your head. On a good day, you're next to impossible to read. And this—whatever this is—is too crazy not to question," she said defensively.

"It's not crazy," Alex replied steadily.

"Yes, it is. And it's weird."

"Weird?" His voice sounded odd.

"Yes, weird. On what planet would anyone ever put you with someone like me?" she said, throwing up her hands.

"What does that mean?" he asked, his forehead wrinkling.

"I mean you're Alexandros the Great. And I'm...I'm just me," she said, standing up and backing away from him. "There is no way a relationship between us makes sense."

Alex looked at her with a slightly softened expression. "It makes sense to me. And I'm the only person you need to be concerned about. What everyone else might think doesn't matter. And there isn't a man I know that wouldn't try to steal you from me given half a chance. You're smart, funny, and sweet. And you have no idea how beautiful you are—which is just crazy."

Elynn's cheeks burned, but she ignored the compliment and thought, choosing her words carefully. "So...this isn't some secret fling or something? You intend to let people know you're seeing me?"

"Of course." He stuck his hands in his pockets and shifted around uncomfortably. "When the time is right. For the moment, I do think we should keep things between us. It would be difficult if our parents were to learn of this before we get...comfortable with each other."

Well, that was a damn fine argument. She didn't want to picture her mother's face when she found out her little girl was in an intimate relationship with Alex. Mary was still intimidated by her powerhouse of a stepson. And Costas would literally explode if he found out.

Alex thought of his father as a mild, softhearted romantic, but Elynn knew better. Her stepfather was an old-fashioned man with old-fashioned values. He had a temper, too. It was just less obvious compared to his son's more volatile one.

Alex got angry easily, but he controlled himself and didn't rage or lash out. Not at strangers anyway. Instead, he would become cold and grim, choosing to tear down the offending party with a few devastating words. If he did lose his cool enough to yell, it was usually with someone he was more familiar with, one of his staff or with a friend or the family. Elynn had always been exempt, but now she wondered if she was going to find herself in the same league as everyone else, no longer off limits when it came to the harsher aspects of his personality. There was definitely a downside to getting closer to Alexandros the Great.

She had been quiet for so long that he grew anxious enough to break the silence. "What are you thinking about?"

"I'm...I'm afraid," she said honestly.

"You never have to be afraid of me."

He sounded hurt.

"That's not what I meant. I mean, yes, I'm a little afraid of that. It's intimidating. Even looking at you now, I can't picture it. Intimacy. With you. But that's something else entirely. I'm more afraid of changing things between us. I liked the way things were. Even if there was...you know...some distance. I've always known that you cared about me in your way, that I'm important to you. It made me feel special. And I don't know if you will still feel the same way about me after this."

After a beat, Alex let out a husky laugh and enveloped her in a tight hug. "You should stop worrying so much. I admit that this is new territory for both of us, but do you really want to go back the way things were?"

"No," she admitted, and his shoulders relaxed.

"Good. So why don't we just take it one day at a time?"

"Does that go for sex, too? Can we take it slow?" she asked, blushing again, eyes squeezed shut.

"That is exactly my plan," he said tracing along her cheek with his index finger. "Slow and steady wins the race," he murmured softly.

"Okay," Elynn said, feeling a little calmer. "So now what?"

He flashed her that sexy smile she was barely getting used to.

"Unfortunately, I have a few calls to make right now. Why don't you get acquainted with this," he said, walking to a pair of doors and throwing them wide.

Curious, she followed him into a large walk-in closet full of new designer clothes and shoes. There were three racks lined with a rainbow of fashionable and expensive dresses and skirts with their price tags still attached. One wall was lined with cubbies for shoes, and each one had a pair of fancy shoes; delicate heels and ballet flats in a soft supple leather. There were even several pairs of knee high boots in their own specially made shelf.

"What the hell is this?" she asked perplexed, turning around in a slow circle.

"New clothes in your size. Anything you don't want we can send back."

Elynn's chest tightened in dismay.

"I thought you would enjoy this," he said, his smile fading as he read her reaction.

Feeling guilty, Elynn fidgeted. "I know you did. It's just that I'm not sure how I feel about you dressing me. I mean, the clothes are nice. Lovely. And they obviously cost a fortune. But they make me uncomfortable."

"Why is that? It's a gesture. I thought it was a nice one. You enjoyed the other things I bought you," he said, rubbing his forehead.

"I did. I do. I know you think it's a nice gesture. And it is. But you picking out my clothes feels like...like I'm on my way to being kept by you. I don't want that. I should have said so before about the other clothes. But you didn't give me a chance."

"*Okay,*" he said carefully, making a visible effort to stay calm. "That's definitely not the message I'm trying to send here. You're not a mistress. I just thought you would appreciate some new things. Some feminine things."

Elynn's face fell. "*Feminine things*? I guess I don't have to ask how you feel about the way I usually dress."

Alex threw up his hands. "I just thought you would appreciate some nice things for when we go out."

"Cause otherwise I'll look wrong with you, right? I don't dress like your usual women after all. But it's hard for me to wear something showy. I prefer to blend in," she said, frowning.

She knew she shouldn't feel hurt, but it was hard not to be. Elynn didn't need Alex to tell her that she wasn't up to his usual standards. A Pretty Woman style makeover was not an aspiration of hers. But he seemed to expect that she would wear what he wanted from now on and that she should like it.

Alex sat her back down and crouched in front of her. "Please stop talking about my women. There's just one, and it's you. And I think you would look gorgeous in a paper sack. If you want to wear one, I will go out and get you one. This," he said gesturing behind him to the closet, "well, it's just me being selfish. I think you would look even more amazing in these. But if you don't want them, don't wear them. Honestly, it will make my life easier."

Elynn was still upset, but the liberal use of the word gorgeous did a lot to mollify her. "What do you mean it'll be easier?"

He snorted. "I bought them before the parents had their party. If you wear these things, you'll get a lot of male attention. I learned my lesson after the blue gown. I don't think I can stomach the competition. We'll just send everything back. I can get my security chief to send someone to your place for your own clothes. It's fine."

Alex being Alex, he picked up the bedroom extension to relay those instructions immediately.

Elynn felt terrible. She wanted to be here with him, and she hadn't meant to pick a fight right away. Staying meant she had to be prepared to leave her comfort zone in a big way.

"I didn't mean to sound ungrateful," she said when he hung up. "You obviously went to a lot of trouble. I should keep some of these things. I don't want to look out of place when we go out."

He shook his head. "Forget it. You have plenty of stuff from shopping with Mary that will do nicely," he said, rubbing his temple with the heel of his hand again.

It was something he did when he was frustrated. Stiffening her resolve, she changed her mind. "I think I should look at some of these.

It wouldn't hurt to look amazing around just you, right?" she said with a little smile.

He smiled reassuringly. "You always look perfect to me, but if you want to keep a few of these then that's okay. But you don't have to," he said drawing closer and putting his arm around her.

"I know. But a few dresses couldn't hurt," she said, and was rewarded when he bent down to kiss her deeply, teasing her lips apart to get a quick taste.

But he raised his head too quickly. "I'll leave you to find some way to amuse yourself. Your laptop is not ready yet, but the TV remote control is on the bedside table and the Jacuzzi tub hasn't been broken in yet. I just had it installed," he announced before walking to the doors.

Elynn chased after him. "What do you mean my laptop is not ready yet?"

Her laptop was in the bag the bodyguard had taken off her.

"I'm having it upgraded," he said with a casual wave as he made his way to the stairs. "We're staying in tonight, so don't feel like you have to dress up."

And then he was gone.

Elynn felt a whole stream of swear words bubbling to her lips—words she would never say out loud. She vented them to herself in an undertone while she stomped around the suite. Her usual mild temper was being seriously taxed by Alex's high-handedness. Admittedly, it was hot when they were in intimate situations.

Really hot.

But her laptop didn't need an upgrade. If his people messed it up, she was going to be pissed. *Not that they would, he only hires the best...but still.*

After a few minutes, she calmed down and picked up the extension to ask about her computer. Someone she didn't know told her it would be ready by evening.

At least Mrs. Braden isn't here, Elynn thought in relief. Of course Alex said he didn't want their parents to find out about them yet, which explained why they were here in this new house instead of the one in Oxford. He was probably regretting hiring his old nanny and housekeeper away from Costas now.

She ended up taking a soak in the Jacuzzi tub, letting her burst of temper fade away in the bubbles. Afterwards, she put on a soft dress that matched her eyes.

She wouldn't have admitted it for the world, but trying it on—knowing it was just for Alex—was actually fun. Her days were usually filled with work or thoughts about work and it was nice knowing she had some leisure time. In a week's time, though, she would probably be crawling up the walls with boredom.

What the hell am I thinking? she thought as she lay down on the bed.

In a week, she would definitely be Alex's lover. Maybe even tonight, despite his assurance that they would take it slow. Life was about to become thrilling, in the truest sense of the word. Both exciting and terrifying. Once again, she wished she had someone she could confide in. This was an unprecedented step for her, and given her history, it was in some ways a leap of faith.

Faith in Alex and in herself.

Alex walked into the bedroom with Elynn's laptop in hand. He smiled when he saw her asleep on the bed wearing the green dress. No other woman he knew would have gone to sleep wearing a dress worth more than a thousand pounds. Not that he planned on telling Elynn that.

Setting her computer aside, he decided to live out one of his more tame fantasies. He called downstairs to delay dinner, took off his shirt and shoes, and climbed into bed. He would have taken off his pants as well but he didn't want Elynn to wake up and get freaked out. There was no need to rush now that he had her here with him. For now, he was content to lie next to her, his arms around her.

CHAPTER 10

Elynn woke slowly, registering an odd weight on her stomach. She looked down to see a large heavy arm thrown over her body. Alex's warm chest was pressed against her back. So were his legs and groin, but he was soft in his sleep. His breath puffed into her hair. Slowly she turned her body to face him, but her effort at stealth failed. He made a muffled sound, and then his arms tightened around her.

"Hi," he said, his voice still hoarse from sleep.

"Hi. When did you join me?"

Alex glanced at his watch. "Only about an hour ago. I was going to wake you, but you looked so peaceful. I had dinner held back. Should be ready soon if you want to go down to the dining room."

Feeling a little shy, she nodded and allowed him to guide her downstairs. She laughed aloud when she saw the elaborately set table for two instead of the large formal dining room table the room was meant to have.

"The room dwarfs the table, but I like it," she said, smiling at him.

Alex's chef had taken up residence in the new kitchen and had expressed his joy in his new surroundings by preparing them a mouthwatering meal of duck confit served with polenta and braised potatoes. Dessert was homemade ice cream and French macarons topped off with a sweet white port wine.

Throughout the meal she snuck glances at Alex's handsome face. It was embarrassing to admit, even to herself, but Elynn really wanted a physical relationship. She had always felt the normal desires and urges a woman her age had. But her fear had always held her back. She had little trust in the opposite sex. But this was Alex. Arrogant, uncompromising, beautiful Alex.

His touch was electrifying. She honestly hadn't expected that. All he had to do was put his hands on her, and she melted into a puddle at his feet. It was no wonder that women chased after him. Having Alex as her guide into the sexual realm was going to be amazing. And she didn't want to wait any longer.

Did she have to? She already knew Alex wanted her. And when she thought about it, were the things that had already happened between them so much different? She might not be a virgin anymore, if you went by the strictest definition of the word.

Her decision made, she found herself growing a little tongue-tied in his company, trying to decide how to tell him. She decided to have several glasses of wine to help her relax, but when she poured a third glass he swooped in and removed it from her hand.

"That's enough, baby. You don't need to get drunk. There's no reason to be nervous. We agreed to go slow remember?" he reminded her.

She shifted under his gaze, flushed and warm with arousal from his physical closeness. "Yeah. About that. I changed my mind."

Alex stilled.

"I think we should be together...tonight," she said slowly.

Elynn felt the blush all over her body. She couldn't quite bring herself to look into Alex's eyes, so she focused on his Adam's apple instead.

"Tonight?" he echoed, sounding slightly thunderstruck.

"Yes. And this is not so much liquid courage as muscle relaxer," she said, gesturing to the empty glass.

"You think you need that?" he asked, lifting her chin with a finger to force her eyes up.

"Well, it can't hurt right?" she said with a sheepish smile.

Alex's smile was hesitant. "You don't have to do this right now. We can wait."

"I don't *want* to wait," she breathed before stepping out of her chair and walking toward him.

That was all the encouragement he needed. His arms wrapped around her at the same time his lips came down to cover hers. The heat and arousal rose so fast, it was all she could do to hold on when he picked her up. He carried her upstairs, using the service elevator as a shortcut.

ELYNN FINALLY REGISTERED that they were in the bedroom when Alex kicked the door shut behind them. He slipped off their shoes before laying her on the bed and following her down, covering her body with his. His lips parted hers for a series of deep drugging kisses, his large hands skimming over her body. Even the way his weight felt on top of her was beguiling, his heat warming every part of her. She loved the reverent way he touched her, the way his breathing became heavy and fast, proof that he was as excited as she was.

She barely noticed his hands starting to remove her dress. The only thing she could hear was the drumbeat of desire in her blood. She must have murmured something about being drugged aloud because he raised his head to give a husky laugh before moving the dress down and off her body. His dark eyes flared at the reveal of her simple satin bra and panties in the same color as her dress.

Dazed, she tried to help when he started to open the buttons of his shirt, but her fingers wouldn't work properly. It was faster to let him do it himself. He tore the shirt open, revealing a dark tanned torso straight out of a men's magazine. Fascinated, she moved her hands up to trace the ridges of his sculpted six-pack.

Alex inhaled sharply, and then he stood up and got off the bed. He slowly undid the fastening of his pants and pushed them down, taking his silky looking boxer briefs with them.

Elynn stared at Alex's arousal, her heart hammering in her chest. It was her first look at a naked man in real life. She didn't think anyone else could have looked so beautiful—or more intimidating.

He didn't move, he just stood quietly studying her expression. If he wondered if she'd seen any man naked before, he would have found the answer right there in her wide eyes. Embarrassed, she made an effort to stop looking so stupefied. But she had to be honest with him.

"Alex you're never going to fit," she said quietly, her eyes never straying from his large erection.

He laughed that husky laugh again, but it subsided when her worried eyes met his. Leaning down he took her hands. "I will fit. Your body will adapt. You'll stretch and become accustomed to me. But you're petite, so the first time, maybe the first few times, it will be a little uncomfortable. I will be as gentle as I can," he said, "Okay?"

"Okay," she whispered, feeling a little light-headed.

Pushing her down on the mattress, Alex kissed her parted lips until she relaxed. Without looking, he undid the front clasp of her bra and pushed the satin cups away. He stared down at her exposed breasts in fascination and bent over to take one of her nipples in his mouth. He sucked and licked one and then the other with a gruff little sound of pleasure that joined hers in concert.

His strong hands moved down her body to her panties. He slid them off slowly and moved between her legs, pressing his erection against the entrance to her softness. He shifted, stroking the broad head of his shaft up and down against her moist inner lips and clit, building the ticklish pleasure up until she was desperate—bucking against him in an uncontrolled motion.

"Alex!" she gasped.

He stopped moving until she met his eyes. "Keep watching me," he whispered as he began to slowly press inside her.

Elynn tried to relax but Alex was so large that all she felt was pain as he eased into her. Her face stiffened and a soft whimper escaped her before she could stifle it.

"I'm sorry baby," Alex breathed, his voice strained. He sounded as if he was in more pain than she was and that made her feel better. "Elynn I'm going to push through now."

"Through where?"

It already felt like he was tearing her apart. How much farther could he go? Suddenly, Alex surged forward, his movement accompanied by a blinding flash of pain that made her cry out. Gasping, she grabbed at his forearms braced on either side of her.

"I'm sorry. I'm so sorry." He grimaced, covering her face in kisses. "You were so narrow. I had to open you up. I'm sorry."

Elynn shifted uncomfortably. She felt so strange—so full and stretched.

Alex hissed. "Baby please don't move. Not yet," he said, the cords on his neck standing out while he fought to stay perfectly still above her.

"All right," she whispered back.

The pain was starting to fade. Restless, she wanted to move too, but when she tried, the burning sensation returned. Instead she focused on Alex, moving her hands from his forearms to his face. She traced the hard planes of his cheeks until he turned his head to kiss her open palm. His lips moved to hers, tongue in and out in a parody of what he was about to do.

"Does it feel better?" he asked after few dizzying minutes.

"Yes." It was mostly true.

"Okay," he whispered. "I'm going to start moving."

He shifted his weight, moving slowly in and then withdrawing until just the tip of him rested inside, keeping his eyes trained on her face. She tried to hide it from him, but the movement made the burning sensation worse. He repeated the motion until he was rocking in and out of her slowly. It wasn't unbearable, but it was an effort to stop from grimacing.

"Alex do you think you could finish?" she asked him in a low voice after a few minutes.

"I can stop," he said, starting to pull out.

"No!" she said, grabbing at his shoulders. "I want you to finish. Inside me. Please Alex."

Instinctively she knew that she had to continue. Her hands tightened on him, desperate to make sure he would not pull away. She didn't care if it hurt a little; she needed him to finish, to make this moment complete.

"I don't want to keep hurting you," he said.

"I don't care. I want this to be special for both of us. I need you to finish what we started. Please."

Alex took a deep breath and pushed back inside her. He tried to be gentle, but she urged him on with her hands and her lips until he was thrusting faster, moving in and out of her with harsh ragged breaths. The more he moved, the less it hurt, but it wasn't exactly comfortable. A minute later, his hands fisted in her hair, and he gave a hoarse groan.

Elynn felt a warm wetness as his cock jerked inside her, touching a spot that gave her a twinge of pleasure. She held onto him, pulling him down over her until he collapsed on her body, softening inside her. One of his hands was still gripping her waist possessively as he shifted so more of his weight rested on his side, off of her.

Alex had never looked so vulnerable. She felt so close to him. Raising a hand, she brushed the hair off his forehead. Her heart gave a little squeeze as a worrying thought came into her head. It was so easy to see why women fell in love with the men they were having sex with. She would be no exception. Elynn was half in love with him already. There was nothing she could do about it.

Could she hope for a permanent place in the life of Alexandros the Great?

Eventually, Alex stirred. With a kiss he eased completely to the side. Elynn flinched a little as he withdrew out of her body, his arms reaching out to wrap around her and draw her close to him. This is spooning, she thought with drowsy pleasure, pushing her worries aside.

"Are you okay?" he asked, his lips in her hair.

"Yes. I feel good."

"Baby, you don't have to lie. I know I hurt you. I feel terrible, more so because it was just incredible for me."

Elynn grinned, proud of herself. She hadn't imagined he would feel that way the first time when she was so new at this.

"I'm fine. It did hurt. I didn't think it would be that bad, but you're just ... big. But it did get better. I felt all tingly at the end."

He laughed. "That's good. I wish I could have lasted longer to build on that, but it was too much for me," he confessed with a grin before sobering. "I'm sorry I hurt you. But I have a confession—I love knowing that I'm your first. I'm going to be reliving that moment, when I opened you up and made you mine, over and over again," he whispered, trailing a possessive hand over her chest. He stopped and his mouth quirked. "Does that make me a pervert?"

"Yes," she laughed. "I guess I don't have to ask if I'm your first virgin."

"First and last."

"Damn straight," she said, giving him a hard spank.

He grabbed her hand and turned until he was on top of her again. "Despite your obvious interest in S&M, you're still a novice so I'm going to go easy on you."

Elynn's smile faltered. "Alex, I'm sorry. I don't think I can do it again."

"I know," he said, an understanding light in his eyes. "You might be sore for a little while but don't worry. I'm going to make you forget you felt even a second of pain," he assured her confidently as he moved down her body to press his lips to her aching flesh.

CHAPTER 11

Elynn woke to bright sunlight and an empty bed. Confused, she sat up and looked around. The bathroom door was open, but she couldn't hear Alex moving around inside. She hopped out of bed and started hunting for a robe. Eventually, she finally found a short silk wrap. It was very short.

I'm going to have to speak to that man about his refusal to see me appropriately dressed. You would think he would mind if the staff saw me like this, she thought, looking down at her barely covered thighs.

The door opened and Alex swept in with a full tray in hand. "It won't be breakfast in bed if you don't get back into bed," he said, shaking his head at her.

Elynn smiled despite the urge to berate him for his choice in robes. He looked amazing, but she was disappointed to see he was already dressed in beige chinos and a black shirt. She hopped back into bed and he followed, putting the tray across her lap and adding a few pillows so she could sit upright.

"I made this myself," he said proudly, removing lids to reveal scrambled eggs on one plate and cinnamon raisin English muffins with butter on another. "Scrambled eggs that are runny with a little salt and a lot of pepper," he announced with a flourish as he kissed her forehead. "Lucky for me you prefer sloppy ruined eggs, or I might not have managed," he added as he took one of the four muffins.

She grinned at him, pleased that he remembered that she liked her eggs undercooked. The embarrassment she'd felt upon waking melted away as he chatted about his upcoming business meetings and travel plans. Evidently, he intended to take her everywhere with him.

"The next few weeks will include trips to New York, Rome, and Shanghai," he said.

"And you want me to come?" she asked, confused. "Won't you be too busy with work?"

"I'll be occupied during the day, but we'll have the nights," he said suggestively before he bit into the muffin with mock aggression.

Elynn burst out laughing. She completely forgot about her reasonable plan of maintaining separate residences while they got to know each other in their new state of intimacy. She wanted to stay with him.

He took the empty breakfast tray when she was done. "How do you feel?" he asked, studying her intently.

"Good," she said a little awkwardly.

"Not sore?"

She did feel something, but it wasn't soreness exactly. Just an awareness that she was different, that he had been inside of her. But she wanted him again. Her body was growing warm and moist at the sight of him. She shook her head and Alex practically ripped his shirt and pants off. Giggling, she welcomed him with open arms as he climbed over her with flattering haste.

"You're sure?" he asked, his forehead creased.

"Yes," she whispered back.

He took hold of the belt of the robe and tugged on it so hard one of the belt loops ripped.

"Sorry," he said before pushing the robe off her body. "Little carried away."

He didn't sound all that sorry. But she decided now was not the time to make an issue out of it...

Alex groaned aloud when he felt how wet Elynn was. She was so hot and ready for him. *Thank god.* Hungry for more, he nudged her legs open wider, moving one hand next to her on the bed to brace himself. With the other, he took his shaft in hand and guided himself to her small entrance. Holding his breath he pushed inside her, trying to be as gentle as possible. Elynn's eyes were wide as he moved forward, digging her fingers into his shoulders as he adjusted, moving back out until she was more comfortable.

He made a soothing sound in his throat. "Is that better?" he asked.

"Yes, don't stop."

"So glad you said that," he said out of breath before he bent and took her lips, sucking her tongue inside his mouth.

Moving slowly at first, he began to pump in shallow strokes. She was so tight around him, gripping him like a velvet vise. It was exquisite, and from the sounds she was making, she was definitely starting to enjoy herself. Struggling to maintain a gentle rhythm, he kept going, testing and exploring as he studied her face to see what she wanted.

It wasn't difficult to figure out. Elynn let him know exactly what she found most pleasurable. His girl was surprisingly vocal.

"Alex, oh God," she cried out in between delicious little moans that were building up in crescendo.

"That's it, baby, come for me," he murmured as he urged her to wrap her legs around him.

Instinctively catching his rhythm, she started to meet his body, rocking with him as he strained against her. He stroked in and out of her, restraining the urge to pound harder until he felt her whole body tighten around him.

He felt like a superhero when Elynn let out a surprised and rather loud cry of pleasure. Her pussy throbbed, clamping down on him. Losing control, he rocked in and out of her forcefully until the tingling pressure at the base of his skull signaled his orgasm. The next moment, it burned through him, utterly divorcing him from reason and reality.

When awareness returned, he shifted down enough to withdraw, conscious that he might be crushing Elynn. She had recovered, too, suggesting he'd been lost in that mind blown state for longer than he'd realized. His head was resting between her breasts and her hands were stroking his hair, running her fingers through it. Her legs were wrapped around his back now.

Should I tell her I love her? Or was it too soon?

He'd never felt so complete and happy. And it wasn't just because he was having the best sex of his life with her. That part was only going to get better the more experience Elynn gained. In fact, at this rate, she was probably going to kill him.

"That was amazing *agape mou*," he murmured, eyes closed, utterly content.

"For me too. I mean...wow," she said in a wondering tone.

He looked up and gave her a smile of deep male satisfaction. "I love feeling you come around me," he murmured, moving a hand to trace her pouting nipples. "It was incredible; it just pushed me over the edge. I hope I didn't hurt you there at the end. I sort of lost control."

Elynn took a deep breath and said shyly, "No, I was fine. Stunned, but fine. Is it always like that?"

"As good or even better. It's how I wanted last night to go," he said, taking her fingers so he could nibble and suck on them.

"You made last night amazing, too, don't worry." She gasped as he ran his tongue over her fingertip before moving his attention to her chest.

Alex was too busy kissing and sucking on Elynn's glorious breasts to answer, but that was good to hear. He'd worked hard to please her with his mouth and hands. He just hoped it was enough to wipe away any memory of the pain that had come with losing her virginity. *Jesus.* Just thinking about it made him grow hard against her thigh. His exploring fingers found her pussy lips again and slipped inside, but she flinched, and he withdrew them.

"Umm. Going to have to wait," he said, as he lifted off her reluctantly.

"No, I don't want to!" Elynn said, grabbing at his retreating body.

Gratified, he smoothed a hand over her hair. "I know baby, I want you again, too. But we should probably pace ourselves, at least till you've recovered," he said before scooping her into his arms and carrying her to the bathroom. "I think a shower would be very helpful right now."

He kissed the top of her head before proceeding to show her how hot a cold, or room-temperature, shower could be.

Inside the stall, Alex ran reverent hands over Elynn. Her form was slim and petite, but it curved in all the right places. And those perfect breasts—they were enough to bring a grown man to tears. Impulsively, he lifted her high against the wall of the shower and until he was level with them. He grazed her nipples with his teeth and, unable to restrain himself, he bit the fleshy underside of her right breast hard enough to leave a faint mark.

Moaning, Elynn grabbed at him, pulling him closer until her legs closed around him. Her hands wound around his neck. Working a hand between them, he stroked her clit, rubbing and pinching lightly while the other cupped her bottom, holding her up against the wall. Moving the hand on her bottom slightly he was able to use his index finger to push directly against her rosette. He rubbed it, probing slightly while his other hand worked Elynn's clit faster under the stream of rushing water. Startled, her eyes opened wide, but soon the combined assault drove her over the edge, and she came, breaking apart in his arms.

"I love watching you come," he whispered, his head against hers as Elynn struggled to catch her breath.

He held her pressed against the wall until she recovered. Finally, she looked up at him with a wicked glint in her eye. "Turnabout is fair play," she said, taking the soap and sponge from the rack to their side, motioning for him to put her down on her feet.

Amused by her playfulness, Alex kept his hands to himself as

Elynn ran the soapy sponge over him. She was humming a nonsensical tune, washing his entire body carefully, paying special attention to his shaft and balls. Handling him as if he was made of porcelain, her ministrations got him hard, but weren't enough to make him come without encouragement.

Leaning against the wall of the shower stall, he whispered instructions. "Hold me tighter, yes, just like that," he said, hissing slightly when she began running her soapy hands over him with just the right amount of friction and speed. "Now squeeze my balls a little."

Elynn was a fast learner. Cupping his balls, she made a circle with her thumb and forefinger, squeezing and pumping him with both hands. He tried to hold on, but the sight of her exactly where he'd wanted her for so many years was too much.

"*Shit, shit, shit,*" he groaned as he pumped his warm seed into her hands while he leaned against the wall for support. Sliding down it, he sat on the floor, the water pouring over him until his vision cleared.

"Are you okay?" Elynn was leaning over him with a concerned expression.

"Oh, hell yeah," he said with a tired grin. "I just got to live out one of my sexual fantasies."

Relieved, Elynn chuckled. He stayed put a few minutes longer, until he felt strong enough to get up. "You're going to be the death of me," he said, holding her to him as he turned off the water.

Alex led her out of the shower stall and grabbed a towel for each of them. He threw one around him before wrapping the other around Elynn. Tired, but satisfied, he ran the towel over her smooth skin, drying her as if he were a devoted servant. He was about to start on himself when he felt her stiffen, then shudder slightly.

"Baby what's wrong?"

Elynn didn't answer him. She was staring at herself in the mirror. Her reflections showed signs of his ravishment. Her lips were swollen and there were red marks on her throat and breast from his stubble and little bites. "I'm sorry. Your skin is sensitive. I'll be more careful next time," he said apologetically.

Her eyes closed. Dropping the towel, he put his hands on her shoulders and was stunned when she pushed him away. Breathing loudly, Elynn walked blindly away from him, accidentally hitting the counter hard with her hip. Crying out, she crumpled to the floor.

"Elynn!" he bent down, trying to hold her, but she waved him away. Alarmed, he grabbed her flailing hand. "Elynn, baby, it's just me. It's Alex," he said reassuringly.

"I'm okay. It's okay," she mumbled, shaking all over.

Scared out of his mind, Alex hovered over her. He didn't know what to do. Elynn was sitting on the floor rocking back and forth, but she was finally making eye contact, and she kept repeating that everything was okay—when things couldn't have been worse.

"Baby, stay right here. I'm going to call the doctor," he said, starting to get up so he could go get his phone. Elynn grabbed him, holding onto his leg.

"No, no doctors. I'm sorry," she said, her amazing green-gray eyes filling with tears.

Alex shook his head. "You need to talk to someone. This is all my fault. I pushed you too far too fast," he said reproachfully as he crouched back over her.

"No, it wasn't too far. I'm being stupid. I don't know why I freaked out like that. I'm so happy with you," she said, throwing her arms around his neck and clinging to him tightly.

Alex didn't say a word to contradict her, but he knew he'd done something unforgivable. Elynn looked so lost and afraid. He'd pushed her into a sexual relationship before she was ready.

You even bit her, you piece of shit. Stiffening, he remembered that picture of Elynn in the hospital Costas had shown him so long ago, the one that showed a bite mark on her shoulder. He'd just meant it playfully, and the mark he'd made was almost gone already, but the fact he'd even had the impulse proved what a fucking idiot he was.

Picking Elynn up off the floor, he wrapped the towel around her more securely before kicking open the door to the bedroom. His heart ached at the way she was holding on to him, as though trying to absolve him of any guilt. He moved to the bed, wrapping himself around her and pulling the covers over her shivering body.

"It's not your fault. Don't ever say that again," she whispered hoarsely.

"It was too soon."

"No, it wasn't. I just had a stupid panic attack. I used to get them all the time."

Yeah, used to. But she hadn't had one in years. Even though Alex knew he should get his fucking hands off her, he squeezed Elynn tighter. She turned her face into his neck and tried to cover him with her slim body, slipping one smooth leg between both of his.

"No doctor," she whispered.

"Okay. For now..." he said quietly, holding her until she fell asleep.

IT WAS afternoon when Elynn awoke. Groggily, she turned in bed, surprised to see Alex sitting in a chair by the bed, fully dressed in a silver-grey suit.

"Where are you going?" she asked.

He wasn't dressed for a day at home.

"I'm moving up the trip to my office in Greece," he said before hesitating. "And I think you should stay here."

Elynn sat up, hurt radiating through her. "What the *hell?*"

He flinched but continued gently. "I think you should stay and see Dr. Greene today."

Dr. Greene. She hadn't seen her former London therapist since she started at Oxford. She'd found someone local to talk to. She'd visited Dr. Andre regularly until last year when she'd been too busy to keep regular appointments.

With a pang, she realized she hadn't even known that Alex knew her therapist's name. Which meant he knew exactly why she was seeing a therapist.

Well, you knew that was the case already... But she'd been hoping they wouldn't ever have to talk about it.

Suck it up, she told herself. *He has a right, he needs to understand.*

"You know everything, don't you?" she asked, looking at him miserably.

"I know how brave you are. I know how proud I am of you," he said evasively.

She shook her head and smiled resignedly. "I know Costas told you...about Stephen."

It was the first time she'd said his name aloud in years. Her counseling sessions had long since gone past the attack to focus on her life and schoolwork. But her continuing issues with men were tied to Stephen, so she was still dealing with him, albeit indirectly.

"I forced it out of him," Alex admitted eventually. "I'm sorry if you aren't comfortable with that. But I wouldn't let Dad keep anything about you from me," he said before running a hand over his face. "Hell, I don't know why I just admitted that. I'm just digging the hole deeper. Look, I called Dr. Greene while you were asleep, and I got an emergency appointment for today. If you don't want to see her I can get your Oxford therapist up here tonight or tomorrow on the helicopter."

He bent down to kiss her forehead, and when she didn't say anything, he continued. "I'm going to wrap things up in the Greek office as soon as I can instead of making it an extended trip like we planned. I'll be back in three days. I rehired Andrea, by the way. I know she was your favorite bodyguard. She'll go with you to the doctors and anywhere else you want to go. Okay?"

For a second, he hovered, but he didn't wait for a reply. She watched him leave without saying a word.

The rest of the day passed by in a self-recriminating haze. *Why the hell did I lose my shit that way?* It had been years since she'd had a panic attack. And now she'd had one in front of Alex at the worst possible time. Their physical relationship was just starting, and she wanted it to keep going.

She couldn't help being hurt that Alex's first reaction was to leave the country, but she mostly blamed herself for freaking out in the first place. Irrationally, she wasn't angry with him for calling her doctor. Though he should have left the decision to her, she didn't resent his action. Alex had always watched out for her. In fact, that knowledge was the only thing that was comforting her in the face of his sudden abandonment.

CHAPTER 12

Dr. Greene was a friendly middle-aged woman with a distinctly maternal air. Her appearance was a total deception, however, as the woman had more degrees than anyone else Elynn knew. She also had a tendency to be blunt, but Elynn liked her for it.

The doctor had been very concerned to hear from her again so suddenly for the first time in years. "Tell me what's bothering you," she said, a tiny frown puckering her forehead.

Elynn blushed and stared down at her hands before speaking. She cleared her throat. "I've started a relationship recently. A sexual one. It's my first and it's...a little overwhelming."

The doctor nodded. "It's perfectly normal to have those feelings even under the best of circumstances. But with your history, you are bound to have even more conflicted emotions. Is your partner aware of your issues?"

"Yes. He made it his business to know," she said with a wry smile.

Dr. Greene was puzzled. "What does that mean?"

"The relationship. It's with my...my stepbrother, Alex. I think he's known about my history for a long time."

The usually unflappable doctor betrayed her shock. She froze, her mouth a little open. It wasn't much, but it was the biggest reaction Elynn had ever gotten from her. She gave the doctor a wry smile and the woman snapped her mouth shut, her professionalism returning quickly.

Dr. Greene cleared her throat. "Yes, you told me as much. Can I assume Alex is the one who initiated this relationship?" she asked.

The doctor knew enough about Alex's reputation from their past sessions to know what a dominant and forceful personality he was. Even Alex's own father deferred to him in most situations.

"Yes," Elynn confirmed, smile still on her face.

"Judging from that smile, I'm going to assume you're happy."

"You would assume right," Elynn nodded.

"But this is Alex Hanas you're talking about. He's a very powerful man, a bit of a bulldozer, if I can quote you and your impressions of him from our past sessions. Are his aggressive tendencies leading to these feelings of being overwhelmed?"

She struggled to find the right words. "Yes and no. I mean Alex is a force of nature, but over the years, I've gotten used to handling him pretty well. We've always been on good terms. I consider him my best friend now. But now we're involved—very involved. There have been some bumps in the road, but my issue, why I'm here, isn't really because of Alex. It's because of me with Alex."

She explained, a little ineptly at first, about the aftermath of their first night together and how she had reacted when she saw herself in the mirror. Understanding the situation quickly, the doctor analyzed her reaction.

"I find it very telling that you weren't looking at Alexandros, but at yourself when your panic attack hit. In fact, you turned your back on him. You didn't identify him as a threat. It was the sight of yourself that triggered the panic attack," the doctor said.

Elynn shrugged. "I trust Alex. I always have."

"But that doesn't mean you're not going to have misgivings about being in a sexual relationship with him. At first anyway," the doctor added.

They continued to speak about trust and inevitably about how

Elynn felt about being involved with an older and extremely powerful man. The conversation about power stuck with her long after the session was over.

She returned to the London house in a pensive mood. Her spirits lifted slightly when she walked into the living room. A huge bouquet of blood-red roses was sitting on the coffee table. Smiling she walked up to admire the flowers.

Alex had always given her white roses because he knew they were her favorite, but red were for passion weren't they? Maybe the change was commemorating their new state as lovers. Lifting the card tucked into the bouquet, she read his message.

Thinking of you.

A little generic for Alex, but he probably didn't know what to say. Elynn sighed and sat down on the couch. The doctor had been right about so many things. Alex was *still* a bulldozer, and unless she took a stand early, he was going to run roughshod over her if they continued their relationship. Like the way he had decided that it was in her best interest to leave her behind and insisted she see her former therapist.

True, the session with Dr. Greene had been helpful. Elynn still felt as if things were unresolved, but that was typical after a therapy session. At least she'd finally been able to confide in someone, and conveniently in this case, it was someone bound by law to keep the conversation confidential. The last thing she needed was for gossip to reach the tabloids, or heaven forbid, their parents.

The session with the doctor had also given her perspective. She was now starting to think beyond the immediate future. Despite the 'bathroom incident', as she was now referring to it, Elynn didn't think Alex was going to back away. Not now. If he tried, she was going to take a bat to his kneecaps. So she had better decide what she wanted out of their relationship.

Sex. Lots of it, she admitted to herself. Something told her Alex wasn't going to have a problem with that. Getting comfortable with the idea, she mulled it over. This might be her one chance to live out her fantasies. There were lots of things she had secretly always wanted to do once she was finally involved with a man. In her vivid imagination, she had an adventurous relationship with a nameless, faceless lover. Now her lover's image was very solidly Alex.

A scientist to the core, Elynn decided it was time to do a little research. She looked over the eBook collection on her laptop as well as a number of websites she would never admit to visiting later. By mid-afternoon, she had formulated a plan—a series of experiments she was going to need all of her courage to carry out.

She buzzed Andrea, the female bodyguard she had been so happy to see again, and asked her for a favor.

ELYNN HAD NEVER VISITED the Greek office of Hanas industries in Athens before. It was more utilitarian than their posh London offices, at least on the exterior. Most of the buildings in town were nondescript white boxes that didn't stand many stories high, but collectively they formed a ring of white that circled the ancient historic site of the Acropolis like sea foam. Individually, Elynn didn't find them attractive from an architectural standpoint, and the Hanas building was no exception.

The interior of the building, however, was a completely different story. It was an Art Deco dream. She could see Costas' touch in the clean lines of the reception area. He was nostalgic for the 1920's and had several important pieces of art and artifacts from the period.

Smiling, Elynn spun around to take it all in. The reception area resembled the outside of the Chrysler building. The green panels on the walls curved in graceful arches that gleamed with gold trim under the overhead lights, and the shining black marble floor was regularly interrupted with a star design made from other geometrical shapes.

Walking through the foyer to the reception desk, she wondered what the other offices of Hanas Industries around the globe looked like. The Indonesian office must be pretty spectacular too.

She approached the blonde receptionist behind a wide curving glass desk. "Hello, I'm here to see Alex Hanas please," she said.

The receptionist looked her up and down in a disparaging once over. "I'm sorry, but Mr. Hanas is extremely busy. You need to make an appointment months in advance," she said in a nasal tone with a mild Greek accent.

"Just tell him Elynn is here," she said.

"I don't think—" the woman began.

"Just tell him I'm here," she repeated firmly, standing up straight with as much bravado as she could muster.

It wasn't the first time she had been given the runaround by Alex's staff. People not familiar with her usually took one look at her unprepossessing clothes and they tried to send her packing. Elynn had learned long ago that she had to be firm and stand her ground until they gave way. The alternative was for Alex to go off on them. He had chewed out more than one individual for being rude to her.

The receptionist grudgingly put the call through and another attractive woman, a brunette this time, came up to join her behind the desk. She too examined Elynn critically. Uncomfortable, she looked away, pretending to examine the decor some more.

She had hoped that the fine green summer dress and expensive coat she'd chosen from Alex's closet of gifts would be enough to avoid getting the stink eye. But she wasn't blonde, she didn't have big boobs or endless legs, and she was wearing glasses. Not for fashion, but to actually see. Obviously someone like her could be nothing to Alexandros Hanas.

"I'm sorry, but Mr. Hanas is in a meeting and can't be disturbed," the receptionist said in a smug tone.

She turned to her colleague, and the two began whispering conspiratorially in Greek, obviously amused with her naiveté.

Elynn sighed and whipped out her smartphone. "Fine. I'll text him, but you're ruining my surprise," she said with a gesture at the high-end shopping bag she held.

She sent her text, and within two minutes, Alex was striding out of the elevator, to the jaw-dropped amazement and distress of the two women behind the desk. He scooped Elynn up in a bear hug before ushering her into the elevator.

"I would kiss you, but there are cameras, and my father would be sure to hear of it immediately," Alex murmured in her ear, pulling her close with strong hands on her waist. "The staff here in Greece is completely loyal to him."

"He might hear of it anyway given where your hands are," Elynn said cheerfully.

She had been afraid that Alex would be worried or reserved given the way he had left. His warm welcome was a huge relief to her.

"Are you going to tell me why you're here?" he asked and then didn't bother to wait for an answer as he guided her to his office with a hand on the small of her back.

Various heads turned to watch their progress. A whole crowd of people watched with surprise from the double doors of an imposing conference room on the left. *Uh oh.* Alex had obviously been in the middle of an important meeting. At least the receptionist hadn't lied about that.

He closed the door to his office, and she had a quick impression of dark leather furniture and heavy wood accents before she was pressed against the door and passionately kissed. Heat flooded her body as Alex pulled her up against him, suspending her in the air as he guided her legs to wrap around him. His hands were lifting her skirt and tugging at her panties before he froze and turned his head away.

He coughed and after a few deep breaths said, "I'm sorry about that. I shouldn't have grabbed you. I forgot—I was just so happy to see you."

He put her down and backed away rubbing his temple with the palm of his hand. Elynn stepped forward to grab his hand. "I'm not sorry. That's the kind of welcome I was hoping for," she said with a big smile.

"Why didn't you wait for me in London? I was going to fly back tomorrow," he said with a little shake of his head as he leaned on the surface of his desk.

"I didn't want to wait. I saw Dr. Greene, and we had a good talk."

"What did she say?" he asked, shifting his weight apprehensively.

"Well...I told her about us. I kind of had to," she admitted with a little shrug of discomfort.

"Of course you did. What did she say?" Alex sounded worried.

"Lots of things. Our chat was helpful."

She took the package out with hands that weren't completely steady and went to sit on a long leather couch on the left. She looked up to find him studying her.

"What is that? What did the doctor say, exactly?"

Stroking the plain brown wrapping of the big box abstractedly, she chose her words with care. "She suggested that the 'bathroom episode' might have been a symptom of my own insecurities. I didn't really need her to tell me that. But she made me think about things in more detail."

"So she doesn't blame me for making you do stuff you're not ready for yet?" he asked softly, looking torn.

"No, and neither do I," Elynn assured him. "I am ready. I may even be overdue," she said with a laugh, stroking the box again with restless fingers. "It's just..."

"Just what?"

"It's all happened so fast. Like zero to sixty. Making up for lost time. But that's what I want. To keep moving forward," she said, searching his eyes for his reaction.

He looked relieved, but then his expression closed down, making his face forbidding and intimidating.

"You can't be sure what you want. I've pressured you into this, and now you're afraid to tell me you want me to back off," he said as he pushed away from the desk and rubbed his temple again as he paced in front of his desk.

"Alex, come sit with me. I need to show you something." She tapped the box with both hands.

Reluctantly, he came over and sat next to her with a furrowed brow. "Did you buy me a present?"

"I bought us something. Or some *things*. I...um...well, I've been thinking a lot about us, and what I want us to be. And I think some of these would be useful."

Elynn was beet red by the end of her explanation. Feeling giddy, she pushed the box into his hands and took a deep breath.

He tore the box open and his eyes flew up to meet hers in complete shock.

Oh God. I've miscalculated, she thought with a silent groan. Alex reached into the box and with a completely bewildered expression picked up a leather restraint. His wide eyes and dumbfounded expression would have been comical under other circumstances.

"I've offended you. I'm so sorry," she said, feeling a wild impulse to run.

She grabbed the leather strap from his hand and shoved it into the box. Slamming down the lid, she slid away from him on the couch. His large hands stopped her progress.

Alex pulled her back towards him, holding her tight against his body. "What possessed you to get *those* kinds of things for us?" he asked. She buried her hot face in his shoulder. "Elynn?" he asked, giving her a little shake.

She took a deep breath, grabbing a fistful of his shirt in her hand. "I thought it might be a good idea to do some experiments."

"What kind of experiments do you need those for?"

She let go of his shirt and met his eyes. He still looked surprised, but there was also expectation there.

"I trust you," she said. "More than anyone else in the world, but I thought maybe it would be a good idea if I could prove that. To reinforce that in my head in a more obvious way." She shrugged helplessly. "I'm not explaining things right."

"No, I think I understand. So you think that using those would be effective?" he asked, gesturing to the box.

Elynn blushed and looked away. "Yes. And you know, kind of exciting."

He didn't say anything for so long that she finally risked a quick glance at his face. His expression hadn't changed much, but he was a little flushed. Anxious, she tried to stand up, but he restrained her. Closing his mouth, he gave himself a little shake before breaking into a large and deeply sexy grin.

"See I did some research on the kinds of things I thought I might want to try from stories I've read," Elynn said quickly, her words running together. "Things I didn't think I could ever do with anyone until now."

Alex leaned back on the couch with a little thump, taking her with him. His hand moved to her hair as she waited for him to respond. He didn't, but he was still smiling and shaking his head. The smile was comforting, but the headshake was not.

"I thought maybe given how you are, you might enjoy this stuff. You've probably done this before," she said in a little whisper, sudden anxiety twisting her stomach.

He was such an aggressive alpha male. He had probably played lots of dominance and submission games with those models and actresses.

"No," he said, immediately contradicting her. "No, I haven't, but now I'm wondering why the thought never occurred to me. Jesus," he said, shifting uncomfortably. "What do you mean how I am?"

She shrugged, "You're so strong. Dominant. It just seemed to fit that you might be interested in that sort of thing..."

He laughed, a sound of wonder and surprise. "I hadn't ever thought about it before. I don't think I would have with anyone else. But baby, I think you're too innocent for what you're proposing."

Elynn's stomach gave a short sharp drop. "Is that what you like about me?" she asked in a little whisper. "My inexperience?"

"No!" He scowled. "I mean, yes. Sort of. I do enjoy that everything is new for you," he said, squeezing her a little too hard. "Honestly, if there had been anyone else in your life, a lover, well let's just say I would have made life very difficult for him. I'm a jealous bastard, I admit it freely. But I would never let something like your virginity get between us. Whether or not I'm the first or the hundredth, nothing would keep me from wanting you."

"Hundredth?" she repeated with distaste.

She didn't want another lover now. She probably never would. Even the thought of someone else touching her made her skin crawl.

"Well, not the hundredth. Seeing you with someone else would have been impossible. Your poor friend Eric came pretty close to getting his clock cleaned. But that's just jealousy. It had nothing to do with a need to...keep you pure. Just to keep you as mine. Even before you actually were mine."

Mulling over that too fine distinction, Elynn frowned. She was about to ask him what he meant about Eric, when Alex suddenly cursed in Greek and looked at his watch. "I was supposed to be back in that conference room five minutes ago!"

He took the box lying at her feet and slipped it back into the shopping bag. He pecked her on the cheek and swiftly shifted, putting on his forbidding business face while straightening his coat and shirt as he went to the door.

It was a little unsettling, the way he could slip on that expressionless mask.

"I'll send Magda, the office manager, in with some coffee," he said. "I'll try to make this quick. Did you bring a bag with you?"

"My suitcase is in the car. The driver is waiting for me. Should I head to the house here?"

Costas kept a sumptuous house in the hills. She'd stayed there once before with Mary, but not with Alex. He had been away on business and hadn't been able to stop by during that trip.

"No. I have a different idea. Wait for me here," he ordered as he left.

Elynn rolled her eyes as the door closed behind him. She needed to talk to him about the tone he took with her, but how could she explain to him that she wanted him to dominate her in bed but not outside of it?

Well, I should probably start by telling him that.

A few minutes later, there was a knock at the door. It was opened by an attractive woman in her late forties. She smiled politely and set down a silver coffee service.

"I am Magda. Welcome Elynn," she said, setting down the tray on the desk. "It is so nice to finally meet you. Both Costas and Alexandros keep a photo of you on their desks," she said, gesturing at a frame behind the tray with a polite nod.

Smiling back, Elynn stood to take a look. It was the same photo of her and Alex that she kept on her bedside table. One of the staff had taken it on her birthday when Costas and Mary were not around. Looking at it now, she wondered.

In the photo, Alex was gazing down at her with an unguarded expression while she grinned directly at the camera. She had seen that look on his face recently. When he got that look now, it meant he was getting ready to take her to bed. But maybe she was misinterpreting him if that was how he had looked at her so long ago. It had always been her favorite picture of him, though, despite the fact he was partly in profile and she had many others.

Dismissing the thought, she focused on Magda. The woman was talking about Costas and Mary warmly. Her mother had hosted several business functions here in Greece, events Magda had helped her organize. Elynn hadn't been around for any of those parties. She didn't know any of the staff based in these offices.

Assuming she was here as a tourist, Magda made a few friendly suggestions for outings. They continued to make small talk while Elynn sipped the delicious coffee. It was lightly flavored with green cardamom, just the way both Alex and Costas took it.

After a few minutes, Magda excused herself, but before she left, she leaned in with a conspiratorial air. "Can I assume that you and the boss are planning on a special surprise gift for your parents?" she asked with a nod to the box on the floor.

"Um, not exactly a gift per se...but we are definitely planning on surprising them," Elynn said noncommittally, praying that the woman wouldn't ask to see what was in the box.

But Magda just smiled before taking her leave, letting Elynn finish her coffee alone. Half an hour after Alex had left, he came back in, spitting orders at a few harried assistants who entered at his heels. They were followed by a few members of the local staff who wanted to introduce themselves.

Embarrassed, Elynn flushed. Everyone was staring, looking at her approvingly and telling her what a wonderful thing it was that they were planning to give their parents a surprise gift. No one was presumptuous enough to ask what the gift was, but Elynn still broke out into a cold sweat. Coughing slightly, she snuck several nervous glances at the box at her feet.

"Don't worry," a young man assured her comfortingly as he sat next to her on the couch. "We won't spill the beans about your visit or your surprise to Costas."

"Good," Alex said in a cold tone, after he dismissed his assistants. "Why don't you start on those figures. I want them on my desk by tomorrow morning, Damon," he said briskly.

"Oh, err...of course," Damon said, springing back up to attention. "I will work on them tonight," he said nervously. "All night," he added as he rushed out the door, presumably to escape before he was given more work.

She frowned at Damon's retreating body, before swinging back to look at Alex. He was still busy, continuing to fire off directions at the remaining employees. After a few minutes, they scattered, rushing off to carry out his orders like good little soldiers.

Finally, they were all alone. "Come, we need to catch the helicopter in half an hour," he said, gesturing to the door. Elynn grabbed the bag. "I had your suitcase transferred to my car and sent the driver off with a big tip," he added as he led the way out of his office.

The executive floor was busy, even this late in the day. Despite that, the staff wasn't shy about loitering to take a look at her. One or two might have wondered just how brotherly Alex's affection for her was from the possessive hold he kept on her as he guided her to the elevator. These observant souls wisely averted their gaze when the two of them passed.

When they reached the ground floor, the two women at reception stumbled over each other to open the doors and wish them a good evening. Elynn refrained from smiling cynically, focusing on Alex instead. He was playing the arrogant captain of industry to the hilt, but his remote manner lasted only as long as they were out in public. Once the door to the limousine closed, he dropped his reserve and pulled her towards him with hard, hungry arms.

Grateful that the privacy partition was already up, Elynn crawled onto his lap, trying to press herself as close as possible to him. When he withdrew to draw in more air, she decided to ask him about a suspicion she'd had upstairs.

"Alex. Were you jealous when you saw me talking to Damon?" she asked.

"Why do you think that?" he asked, his expression shutting down.

"You went all cold. Kind of like now," she added a little sarcastically before shaking her head. "How could you possibly feel threatened?"

"I wasn't *threatened,*" he said. "But he was standing too close to you. Damon's the local office Lothario...and he's asked about you before. I've found him looking at your picture on Costas' desk more than once. He probably thinks marriage to you would be a good career move," Alex said with a small sneer while stroking her cheek.

Elynn laughed. She hadn't gotten that vibe from Damon at all, but she didn't make it a habit of examining men too closely. And that was clearly a mistake, she thought when Alex squeezed her arms a little tighter.

"That laugh better not indicate you were flattered by that little weasel," he said from behind gritted teeth.

She took his face in her hands and kissed him. "I'm not flattered by his attention. I'm flattered by your jealousy."

"Don't make a habit of poking the bear, Elynn," he said before pulling her in for a kiss with a hand on the back of her head.

Pulling away she laughed, again. "I really don't think I have to poke it to get it riled up."

Alex relaxed. "That's probably true," he admitted before sighing. "It's just that Damon is a lot closer in age to you than I am. So forgive an insecure old man."

"Alex, you're thirty-one."

"That's ten years older than you," he scowled before changing the subject. "Baby, I'm pleased that you couldn't wait another day to see me, but I'm not happy you came without Andrea. Where is she?"

"Home," Elynn said pointedly. "I'm perfectly capable of getting on a plane by myself. And it's nine years and eight months."

He scoffed. "That's close enough to ten. And I know you're more than capable," he said eventually. "But I would feel a whole lot better if you didn't travel alone. Andrea gets a handsome salary to watch out for you. Let her do her job. Humor your old man, okay?"

Elynn sighed. "Next time. And Andrea did put me on the plane. She also arranged for the driver who picked me up. He was thoroughly vetted and approved, and I had a picture of him in advance. Satisfied?"

"Not entirely, but I won't dock Andrea's pay, if that's what you're worried about."

She rolled her eyes, but decided she would rather spend this time kissing him than arguing. Before Elynn knew it, they were at the airfield. She was buckled in on the helicopter before she thought to ask where they were going.

"It's a surprise," Alex said with that small private smile she now loved.

Closing her eyes in anticipation, she leaned against him for the duration of the flight.

CHAPTER 13

Some thirty minutes later, they landed on a small jewel of an island. The security men who had accompanied them melted away while she took a look around. "Where are we?"

"This is the island where I was born. I thought we could stay here for the next week."

"But there's no house here anymore," Elynn protested.

Costas had grown up on this island. The Hanas family had once owned a large estate here, but a bad storm had done a lot of damage to it. Due to the lack of funds during his youth, Costas had been forced to abandon the family's rambling ancestral home and sell off the property. Alex had always talked about buying back their land and restoring the house, but as far as she knew, it had only been talk.

"Did you do it? Did you buy back the property?" Elynn asked excitedly.

"All the land we owned and then some," he said with satisfaction. "The house was a total loss, however, so I just built a new one on a slightly better vantage point."

They turned the corner, and Elynn gasped. The new 'house' was a gorgeous sprawling Mediterranean mansion high on the cliff ahead. Wrapped around the house was an exotic snaking garden that was designed to blend in with the hillside's natural conformation. A more direct path up to the house was on their right along the cliff's edge.

The interior of the house was beautiful—warm and open with comfortable-looking furniture and beautiful paintings and antiques. A matronly Greek housekeeper Elynn had never seen before appeared halfway through their exploration of the house. She smiled and said something to Alex in soft Greek before she retreated.

"Dinner is ready," he translated.

He took her hand and showed her to a terrace with a spectacular view of the sea. An elegantly set table for two was waiting for them.

"When did you finish this place?" Elynn asked in between bites of a to-die-for shrimp saganaki.

"Last year," he said, looking around appreciatively. "You know, I used to think Costas was too sentimental about this place. He used to drag me here all the time when I was younger to keep us in touch with our heritage. I hated it when I was a teenager. The old house was a mess and there was no semblance of a social life. It wasn't until a few years ago that I realized the privacy we could have here was worth more than gold. That's when I started construction. I've come here a few times to relax in between trips. Costas knows about it, but he and Mary are more concerned with traveling right now. He wants to show her the world. I understand the feeling."

Elynn answered with a smile. She hoped he meant to follow in his father's footsteps and would soon be globetrotting with her. Traveling the world with Alex was a tantalizing prospect. When she had time away from work that is.

Dinner was followed by a leisurely dessert, but soon the light faded. When servants came to light candles on the tables, he waved them away.

"I think it's time you saw the master bedroom," he announced before showing her upstairs.

He opened the door to the bedroom with a flourish worthy of a game show hostess. Elynn's mouth dropped open. It was breathtaking. White walls contrasted with graceful rosewood furniture and one entire wall was made of glass. Built-in doors slid back automatically to allow access to another terrace with a spectacular view of the ocean lit by a full moon.

"Isn't this meant to be our parents' bedroom?" she asked apprehensively.

"No, father preferred the old house, so I am having it rebuilt for him. It should be done early next year. This is our house."

Elynn had never been so thrilled to hear anyone say 'our' before. A little dizzy, she gave him a glorious smile. But it faltered slightly when another thought occurred to her. "So you've never brought anyone here before?" she asked.

"No, of course not. This is our sanctuary." He cleared his throat and walked to the side of the bed. The staff had put the bag with Elynn's surprise there. Picking up the box, he gave her a sheepish smile. "I should have put this away myself to make sure the staff didn't open it. Imagine their surprise if they had."

"Who's to say they didn't," she said with a raised brow.

He laughed at her sour expression. "True. Come here," he said, holding out his hand to her as he sat on the bed.

ELYNN CAME to him without a moment's hesitation. It was an intensely gratifying moment. After all these years, Alex finally had her right where he wanted. Already getting aroused, he gathered her in his arms and kissed the top of her head, breathing in her sweet citrus scent.

"I've been thinking about your...proposal. I think we should start out a little differently than how you described."

Reaching over, he opened the box. He was incredibly impressed, and damned surprised, at the variety of things inside. How she had found the courage to go into a store and buy all these things was mystifying. Even he probably wouldn't have done that.

"Different how?" Elynn asked.

"Well, for one, these are conveniently adjustable," he said, grinning as he lifted a leather restraint. "I think before you prove that you trust me, I should prove that I trust you."

Realization dawned. Her eyes widened and her mouth opened and shut a few times. "You would let me do that?" she asked, shocked.

"It's only fair...and it makes sense that I should go first. You can do as much or as little as you want. It's the principle here that matters. It should be easy with this headboard. I can just lie back and you can tie me to it."

"Oh." Elynn sounded intrigued.

Excited, Alex stood up and slowly undressed. He didn't make a move to remove her clothes. He wanted her to have complete control. Lying down on the bed, he stretched out and got comfortable. It might have never occurred to him to do this sort of thing before, but with her it made perfect sense. Putting his hand behind his head, he experimentally gripped the headboard.

"Okay, I'm ready," he announced.

CHAPTER 14

Almost dizzy with anticipation and a heady sense of power, Elynn kicked off her shoes and picked up the soft woven restraints. She scooted up to him on the bed, still feeling a little shy. Heart pounding, she tied one wrist and then the other to the headboard. He tested the restraints. They gave very little.

"Good. You were paying attention when we sailed," he said approvingly, recognizing the knot as one he had taught her years ago.

Their gaze met and they both started to laugh.

"I can't believe were doing this," she said, hands moving to her hot cheeks.

"We're not doing anything yet," he pointed out.

"True," she breathed, kneeling beside him on the bed.

It was impossible not to stare at his long golden body lying there waiting for her. Wriggling out of her dress, she tossed it aside. For the time being, she kept her bra and panties on. They were black lace, part of her new wardrobe, and from the hungry look in Alex's eyes, he approved. Encouraged by his expression, she started touching him, tentatively at first, then with increasing confidence.

Alex closed his eyes, a stupid grin on his face as she explored him with her hands. When she had run them all over his body, she started over again, this time with her mouth. Flicking out her tongue, she licked his pectoral muscles and gently bit the buds of his nipples before moving down to his abs. She traced the grooves on his stomach with a little bit of awe before running her tongue along them, causing him to shift restlessly.

Elynn moved her attention to Alex's steely erection. She could finally look her fill, touch it without his interruption. His shaft was long and seemed terribly broad to her, but luckily it wasn't one of those monsters she'd seen on the Internet.

Still, it wasn't easy to see how he managed to fit inside of her. Afraid of being too rough, she stroked him gently. The soft skin covering him was so smooth and silky but also slightly veiny underneath the broad, purple-tinted head. It seemed so contradictory, that such a thing could feel so soft and delicate, yet so hard.

Leaning over, she took a quick swipe at the tip with her tongue. She liked how he tasted. The small slit seemed to be leaking slightly. With increasing confidence, she took hold of him at the base and gave him a long slow lick, curling her tongue around the ridge.

Alex groaned loudly and the headboard creaked as he strained against the leather restraints. Thrilled at the sound, Elynn used both her hands to fully grasp him. She replayed their encounter in the shower to remember how he wanted to be held. Using her memory and his vocalization as a guide she stroked and caressed him for a few minutes then cupped his balls, testing their weight before squeezing him the way he'd taught her.

The headboard was groaning loudly now as Alex started to struggle to get free. She looked up to see his face taut with tension, jaw clenched as he breathed hard. His eyes locked with hers. Maintaining eye contact, she lowered her head to take him in her mouth.

Alex gasped. "Holy shit."

Fighting a grin, she flicked out her tongue to give the head of his penis a long slow lick, her hands firmly around the base of his shaft. Encouraged by the broken gasp he gave, she wrapped her lips around him and started to lick and suck.

"No, baby, don't. You don't have to," he said tensely.

She paused. "I want to," she whispered before taking him in her mouth again.

Though it was a distinctly amateurish first attempt, that didn't seem to bother Alex. He hissed and moved impatiently under her determined mouth. Using a technique she'd seen online, she used her hands to caress him in time with the movement of her mouth.

Alex was swearing a storm in Greek before he broke off, "Please, Elynn. You have to stop now," he begged.

When she didn't answer, he bucked a little, and with a ragged groan, he climaxed. Elynn's eyes flew open as his hot seed spurted into her mouth, his cock jerking as he took several deep breaths before swearing again.

"Fuck me."

Elynn laughed as Alex's whole body relaxed, his sculpted chest heaving slightly.

He cracked an eyelid open, "You didn't have to do that. But thank you." His voice dropped and grew suspicious. "By the way, baby, where did you learn to do that?"

"The internet," she said, rolling her eyes. "And you're welcome. I felt obliged to return the favor."

"Well, for future reference, you don't have to return anything if you don't want to. Are you going to untie me now?"

She smiled and didn't say anything.

"Elynn?"

She ignored him. He wasn't pleading to be released, so she didn't think she was hurting him. And if he was a little frustrated...well, that was a good thing for her. Feeling wicked, she started to touch him again, teasing him until he was hard again. She wiggled out of her panties and slowly climbed on top of his lap.

"Kiss me," he ordered.

"You are not in charge, remember?" she reminded him, leaning in to lick his full lower lip before backing away.

He swore again, and she fought to keep her face impassive, cocking her head to the side to study him. "You're really enjoying tormenting me, aren't you?" Alex asked, a little breathlessly.

"Very much," she teased, arching her back so her hair touched the tops of his thighs.

"Holy shit," he breathed. "How the hell did you get so stretchy?"

With a wicked giggle, Elynn shifted her hips so that her wet lips rubbed against his straining erection. "Did I forget to mention that I do Yoga?"

Alex coughed. "Oh, hell yes, you did," he said, eyes wide with wonder as she bent back nearly in half while using her hands to rock herself forward.

"And Pilates," she added, straightening back up.

She wanted to laugh at the awed delight in Alex's eyes, but she was too keyed up. Being in charge was uncharted territory. And this was a completely new position for her. Staring deeply into his eyes, she took hold of his shaft and guided him inside her. Putting her hands on his shoulders she lowered herself onto his cock, slowly working his hard length inside herself with a sharp exhalation.

"Oh my god," she said, mouth wide.

He felt so much larger in this position. Tentatively she began to rock against him. His cock filled her so much that this was a little uncomfortable, but she soon learned how to adjust, shifting so his hardness hit a spot that made her tense and tighten with pleasure. The hot pulse intensified as she moved up and down on him, little moans of bliss escaping her.

"Elynn let me go now," Alex begged as he thrust his hips out to meet her halfway.

Eyes unfocused, her hands went to the restraints. She'd only gotten one loose when her body decided it couldn't hold off the ecstasy any longer. Holding his shoulders, she ground down on his lap before convulsing and crying out.

Rapidly working the other tie loose himself Alex put both hands on her hips and lunged upwards, thrusting into her from below repeatedly, extending her orgasm and bringing on his own climax. Grabbing her hair with two fists, he let go with a shout. Elynn didn't complain, though. She simply slumped forward, her face on his neck. Her breathing slowed, and she drifted, only half-aware as he rolled her over until she was underneath him. Gently, he withdrew and moved to her side, putting an arm around her.

"Sleep," he whispered, and she obediently closed her eyes and slipped away.

THE NEXT MORNING, Elynn awoke to an empty bed. She was disappointed until she spotted the white rose on Alex's pillow. There was a note next to it.

Had to make some calls. Come find me for breakfast when you're ready.

She shook her head in wonder. It was amazing how little sleep Alex seemed to need. He'd woken her late last night to make love again. And again just before dawn, she'd drifted awake with him already inside her. At the time, she hadn't had any complaints. She'd simply lain back and enjoyed his sweet, slow lovemaking.

Of course, that meant she'd overslept. The clock said it was after eleven AM. Alex had probably been up for hours. This is why morning people rule the world, she thought as she stretched and jumped out of bed. Energized, Elynn took a shower and put on a dress in the shade of green Alex seemed to favor before going to find him.

Breakfast was waiting on the same terrace where dinner had been served the previous night. When he saw her, Alex cut his call short.

"Who was that?" she asked curiously.

The conversation had been in English, but he'd said a few foreign words at the end of it that she couldn't make out.

"It was Sergei."

"Your Russian friend. I didn't know you spoke his language."

Alex smiled disarmingly while he poured her a cup of coffee from a nearly empty carafe. He'd already had several from the looks of it.

"I'm not actually all that good. Calen, who roomed with him, became quite fluent. I only picked up a little in comparison."

"Right," she said, a little sarcastically.

"There's no need to be jealous," he said smugly.

Elynn's grades in school had always been better than his, especially in math and science. Costas used to tease him mercilessly about it. Alex's saving grace had been his expertise with foreign languages. Compared to him, she had a tin ear. Her efforts to learn basic Greek had been a spectacular failure. She'd barely squeaked by with enough Spanish to pass her foreign language requirement in school.

"I'm not jealous. I'd rather be better at Calculus than Greek." She sniffed before taking a long sip of coffee. "Math is the universal language after all."

"Only if you're planning on talking to aliens," he said laughing, turning around to make sure they were alone before handing her something. "Don't forget to take these."

Elynn stared down at the packet of birth control pills in her hand rather dumbly. It had been in her purse. Except now that she thought about it, she had no idea where that was. Her suitcase had been unpacked by the housekeeper. Alex had obviously gone through her things.

Her heart gave a funny little lurch. "You went through my purse?"

He was caught off guard. "Um. Yeah. I didn't want you to be without these. I'm sorry. I won't do it again."

"How did you even know I take birth control pills?" Elynn shook her head before realization dawned.

Of course he knew. Alex didn't use protection with her. Ever. He wouldn't have taken that chance unless he'd known she was on the pill. Annoyed, she scowled at him. "If you tell me that you have my medical history in one of your files, I'm going to smack you."

"No!" he said, his expression unsure. He was starting to understand that he was on thin ice. "I've known you were on the pill for years."

When that just made her scowl deepen, he rushed to explain. "I didn't spy on you, I swear. Remember that vacation cruise we took a few years ago as a family? You were so sick, I wanted to turn the boat around. But your mother said you would be fine. You'd just forgotten something. I wanted to send the helicopter off for a doctor, but she said you would find that too embarrassing and that ibuprofen would do in a pinch. I got the picture then, that you have bad side effects with your period unless you're on the pill. It's nothing to be embarrassed about. I hate seeing you in pain. And we don't want to get pregnant yet, do we?"

Elynn's stomach dropped to her knees. Alex seemed perfectly serious.

"Yet?"

He smiled sheepishly and changed the subject. "Why don't we have breakfast now?" he suggested. "I could use a second one. Burning a lot of calories lately," he said suggestively, his shoulders easing when she cracked a smile in response.

For the rest of the meal, they avoided further talk of the future, even when she took her pill in front of him. Instead, he distracted her with entertaining stories and eventually took her back to bed to make love again. Afterwards, they showered, and he watched her carefully as she dried off with a towel in front of the mirror. She didn't feel a panic attack coming along, but something was wrong, and she couldn't hide it.

Troubled, Alex put his hands on her shoulders. "Is everything all right?"

"I'm fine. Well, mostly fine. Look, this is rather stupidly after the fact, but we need to talk," she said, slipping on a robe.

Male panic seeped into Alex's eyes. "About what?" he asked cautiously.

Elynn took a deep breath. "A few things actually. There's this not so tiny issue about boundaries. And birth control. I don't mind being the one to handle that. It's fine as long as we're together exclusively, but what about—" She broke off and looked away, running her fingers through her wet hair.

His brow furrowed. "What about what?"

"What about your past? If you didn't use protection, how can I trust that you're safe?"

Alex frowned as he turned her to face him, "Hey, I would never put you at risk. I have always used condoms with everyone but you, and I got a full checkup before we started seeing each other."

"Oh."

"Do you want me to call my personal physician? Have him talk to you?"

Elynn inhaled and shook her head. "That's not necessary. I believe you. I guess it's redundant to add that you don't have anything to worry about with me, right?"

Alex relaxed. "Of course. And about boundaries, I won't look through your stuff again. I promise."

She rolled her eyes. "It's not just that. Not really. I've been meaning to tell you that, while I love your whole agro alpha male thing in bed, in real life, it's a bit much sometimes."

His mouth quirked up a little. "Okay. I'll keep that in mind."

She raised her brows. "You'll have to do better than that. From now on, we make more decisions together. You'll have to start consulting me on my preferences. Ask me what I want to have for dinner every once in a while. And stop laying out my clothes. I'm not four. I can dress myself. Little things like that. Don't get me wrong, you do a damn good job at guessing what I want most of the time."

"That's 'cause I'm not guessing," Alex said smugly, crossing his arms and smiling down at her.

"Yeah, yeah, you're a magic man," she said with a dismissive wave of her hand. "I just want to be consulted every once in a while."

"I can do that," he promised softly. "But you have to promise me something in return."

"What is it?"

"Never say 'we need to talk' again. Those are the worst words you could ever say to a guy."

Elynn giggled. "All right. We have a deal," she said putting out her hand.

With a grin Alex took her hand and they shook on it before he pulled her against him for another scorching hot kiss.

CHAPTER 15

The weeks that followed were long and happy. Each gorgeous day blended into one another as Elynn and Alex got to know each other in a totally new and different way. They walked on the beach, picnicked in the garden, and made love just about everywhere he could ensure they had privacy.

Elynn blossomed in the warmth of Alex's unreserved affection. He showered her with gifts, spoiling her, because as he put it, her mother had clearly failed to do so. She explained that this was a good thing, but he waved off her assurances and protests before presenting her with yet another gift.

He was also teaching her how to sail. One morning, he took her down to the dock to surprise her with a brand new twenty-foot sailboat. The name on the hull was the *Elynn*^{2}. After getting over her shock and surprise, Elynn scratched her head.

"Why is it the Elynn two?" she asked puzzled.

"That's the Elynn squared," he corrected with a grin before shaking his head at her. "And you thought you were so much better at math than me."

"I am," she said, hands on her hips.

"Yeah, yeah. But it's squared, because I've decided to rechristen the yacht the *Elynn*," he announced.

"What! You can't do that. Isn't it Costas' boat? Shouldn't we name it the *Mary*?"

"I bought the boat, actually. Costas doesn't mind cruising around occasionally, but he's not into it enough to buy a yacht," he explained as they made their way back to the house. "But in my early twenties, I wanted a way to escape, so I got the first one back then. It was a convenient way of getting away while protecting my privacy."

"Uh huh. It had nothing to do with having a place to hold wild parties away from the prying eyes of the paparazzi."

Alex wagged a finger at her. "You know perfectly well that there have been no wild parties on our yacht. Those days were long over when I got the current one. Do you think Dad would have consented to sail around on a boat that had hosted one of...*those* parties?"

Elynn narrowed her eyes at him. "Those parties," she repeated. "You were going to say orgies weren't you?"

He scowled at her. "I have never participated in an orgy. I would never be that indiscriminate."

"Right," she said, laughing it off before heading to the pool for a swim.

Despite their little talk about boundaries, Alex was a complete dictator about one thing: her safety. He never let her swim in the ocean, saying the surf near the house was too harsh. When she pointed out she could swim off the boat, he hummed the Jaws theme until she gave up the idea. He also wouldn't let her go swimming in the pool until an hour after she'd eaten. It would have been ridiculous if he wasn't so genuinely concerned about her.

Alex was also still cautious about their intimate relationship. When they were together he would observe her carefully, especially after they had sex, even though she no longer froze up on him. She would tell him over and over again that she was fine, but he would just smile and nod and go back to watching her like a hawk, searching for minute signs of anxiety or discomfort.

He must have been satisfied with what he saw, because he didn't bring up the 'bathroom incident', nor did he mention therapy again. Instead, he made plans for the rest of the summer and when they should tell their parents. He wanted to do it soon, but she wanted to wait. She won that argument, but he punished her for it later in bed… and she loved it.

Alex hadn't actually restrained her as she had done to him, but he took full advantage of her box of gifts. He used the toys with great enthusiasm, even though he continued to swear that he'd never used that kind of thing before. But he was a quick study, and an expert in every other possible respect.

He introduced her to a wide variety of sexual experiences, things that made her blush when she was thinking about them later. He was intrigued when she confessed about the 'research' she had done and insisted they do some together. He got very enthusiastic about the project and insisted on trying several extremely daring and acrobatic positions. A few were so undignified that she broke down in hysterical giggles when they attempted them. They laughed a lot together.

After two weeks of uninterrupted bliss, Alex announced that he needed to resume work and they started traveling. They went to New York, Munich, Rome, and Hong Kong. She had assumed he wouldn't want to take her near his work in order to keep their affair quiet, but she was wrong.

He took her everywhere he went, to work functions and dinner meetings. When they visited cities where Hanas Industries had an office, he took her with him, insisting on getting her up at ungodly hours of the morning so he could have her at arm's reach all day. She would work on her laptop doing research from the couch in his office while he made calls or read reports.

Seeing Alex at work first hand was an eye-opening experience. His reputation as a slave driver was well-earned. He was so demanding of his employees that she often felt sorry for them, but she worried most about him. He was hardest on himself. Though he was a born multitasker, Elynn thought he tried to do too much.

"Alex, you have to trust your employees," she said one night after a long day at the office.

He looked up from his desk with a puzzled frown. "I trust them," he protested.

"Not enough," she said firmly. "You hired the best people in the world to work for you, but you don't trust them enough to do your bidding. If you think something is important, you insist on doing it yourself. Which would be fine, but you think *everything's* important. You need to delegate more."

Alex broke out into a wry, but tired grin. "Elynn, no one has ever accused me of going easy on my staff."

"I know that. Believe me. It's obvious why so many of them quit. But I'm not talking about your personal team. I'm talking about the management and personnel in your local offices. Like today with the deal your VP brokered. You insisted on taking over the negotiations in the final step."

He frowned. "Those were sensitive talks."

Elynn rolled her eyes. "I know, but your man here knew the deal inside and out. He didn't need you to come in and finish for him. He was capable of doing it himself—but you can't help yourself. It's not a criticism. I'm a perfectionist, too. But that's why we're still here at ten PM at night."

Guilt flashed across his face. "Oh, I didn't realize it was so late," he said. "*Shit*. I forgot about dinner."

She smiled benignly. "Alex, we ate. You had dinner brought in, remember?"

Guilt was briefly replaced with confusion. "Oh, yeah. Chinese."

"We are in China," she laughed.

There was a flash of surprise before he rubbed a hand over his face. "Okay. Maybe I see your point."

She cocked her head at him. "You forgot where we were, didn't you?"

"Guilty. Sorry. Why don't we get out of here?" he said, dropping his pen.

Elynn stood up quickly. "Wait," she said, walking over to him and pushing his papers to the side of the desk and hopping onto the surface in front of him. "We are here all alone with this big ol' desk. May as well take advantage," she said huskily before grabbing his tie and using it to drag him to her.

CHAPTER 16

Things between Alex and Elynn were going so well their first real argument blindsided them both.

He had surprised her with tickets to a masked ball in a real palace in Prague. Excited by the idea of being anonymous, she decided to wear the most revealing dress in her closet, the one Alex had taken one look at and said she couldn't wear in public.

Feeling daring, she met him at the ball in the wine-colored satin gown. It molded to her hips in a sensuous fall of fabric and revealed her cleavage with a plunging neckline fit for a red carpet. She had never worn anything resembling it, but under the anonymity of the mask she was a different person. A braver one.

Alex was also feeling brave. He wasn't normally one for public displays of affection, but tonight he was different. He caressed her in a way that made their status as lovers clear to everyone. Unfortunately, that only seemed to bring out a competitive streak in other men.

The first time Alex stepped away to refresh her drink, a tall, dark-haired man approached her and asked her to dance. It was a fairly benign exchange, but when it happened a second time, Alex refused to let her out of his sight.

"We're burning that dress when we get home," he growled as he swept her onto the dance floor.

Elynn laughed it off and all was well for a while, until another foolishly brave, or incredibly stupid, man tried to cut in. Before she could turn him down herself, Alex growled something in another language at the offender before ushering her up a cordoned off staircase with a prominent 'No Visitors Beyond This Point' sign.

"I don't think we're supposed to be in here," she whispered as he led her deeper into the darkened rooms upstairs.

But Alex didn't stop moving. He'd snuck them past the velvet rope as if he knew where he was going.

"Have you been here before?" she asked as he continued to lead her through room after room filled with priceless treasures from the royal family.

"Once when I was twelve. And there's somewhere I've been fantasizing about taking you for years," he said. "Here we are," he said when they reached an imposing archway.

Curious, Elynn looked around him. Her breath caught. It was one of the loveliest spaces she had ever seen. Delicate antique tables and sofas littered a room lined with stained glass windows on one side. The ceiling above was one huge skylight.

"It's a conservatory," she breathed, but anything else she was going to say was lost when Alex picked her up and carried her inside the room.

He set her down near the far wall and reached for the zipper of her dress. It dropped to the floor with the kind of rustle only expensive fabrics make. Breathing fast, Alex pulled at her panties, but his hands were shaking so bad she had to help him remove them. Her hands went to his zipper, but he took both her wrists in one hand and tore his pants open with the other.

Elynn shivered. There was something feverish and dark swirling in the atmosphere around them. Alex's possessive nature had been pushed into overload by those other men downstairs, and now he seemed determined to brand her with his touch. And she wanted him to do it.

Without a word, he pushed her against the wall next to one of the stained glass windows. Moving a hand down, he stroked between her legs. He didn't need to test her though. She was more than ready. Putting her hands on his shoulders, she pulled him closer, unwilling to break the spell by speaking.

He pinned her high up on the wall, bracing her with his hands as he entered her in one rough motion. Elynn gasped as he filled her. For a split second, she felt like a butterfly pinned to a board, but the incongruous image faded when he began thrusting hard, rocking her into the wall with each move. His hand moved up to fist in her hair, tugging her head to the side so he could suck on her neck as he fucked her.

Helpless to stop it or slow down, Elynn came so hard her vision blurred. She cried out as the blistering orgasm took hold of her. Out of control, she clawed at Alex's back while he slammed into her. Her pussy fluttered and tightened around him, milking him for all he was worth. He wasn't able to hold on, and he emptied himself into her with a hoarse cry of his own.

Alex held her for a few minutes until he recovered enough to withdraw. He slid to the floor with her in his lap, stroking her hair until they were able to get dressed.

Elynn was quiet on the way back to the hotel. Alex's aggressive claiming had been spurred by his jealousy, but there wasn't any need to be that way over her. There was no one else for her, no one in the world.

The reality of what that meant was starting to sink in. Feeling overwhelmed, she sat, playing with the folds of her dress as she leaned against his chest.

"Elynn?" Alex sounded worried.

"Hmm," she murmured, looking over her shoulder at him.

His guilt was all over his face. It radiated off of him in waves. "Elynn, was I too rough? I don't want to trigger another panic attack."

Startled, she leaned back. "I'm fine."

He didn't look convinced. Reaching out, she took his hand and wrapped it around her shoulders.

"Alex, I think you should know something," she said.

"What?"

"That thing that happened with Stephen...it wasn't about sex. It was about power. Stephen wanted to hurt me because I didn't worship him the way everyone else did. I don't remember everything that happened all those years ago, but I remember enough. He was obsessed, but it wasn't over me. It was never about *me*. All the things he claimed to admire about me weren't real. He didn't know me at all. But you do. You're not like him. Not in any way. I know you're possessive, but it's because you're protective. You would never hurt me. Not on purpose."

Alex absorbed that in silence. "But you freaked out on me once," he said eventually.

She shrugged and grimaced slightly. "And I may again. Sometimes I'm just going to react. But it won't be because of you."

"I still think I was too rough."

She shook her head. "Alex, you're not doing anything I don't want you to do. And the rough handling—well, it's exciting. I like being taken."

He let out a harsh breath. "If you ever start to change your mind about that, I want to know. Don't be afraid to tell me. We'll adapt."

"Deal," she whispered, leaning against him to cuddle for the rest of the drive.

Quiet and relaxed the whole way home, they were back in their hotel suite when Alex went to the closet to retrieve something.

"There's something I want to give you," he said, presenting her with a square velvet box.

He opened it to reveal an elaborate diamond and emerald necklace.

"What is this?" she asked in a mystified tone.

"Just a token of my appreciation," he said, moving around her to hug her from behind.

Elynn felt the floor underneath her give way. "Your what?" she asked aghast, her contentment slipping away like water.

Finally registering that things were not going exactly as he'd expected, Alex took a step back. "What's wrong?"

"How could you ask me that?" she asked in disbelief.

He'd just given her a ridiculously expensive piece of jewelry as if she were his mistress. After the conversation they'd just had, this was grossly inappropriate. He *knew* she didn't believe in jewelry or the worth of diamonds. It was her fervent belief that the overinflated price of such things led to greed and exploitation. And even if the diamonds were no-conflict, as a scientist, she knew that they were overestimated in value.

Diamonds weren't actually that rare. But all Alex wanted was to present her with a costly bauble the way he had reportedly done for all of his former mistresses. But she thought of herself as his girlfriend, not his mistress. When she told him that, he was both mystified and angry.

"What do you mean I'm treating you like a mistress? I just gave you a beautiful gift worth tens of thousands of pounds, and you're throwing it back in my face?"

"You know how I feel about diamonds and jewelry," she protested.

"I didn't think you were serious," he threw back, gesturing wildly. "I just wanted to give you a gift. A nice one. Most women would trample over each other to get their hands on something like this."

"I thought you wanted me because I was different from most women," she said quietly, crossing her arms and looking at the floor.

"I don't believe this," he mumbled as he left the bedroom, slamming the door behind him.

ELYNN WAITED for him to come back, but an hour came and went. She showered and dressed in a numb haze. She wished she'd kept her mouth shut about the necklace. She could have just shoved it in a drawer and never mentioned it.

But he probably wouldn't have stood for that. The thing looked as if it belonged in a museum, and he probably would have insisted on seeing it on her. The thought of wearing it gave her an unpleasant sensation in the pit of her stomach.

She remembered all too clearly the tabloid article about Alex that she'd read as a teenager. It had been entirely devoted to the lavish gifts he had given to his mistresses. Costas had despaired over it during his courtship of her mother. Such an elaborate necklace hadn't featured, but plenty of other jewelry had been mentioned, in addition to fur coats and exclusive designer clothing.

Just like the clothes hanging in your closet.

Elynn sighed. It had been uncomfortable at first, but she'd accepted the new wardrobe as a necessity of being with Alex. When she was at his side, she was scrutinized as if she were a bug under a microscope. And really, what was the big difference between Alex buying her clothes and her own mother? It all got paid for by the Hanas family coffers.

It wasn't a big surprise that he thought she would want such a gift. She should have spoken to him about it more calmly. But his choice of that phrase made her doubt the strength of his feelings for her. Perhaps she had read too much into his desire for a relationship with her. She was completely in love with him, but he just *appreciated* her.

Oh crap. Where did that come from? Did she love him? Was she already in so deep? Yes. Yes, she was. *Shit*. She was in love with Alexandros the Great. Well, she'd known that was probably going to happen when she got involved with him. And Alex cared about her. But his reputation as a womanizer who callously cut off his lovers when he got bored with them came back to haunt her.

I'm different, she told herself. She had to be... *Yeah, and how many of his exes had said the exact same thing?*

After a few more minutes, she went looking for Alex, only to discover he'd left their suite. Depressed, she got into bed. Eventually, she drifted off after having a good cry.

CHAPTER 17

Alex slipped back into their hotel suite well after two in the morning. He'd been downstairs in the bar, trying to get drunk.

He'd sat there alone, despite the offer of one or two very questionable young women to keep him company. He'd repulsed them with a harsh word and proceeded to drink his anger and annoyance away. It didn't take long, and soon he was completely ashamed of himself.

He *did* remember Elynn's earnest conversations on the subject of fine jewelry and diamonds, in particular when she had tried to dissuade Costas from buying that sort of thing for Mary. Her mother appreciated the jewelry, however, so Costas made sure to give it to her when Elynn wasn't around.

But Alex should have been more considerate of her feelings. He had bought the necklace on impulse from an auction catalog. It had belonged to a real princess, and he had looked forward to giving it to Elynn. And although she was completely wrong about his thinking of her as a mistress, there had been a grain of truth in her accusation.

He used to give his lovers gifts instead of real affection or commitment, and the habit was ingrained now. But he loved Elynn. She had to know that she was different.

He almost kicked himself as their argument came full circle. Elynn was different, and he loved her. He had to make an effort to meet her expectations and respect her desires and beliefs instead of always expecting that she would always adapt to his. She had deeply held convictions, and he had better stop conveniently forgetting them when it suited him. Taking one last sip of his drink, he asked for the check.

"It's on the house, Mr. Hanas," the bartender said. Alex nodded in thanks, although it wasn't unexpected.

They knew him here. This hotel was part of the Caislean chain, and he'd been an early investor.

He needed to talk to Elynn. There were things he needed to tell her. And not just his confession of love. He had another confession, one that had been weighing on him for a while. About Wainwright.

For years he'd paid top dollar to have someone monitor Stephen Wainwright. Unable to find anything criminal in his background, he was disgusted when the guy graduated from college with honors from a prestigious university in the states. But when the asshole had decided to celebrate with an extended European tour, Alex had freaked out.

He and Costas had agreed long ago that Elynn needed protection. When she went off to University, she had eschewed bodyguards, but Alex hadn't been able to accept that. It hadn't been enough to have the doorman, a former police officer, keep an eye on her. He'd also had two other men watching out for her, with Costas' blessing. Elynn's security team did background checks on everybody she worked with as well as her friends.

Elynn lived under the carefully crafted illusion that she was a normal girl, living a normal life. He didn't want to shatter her sense of safety. But whenever Wainwright left the states, he doubled the number of men on her.

Right now, Wainwright was in Spain, partying in Barcelona with a group of friends. That knowledge had helped push Alex into his decision to keep Elynn close this summer.

He didn't feel bad for spying on Elynn. What he felt bad about was lying about it. But she needed to know the truth. He had just been trying to protect her. She would understand. Eventually...

Maybe this wasn't the right time to bring up his surveillance. No matter how he spun it, the fact he'd had her watched was not going to go down well with Elynn. And she was already mad at him right now. But he was prepared to apologize. Their argument would blow over. And afterwards, they would carry on with their happily ever after. In the meantime, he wouldn't mention Wainwright. Elynn deserved to live her life out from under his shadow. He'd tell her after they were married. If he had to.

He went back to their suite. Elynn was lying on the bed with the curtains pulled back. She was curled up in a little ball in a patch of moonlight. He felt like a real bastard when he noticed the marks of tears on her cheeks. Mentally cursing himself, he undressed, resolving not to make the same mistake again.

Crawling into bed he wrapped his arms around Elynn, squeezing her lightly until she tensed and her breathing changed.

"I'm sorry," he whispered.

She didn't say anything.

"I'm an idiot," he added.

"Yes, you are," she agreed in a low voice.

"As long as I'm an idiot that is also forgiven," he said, giving her another squeeze. "I promise I won't forget who you are. Not ever again."

He waited. An eternity passed until she finally nodded and returned his embrace.

ELYNN WOKE UP WITH A START. She had been drifting closer and closer to consciousness when she realized she couldn't move her arms. Her eyes flew open to meet Alex's above her. Her wrists were tied to the bed and he was lying between her open legs. She was completely naked, her discarded nightgown lying off to the side. Frowning, she realized the satin nightdress was no longer intact.

"I hope you don't mind that I cut it off you. I didn't want you to wake up yet. I'll replace it," he said as if it was the most normal thing in the world.

She tilted her head back to examine the restraints holding her to the headboard. Though they had discussed it, Alex hadn't tied her up before. Instead, he occasionally used his strength to hold her down when they made love. She had found that incredibly exciting, but this was next-level. Open-mouthed, she gaped at him before he swooped in for a kiss.

"Hmm, still sweet even first thing in the morning. How do you manage that?" he asked in an undertone as he lowered his head to her breasts.

He didn't wait for an answer as he began to suckle on one nipple, then the other. His hands moved to the dresser next to the bed. He raised his head and sat back in order to show her what he had in his hands, a black blindfold. "I think after last night we need a reaffirmation."

"What do you mean?" Elynn asked apprehensively.

Though she had bought the blindfold with the other toys, the prospect of actually using the blindfold and the restraints for the first time was a little nerve-wracking.

"I think we need a reminder that you trust me," he said. "Even when I make mistakes and behave like an ass," he added softly as he leaned over her.

"I already forgave you," she said.

Alex hovered over her, looking deeply into her eyes. "I need more," he whispered.

The intensity in his expression made her breath shorten. "Okay," she whispered, and he tied the blindfold in place.

He kissed her forehead. "Remember our safe word," he teased.

She had insisted he have one when she'd tied him up.

She giggled. "All right."

When Alex was sure Elynn couldn't see, he leaned back to enjoy the picture she made. Her silky skin was such a temptation—one he didn't need to deny. Sliding his hands down the underside of her arms, he reveled in her softness, stopping to kiss her breasts and nuzzle underneath them. He continued down to her waist and hips, measuring her with his hands.

She was so small and delicate. He sincerely hoped she wouldn't have any complications when the time came for her to have his children.

He stroked her thighs and legs, avoiding the area she wanted him to focus on the most. Her rapid breathing turned into moaning when he returned his mouth to her breasts as his hands continued their work. He paused to tickle her feet, and she kicked them wildly. Moving up, he tickled above her hips until she was shouting at him and forcefully struggling against the restraints.

His erection was almost painful as he subdued her, covering her with his body. Playfully he covered her mouth with his hands and whispered in her ear. "I have you right where I want you now...and you're going to give me everything you have."

Elynn's breathing shifted into excited little pants. He waited, but she didn't use the safe word. Excited now, he bent to tease her with his tongue, tormenting her with it, until she managed to use the restraints to pull herself up so she could use her legs to push him away.

Blood pumping fast in his veins, he forgot to cover her mouth as he pulled her back to him. Elynn nipped his shoulder. Surprised, he laughed before moving between her open legs. She continued to struggle half-heartedly as he plunged inside of her. Her whimpered cry filled the room. Hesitantly, he covered her mouth with his hand once more. His impulse paid off. She actually grew wetter, and she moaned aloud.

"You're going to pay for that bite," he gasped as he began to pump inside her.

Elynn seemed as excited by their bondage play as he was. She was like hot silk around him. He wrapped her legs around him, replacing his hand on her mouth with his lips. His tongue teased hers until she responded and the kiss became demanding.

On impulse he lifted her legs so her lower body wasn't lying on the bed and he was on his knees. He held her legs up around him and stroked in and out of her with enough force to make the bedsprings squeak. Making sure his grip wasn't too tight, he continued to rock in and out of her until she bucked and strained in his arms, crying out as a climax burned through her.

"Oh hell," she gasped as the last tremors ran down her body.

Still in a daze, Elynn was soft and limp in his arms as he turned her around so she was face-down on the bed. Her arms were too taut against the restraints so he pushed her higher on the bed until they were slack. Slowly, he covered her body with his own, entering her from behind.

Alex hissed. Elynn felt incredible around him in this position.

Apparently, the feeling was mutual. She moaned loudly as he praised her with hot whispers in her ear. He let her know how much he loved her without using the actual words, worshipping her with his hands and mouth in between penetrating strokes. Eventually, his more aggressive instincts took over. He needed her to understand. And he needed her understanding.

"You belong to me, Elynn. I'm your first and last lover. No one else will ever touch you. No other man will ever know how silky soft your skin is here," he said as he bent to kiss the back of her neck. She gave another broken little whimper as he rocked into her tight little sheath.

"Tell me you love me," he coaxed softly.

When she could only pant in response, he withdrew and turned her around again. He entered her slowly and kissed her deeply. When he raised his head, her green-grey eyes were fixed on his. But she hadn't answered him.

"Say the words, Elynn. I want to hear them," he said, nipping at her lower lip in encouragement. She shook her head. "Say the words. Tell me you love me." She was silent. He rocked into her hard enough to make the bedsprings creak. "Say it, Elynn, or so help me I will never let you out of this bed!"

He was only half-joking, but he was still a little surprised when she started to laugh. He pumped deep into her until she stopped. "You will say the words," he promised her as she moaned and panted in response.

It took two more orgasms before she begged him to stop.

"All right. I love you," she finally whispered before she closed her eyes to sleep.

Satisfied, Alex untied the restraints, rubbing the slight red marks on Elynn's wrists before he gathered her into his arms. He hadn't meant to keep her tied up so long, but lord, she was so stubborn. He wrapped himself around her, completely at peace for the first time in years.

Well, truthfully, he'd felt this strange contentment since the first time he and Elynn had made love. He'd known then that she loved him, but it was still a relief to hear the words. Drifting off, he recalled her reaction to the necklace. He was going to have to do something different now.

The engagement ring he'd bought for her two years ago wasn't going to work.

CHAPTER 18

In the days that followed, Elynn was both happy and terrified. She and Alex skipped across several more European cities, working hard during the days and making love for hours every night. She was sure about her feelings for him and only felt a little bit of anxiety about telling him she loved him. It wasn't like he'd given her much of a choice. But he didn't say it back. She was sure he loved her; he didn't say the words.

Typical.

It was completely unreasonable that he would demand a declaration of love and deny her one in return, but Alex wasn't known for playing fair. Unless...

There was always the possibility he regretted pushing her for a declaration because he didn't intend on ever saying it back. Even if he did love her, that didn't mean he was ready to settle down. Maybe he didn't have it in him, and he wasn't confessing his love so she wouldn't get her hopes up.

She tried to tell herself that her fears were unjustified, but her insecurity about being enough for him was sorely tested one night in Rome. Alex had arranged for a special night tour of the Coliseum and then taken her out to a five-star restaurant for an amazing meal.

After they ate, he was waylaid by a business associate. Full and flushed from the wine, Elynn took the opportunity to get some air. It was warm outside, but she didn't want to duck into the air-conditioned car just yet. Instead, she leaned against it, letting the ambiance of the eternal city soak into her veins while she waited for Alex to come out of the restaurant.

When he did, he wasn't alone. A slinky blonde in a short red dress was clinging to his arm, whispering in his ear. It didn't help that Alex looked furious...Elynn saw red.

The blonde bitch looked over at her before turning away in an obvious dismissal. "Alexandros," she purred. "Why don't you come back to my place tonight?" she said in a voice loud enough to carry to Elynn.

She didn't hear what Alex said back to her, but it must have been pretty harsh. He leaned over and whispered something that made the stranger turn purple. She turned to Elynn and shot her a nasty look, but then her face became calculating. She whispered something to Alex before turning in her direction and laughing derisively, as if she couldn't believe he would waste his time with her.

Elynn felt the sting of that laugh deeply. It touched on her insecurities too closely for her to be able to shake it off. Instead, she focused her anger on Alex.

As soon as they were sitting in the back of the car, Alex instructed the driver to take them to their hotel. He could tell Elynn was furious. A perverse part of him was secretly pleased that she was jealous. It was about time the shoe was on the other foot. But in this case, she had no reason to be upset.

Maria, Gio's ex-wife, had seen them at dinner. She was still angry that he had always refused her attentions, so she decided to cause trouble for him and Elynn. Everyone knew they were together at this point. Despite his attempts to block them, stories of their relationship had leaked to the tabloids in the last week. And Maria, the skank, was a born troublemaker. She had blown up her marriage to Gio with her infidelity, and when he wouldn't take her back, she vowed to get even with him and all of his friends.

I have to tell Elynn about the tabloids.

When the news about the two of them had hit the rags a few days ago, his father had called him several times demanding to speak to her. Alex had managed to put him and Mary off by assuring them that Elynn was happy and they would see the both of them soon—and by turning off the ringer on Elynn's cell phone to buy a little more time.

His future absentminded professor hadn't even noticed. He had promised their parents that they would meet them in Venice ahead of schedule as long as they remained patient. In the meantime, he kept the tabloids away from her, a simple matter since she never bothered to ever look at them.

In the back of the car, Alex studied Elynn's tense profile. She was still seething. He put up the privacy screen before he put his arms around her. Her shoulders were stiff, and again he couldn't stop the satisfaction that coursed through him. His own possessiveness was an angry weight when he saw another man hit on her. The fact that she could be jealous, too, was comforting.

He was starting to explain about Maria when she turned on him suddenly. Her hand shot out, and she gripped his testicle tightly. Surprised, he tried to pry her hand off, but she simply squeezed tighter.

"Elynn!"

"If you ever even think about cheating on me, I swear I will twist one of these off, and I will bury it in the backyard just to see what grows. Do you understand me?" she hissed.

Stunned, but also a little proud, Alex pried her surprisingly strong little hand away. As a precaution, he grabbed both of them and pulled her closer to him.

"I understand. There's no need to rip off my testicles. For Christ's sake, Elynn." He leaned back, taking her with him by the grip he kept on her hands.

"I'm serious, Alex. If you get bored and you start thinking about seeing someone else, you end this first. I won't be deceived. You will break up with me first before you let another woman touch you," she hissed.

He wanted to laugh, but she probably would have broken free of his grasp to hit him. "There will be no other women," he promised. "I waited a long time for you to be ready for me, and I have no intention of letting you go now, or anytime in the future. I have loved you, and only you, since you were seventeen years old."

Elynn stared at him, utterly shocked. He was a little shocked, too. He hadn't intended on telling her that, not right now. More like on their tenth wedding anniversary.

Well, maybe some things shouldn't wait, he thought as he bent his head.

He kissed her still open mouth, slipping his tongue inside until she finally responded. They continued until they reached their hotel. Elynn was still speechless when he led her out of the car and up to their room.

He hadn't expected that. She should have had some idea of how he felt before this.

She was quiet as they went into their bedroom, but enthusiastic when he stripped off their clothing. Elynn put both of her hands on either side of his head and kissed him passionately. They tore at each other's clothes, but this time she took charge, pushing him on the bed and climbing on top of him.

"Fuck," he growled as she lowered herself on his straining cock.

Nothing had ever felt so good, or so he thought. And then she started to move, and he almost bit his tongue. He loved her in this position, watching his shaft as it entered her tight little pussy. And unlike the last time she was on top, his hands were free. He used them to cover her breasts and bring them to his mouth as she rocked against him. Suckling hard, he ran his hands down to cup her bottom as she slid up and down on him.

"I love you," he whispered.

Elynn leaned down to kiss his lips. "Good," she said, making him laugh.

The moment of levity passed, and she arched her back and closed her eyes. His hands moved to her waist, and he sat up to bring them closer. Her hands moved to the back his head, and she tugged on his hair. Unable to hold off, he climaxed inside her, wishing that his seed could take root.

He wanted to put his baby inside her. The idea of it made him shout when he came, shattering him into a million pieces of light. He took her with him, her body tightening around him as she held on to him for dear life as he thrust back at her, his cock jerking as he spent himself inside of her.

Afterwards, Elynn didn't speak until their bodies had cooled and they were lying quietly spooning in bed.

"Exactly how long have you been planning this?" she asked turning her head to look at up at him.

Alex raised a brow. "This? I'm constantly planning this," he said grinning wickedly while running a hand over her bottom.

Elynn punched him in the arm. "Not *this*. A future together."

"Our future. Well that's been my master plan for a long time. Since before it was okay for me to want you. It's still a little wrong now. But I don't care anymore. I love you and you love me. That is how things should be," he whispered into her hair, holding her close.

"It's not wrong," she said. "We belong together. But it's still crazy to think that you felt this way since I was seventeen. And even back then, you knew?"

"Not right away, but soon enough. Too soon, maybe. It made for a long wait. Although it was probably for the best that you were still underage. It meant we had to be friends first. But after a while, I started to worry that you would only see me that way. I told myself if that was the case, I could change your mind. I just had to wait for you to be ready," he said before changing the subject. "I told my dad that we would come to see him and Mary earlier than planned. We will meet them in Venice in a few days."

Elynn gasped. "What are we going to tell them?"

"The truth. But honestly, they already know."

"What?" She twisted around to face him. He turned away.

"Alex."

"All right. So...news about us has leaked to the press."

"What!"

"I'm sorry. I did my best to keep your name out of the papers. Me and Costas have been paying them off for years to keep your name and privacy protected. But we've been seen in public too many times in romantic settings. The story was too juicy to keep under wraps."

"Oh, god," she moaned in embarrassment. "What do they say? I want to see them."

"There's no need. They don't really say anything except that we're together," he said, leaving out the fact that the lurid titles always referred to their status as stepsiblings with a decade of age difference between them.

Seeing the headlines would only upset her. Especially since a lot of them left off the 'step'.

"What are our parents going to say? They know we're sleeping together, even if the articles don't say so explicitly. And I know they probably go into all the gory details, you big liar."

"We were going to tell them soon anyway," he pointed out. "Don't worry. They will be fine with us as a couple once they know how happy you are. How happy I make you."

"Are you kidding? Do you have any idea of what your father must think of me right now? He's going to go ballistic. He's always hated all your girlfriends."

He scoffed. "He's not going to turn on you now just because we're together. He loves you. And don't worry. Costas knows whom to hold responsible for this relationship. He's been aware of my feelings for you. He was furious when he first found out, but he's had a lot of time to get used to the idea. It might be a little awkward at first, but it will get better once they get used to seeing us together."

"What do you mean when he first found out? It wasn't when he saw the tabloids?"

Alex stroked her cheek. "No. My father knew I was in love with you before I did."

Elynn frowned at him until he sighed and sat up so he could take her in his arms. He looked down into her face, kissing her puckered brow. "I didn't realize what was happening right away. Costas is the one who pointed it out. I'd been denying my feelings for a while, but when I flew twenty hours straight to make sure I didn't miss your eighteenth birthday party, he felt like he had to intervene."

"My party?" she asked in surprise. "Wait—you two had an argument that night!"

"Argument is a mild word for it. It was a huge fight. He'd seen the way I was looking at you. He demanded I stay and speak to him after we served the cake. You were finally legal, and he didn't trust me. He should have known better. I wouldn't have done anything you weren't ready for," he said, kissing her forehead again.

Elynn shook her head, her eyes wide. "You really flew *twenty hours* to make it to that party?"

"I flew twenty in, stayed four, and then had to fly twenty back because the meetings weren't actually over yet," he confided.

"I remember the argument, but I had no idea you were fighting about me. You were so angry when you left. I thought maybe you were still upset about my mom or something had gone wrong at work. But things got better right away. You were so kind, and Costas was much calmer."

Alex gave her a sheepish smile. "Costas raged a bit, but we came to an understanding of sorts. You would get a chance to grow up a bit more and choose me. And you did," he added smugly.

Elynn smirked. "I'm not sure I see it that way. I don't think you ever intended on giving me a choice."

She knew him so well. "You would have fallen in love with me eventually. Even if I had stayed away."

"Arrogant ass," she said, wrinkling her nose at him in the most adorable scowl.

"Guilty as charged. But I have my good points. You've always trusted me, and that's the most important thing in the world to me. So trust that everything's going to be great now that we're together. We'll live in the Oxford house full-time once you start graduate school. The commute will be a little longer for you, but on the days you work late,

I'll have a driver come get you or pick you up myself so you won't have to drive tired. I have it all worked out."

"Of course you do," Elynn said in a wry tone before her lips tightened.

She grabbed a pillow and swung it at him as hard as she could.

"Hey!" he said, taken by surprise by her sudden attack.

"That's for sleeping with other women when you were supposed to be in love with me!"

She hit him again and again until he grabbed the pillow from her. He pulled her close to him, forcing her head under his chin.

"I know you're angry. I would be, too. But I didn't know how long it would take for you to be ready for a physical relationship. If it makes you feel any better, there haven't been that many since I met you. About one a year since you turned eighteen. And each one lasted only a few weeks, at most. I tried to be celibate, but it was too...frustrating," he said before letting his head hit the pillow with a thump.

Elynn sat on her heels on the bed facing him. She stared, assessing him in silence. He hoped she wasn't too mad. At this point, she knew better than anyone what kind of sexual appetite he had. For him, one woman a year was a remarkable feat. He made love to her at least two or three times a night, every night. More than that if he could get away with it, but he was making up for lost time.

With a frustrated little grunt of her own, Elynn hit the bed next to him. "You should have waited for me," she said, striking him in the chest with her small fist.

He covered it with one hand and drew her closer. "I know. I should have. But I wasn't sure you would ever be ready. For a while there, it looked like you weren't ever going to want anyone. So I waited. I kept telling myself it was for the best if you got a chance to have other relationships first. That it would be healthier for you. But as soon as I saw you with Eric in the street, I lost it. I couldn't let anyone else have you," he said, stroking her hair.

To his relief, her fist relaxed and she splayed her fingers over his heart.

"When did you see me with Eric?" she asked.

"In London before brunch, just after you gave me the car. He swept you up and kissed you. I was going to punch his lights out. If I had been on the right side of the street, I might have."

"He did not kiss me. Not on the lips anyway. He was hoping you would show up so he could meet you, for crying out loud," she said heatedly, despite a big yawn.

Alex laughed, mostly at himself. "Then it's a good thing for him that I couldn't cross the street in time."

Elynn smacked him in the chest again, and he grabbed her hand.

"Tell me again that you love me," he said, "and I'll let you go to sleep."

She looked as if she was contemplating hitting him again. "God only knows why, but I love you, you frustrating autocrat."

It wasn't quite what he had in mind, but he took it anyway.

CHAPTER 19

Costas and Mary had rented a huge Palazzo on the Grand Canal in Venice. Elynn had never been so nervous to see her mother and stepfather before. She was wearing a russet red silk dress that Alex had laid out for her in the morning. She hadn't even gotten angry—she'd already tried on and discarded three other outfits in her anxiety, so letting him decide had been easier in the end.

Alex did have damn good taste, she silently conceded while adjusting the strappy sandals that he had chosen to go with the dress. Exhaling hard, she straightened up and stared at the house in dread. Smiling commiseratingly, he took her hand.

"It's going to be fine," he assured her as they made their way up the stairs to the beautiful house.

Mary rushed to meet them as soon as they stepped through the door. She embraced Elynn and then held her at arm's length to look at her closely. Elynn knew she was blushing red, but she gamely tried to smile as if everything was normal. Mary gave Alex a nervous appraisal until he leaned over to kiss her cheek. Her mother seemed to relax after that, and she finally let Elynn go.

Alex put an arm around Elynn and led her to the stairs where Costas was waiting. Her stepfather looked grim. It was quite a change from the warm and friendly father figure she was used to. Her smile faltered and fell away.

"Stop looking at her like that or she's going to think you're angry with her, too," Alex drawled.

Costas frowned at his son. "You should have waited until she finished graduate school," he said suddenly.

Alex smiled and shrugged slightly. "I'm not a saint. Come and congratulate us properly," he insisted, making Costas frown harder.

He rolled his eyes at his son but moved forward to hug Elynn tightly. "Are you sure you're okay, sweetheart?" he asked with fatherly concern.

"I'm fine. So is Alex. We're great, actually," she said, taking his hand.

Costas was still angry, but she kept smiling at him determinedly until he broke and smiled back. He swept her up in a big bear hug before setting her back on her feet. Tugging her close to his side, they walked to the dining room.

"He should have waited," he couldn't stop from saying again.

Despite their parents' relatively warm welcome, lunch was an ordeal. And the blame could be laid squarely at Alex's feet.

Mary and Costas danced around the fact that their children were now lovers with determined skill. But Alex was as blunt as a sledgehammer. He alluded to nights spent in different exotic locales in a way that left their parents with no doubt as to their nocturnal activities. Elynn kicked him under the table, but Alex just smiled at her as if he wasn't being an idiot.

"You should come visit *us* at the Oxford estate before Elynn's school starts," he said, casually dropping the bomb on their already tense parents.

She hadn't known he was going to tell him they were moving in together. He should have warned her.

"What did you say?" Costas asked, completely red in the face.

"*Shit,*" Elynn murmured, grimacing.

Costas stood up and shouted in Greek too fast for Elynn to follow.

At the other end of the table, Mary sighed, pouring herself a second, much fuller, glass of wine.

What followed was an excruciating few hours filled with shouting and a lot of arm waving. The argument between father and son started at the table, but soon it raged all over the palazzo as the two men went at each other in a battle that was apparently long in the making.

Resigned to the fact that they were both involved with two volatile men, Elynn and her mother followed the argument at first to make sure the men didn't come to physical blows. At one point Elynn gasped when Costas used a Greek word she recognized.

"Don't worry, love. He's not calling you a whore. He's calling me one," Alex stopped to reassure her, kissing her forehead before he dived back into the argument.

Eventually, Elynn threw up her hands and suggested they leave them to it. The men were paying them no attention in any case. They *liked* arguing with each other. Instead, she and her mother sat down to coffee in a lovely salon with a view of the Grand Canal, waiting for their men to tire themselves out.

"Are you happy, sweetheart?" Mary asked.

She smiled reassuringly at her mother. "Don't worry about me. I know Alex and I are an odd match, but we're very happy. He makes me happy."

"I'm glad, sweetheart. And it's not as if we didn't know this was coming. Costas warned me about Alex's feelings for you a long time ago. I'll be honest—it used to worry me. But nothing happened for so long that I almost forgot about it. I confess, I still have some misgivings, but if you're happy, I'm happy. Besides, I did get involved with an older Greek tycoon myself. I know you'll make him take good care of you," her mother said, patting her hand.

"Thanks, mom. Although, I'm having a difficult time with the idea that Alex felt this way about me, and I was the only one who didn't know."

Mary fiddled with her necklace and shrugged. "Well, I thought telling you might not be wise. It might have scared you…or hastened events. You might have ended up together much sooner. Maybe before you were ready."

Elynn frowned at her.

Mary shrugged. "I am your mother. You can't blame me for wanting you to stay my little girl a while longer."

"I will always be your little girl," Elynn said before hugging her.

Further conversation was drowned out when Costas and Alex burst into the room, still arguing.

"Of course we will be married first. Calm down. Your blood pressure is high enough as it is," Alex eventually shouted in English.

Elynn's head whipped around. *Married*?

"Don't you think she's a little young for marriage?" Mary asked in a strained voice, but it was Costas that answered.

"No! This is wonderful news. Elynn is more mature than most people twice her age," he said, rubbing his hands. "We will start making wedding plans immediately. We'll keep it small and intimate," he said with satisfaction. Once he heard the word marriage, his attitude changed completely. "You can have your grandmother's ring," he added as he sat next to Mary.

"I have a ring, but thank you for the offer," Alex said calmly, using a hand to nudge Elynn under the chin. She finally registered that her mouth was open. He took her hand with a gentle squeeze. "You're making your mother nervous, baby. Try to act happy, or she'll think you don't want to marry me," he whispered in her ear.

When she continued to glare at him, he leaned over to kiss her softly. He sat down next to her, and she couldn't resist giving him a firm pinch.

"You forgot to ask me," she hissed in his ear.

"Later," he whispered back and he turned his attention back to their parents.

THE REST of the afternoon passed with Costas gleefully making wedding plans until Mary also got into the spirit of things and joined him. Elynn sat there, offering the occasional yes or no.

Somewhere, things had gotten away from her.

Alex also listened without offering much. Instead, he simply put a lazy arm around her, making the occasional suggestion and kissing the top of her head periodically. They lingered for a tour of the palazzo, but when Mary started browsing wedding gowns online, Elynn pinched Alex again, and he made an excuse to leave.

The luxury speedboat that dropped them off was waiting for them outside when they finished saying their goodbyes, but the driver was nowhere in sight. Alex stepped inside and gestured for her to join him.

"Can you even drive this?" she asked him behind gritted teeth, biding her time so she could yell at him once they were alone.

"Of course I can. Get in already so you can scream at me properly in private."

Annoyed at how easily he could read her, she got in the boat. He drove them away from the city, so that Venice was in the distance and there were no other boats nearby to witness them.

"Are you going to ask me to marry you?" Elynn asked sarcastically.

"No. I decided asking wasn't a good idea."

"*What?*"

"I decided not to ask you. After months of deliberation, I decided just telling you was a better way to go."

Eyes wide she stared at him. "*Why?*"

"Because you might say no," Alex said with a shrug, as if he was talking to a simpleton.

"Do you know how crazy you sound? You're not asking—you're telling. It's crazy. *You're* crazy. I'm only twenty-one!"

Alex wrapped his arms around her. "You know perfectly well that I would never ask you to move in with me unless we were married. I know you don't pay much attention to gossip, but people will say nasty things if we live together without getting married, especially given our age difference. And you would end up marrying me eventually. You know you would. Plus with my ring on your finger, no other man would dare get near you."

Elynn did start to shout then. There was no one near them, and she didn't want to disappoint him after all. She'd only got a few words out when Alex dropped to his knees in front of her. Thinking he was finally going to propose, she stopped yelling, but he didn't say a word. Instead he parted her legs and put one leg over his shoulder.

"If anyone gets close, tell me, and I'll stop," he said in a low voice before he tore her delicate lace panties off.

He has to stop doing that. She would have no underwear or night-gowns left if he kept ripping them all. She was about to tell him so when he began to touch her, and she lost the ability to speak.

"God, you taste so good. I can't get enough of you," he murmured between long hot licks.

Elynn clutched the rail on the side of the boat while Alex licked and probed with his tongue and fingers. He forgot technique and finesse, consuming her with abandon. Her cries seemed to fuel his hunger, and he fucked her hard with his tongue until she splintered and broke, and finally he had to catch her when she collapsed.

He stood then, carrying her in his arms to the cushioned seat to cuddle her on his lap.

"Say yes, Elynn."

She stirred on his lap, barely able to lift her head and arms. If she was honest with herself, she desperately wanted to be his wife. People would say she was too young, but she didn't care. She felt ancient most of the time trying to keep up with Alex.

"Yes."

He rewarded her with a hungry kiss, one she felt in every cell of her body.

Elynn closed her eyes, almost afraid of the sheer force of her feelings. Alex was an earthquake, a force of nature. But she felt protected in his arms, and eventually her heartbeat slowed. One weak hand moved up to caress his cheek.

"You need a shave," she said in a distant voice.

He nodded and pressed a box into her hand. *Uh oh*. She stared at it apprehensively.

"Go ahead. Open it."

She flipped open the lid and frowned in surprise. There was a silver-colored ring, probably platinum. But the huge solitaire in the middle wasn't a diamond. It was a shiny black stone. Puzzled, she held it up to the light. She had been expecting a diamond or a sapphire of some size, but this ring was unlike anything she'd ever seen.

It was beautiful.

"What is this?" she asked, brow wrinkled.

"It's a black diamond, cut from the heart of a meteor."

Elynn gasped and looked at him with wide eyes. "Are you serious?"

"Of course I am," he said, taking the ring and slipping it on her finger. "It's the only thing I could think of that would be precious and rare enough to be on your finger. I bought the rest of the meteor as well. I think it will serve as an excellent first anniversary gift. But...you have to marry me first."

"I already said I would," she laughed, resting her weary head on his shoulder.

"Yes, you did," he replied with satisfaction as he turned them to face the sunset.

Together, they watched the light fade around them. When the sun had set, he drove them back into town and they spent the rest of the night making love in their hotel room.

Before Elynn drifted off to sleep, a thought roused her. "I guess you are going to win our bet. You'll still be in the Oxford house this fall."

"That's right," Alex murmured with a smile, throwing a possessive hand over her waist.

"Did you decide what it is that you wanted as a prize?" she asked, shifting in the bed to look him in the eye.

He lifted her hand and kissed the ring adorning it before tightening his grip and hugging her closely.

"I already got what I wanted. What I've always wanted."

CHAPTER 20

Elynn could barely believe she was getting married in two weeks.

Not long after she and Alex had returned to London, he had promptly departed again for ten days. He had scheduled a long series of business meetings in order to free himself up to take time off for their honeymoon. They were going to spend several weeks on the '*Elynn*' until it was time for her to start her graduate program.

In the meantime, she stayed in the London townhouse on her own, spending her days shopping for the perfect wedding dress. She also took the time to catch up with a few trusted friends.

Most were stunned when she confirmed that the tabloid stories were true, that she and Alex were a couple. They had believed the stories were faked by unscrupulous gossip sites looking to make money. One even suggested that Elynn sue them for libel, before she admitted the truth and told them she and Alex were getting married.

The tabloids were full of speculation about her and Alex's relationship, but so far none had found out about their wedding plans. Elynn swore her friends to secrecy with the promise of an invitation to the small intimate event. In total, less than fifty guests would attend the ceremony, which would be held on the grounds of the Oxford estate.

Elynn missed Alex fiercely while he was away, but she was consoled by his frequent texts and videophone calls. She didn't know how much comfort she would find in his attentiveness until she went out for drinks one night with Eric and Fred.

Her friends were in fine form that night. They had seen the tabloids, and they didn't believe a word of it. Scanning the darkened bar to make sure no one was within earshot, she leaned in conspiratorially.

"Uh guys...it's true. Me and Alex are together. Like *together* together," she said with a 'yes I'm crazy' look on her face.

Eric choked on his sip of beer, and Fred whistled.

"Damn, girl. I told you to get out there, but when you jump, you go right for the deep end," Fred said.

Eric coughed and scowled. "This better not be big brother looking for some kinky thrill."

She rolled her eyes. "*Don't* call him that, please. And no, it's serious. He told me he loves me. That he's loved me for years—since I was seventeen."

Eric's jaw dropped. "Fuck!"

"I know," Elynn agreed, widening her eyes for emphasis.

"But he did date. Not a lot, but some," Fred said before Eric dug a pointed elbow in his side.

"I know, and I did give him shit for that. But I had some stuff to work through, so I can't really hold it against him. And he does love me. I know for sure."

"Wow," Eric said with a disbelieving shake of his head.

Elynn sipped her drink and nodded understandingly. It *was* unbelievable. "Listen, Alex wants you two to come to a party," she said. "A business thing that he wants to be a little more social than normal. It's the Saturday after next. Will you come? To the estate at Oxford?"

"Will we?" Eric said. "I'll camp out there in the woods if Alex wants us to," he said laughing.

She felt a little bad for lying, but much as she loved the pair, Eric was a terrible gossip and they wanted to make sure no tabloids got wind of the upcoming ceremony. The three of them continued to drink, and Elynn was more than a little tipsy when the driver took her back to the townhouse.

Her happy buzz died quickly as soon as she stepped inside the house. One of Alex's junior security men came up to her to whisper an apology.

"I'm sorry, we just didn't know what to do."

Perplexed, she stepped into the salon. "Sorry about what?"

"What the hell are you doing here?" Sonia Steele demanded from the couch.

STUNNED, Elynn stepped toward the couch.

Sonia was wearing a skintight, barely-there red dress. The sleekness of the gown made it obvious she wasn't wearing any panties. Andrea was standing above the scantily clad woman, scowling as if she couldn't wait to throw her out. Preferably on her ass.

"I live here. What the hell are *you* doing here?" Elynn asked before she could stop herself.

This woman was an intruder. She didn't have to be polite to her.

"I'm waiting for Alexandros," Sonia said, stretching languorously. "I think you should run along to your room while I wait, since I'm apparently not allowed in his bedroom," she added, shooting Andrea a nasty look. "I'll just have to give him his surprise here."

Does she think I'm a guest?

"I don't think I understand," Elynn said.

"Well, let me make it clear," Sonia droned as she leaned back on the couch provocatively. "Alexandros and I got back together a few days ago. He told me to come here and wait for him to get back into town. I would wait for him in our bedroom, but these people keep getting in my way," she said, glaring at the security people.

Elynn's stomach twisted into a painful knot. It took her a minute before she recovered. Sonia had to be lying. She was an actress. It's what she did for a living. Alex had no idea that the other woman was here. There was no way Sonia could have been in contact with him.

This was all a big bluff, an attempt to win Alex over with her daring. Or at least get Elynn out of the way. Sonia either hadn't seen the tabloids about their relationship or she didn't believe them. Eric and Fred hadn't believed them at first, either.

Steeling her resolve, Elynn stood up a little straighter. "*You* don't have a bedroom here with Alex. His room is my room. We're together—a couple. And you have to be on your way now," she explained as calmly as she could.

Sonia laughed at her. "I think it's very sad how you've latched on to your stepbrother the way you have. Oh yes, I know about his little fling with you. He told me all about it. He didn't sue the tabloids that published their dirt about the two of you because he feels sorry for you. But he's already bored. His attention does tend to wander, but I don't mind. Like most powerful men, he doesn't want to be tied down, but then neither do I. It suited both of us to be apart for a while, but he's crazy about me. He wants me back. So I'm back," Sonia said in a husky voice as she leaned deeper back into the couch cushions, her arms resting along the back of the couch in a deceptively casual pose.

She rolled her eyes. "Get rid of her," she said to Andrea.

The bodyguard went from silently hostile to thrilled in the blink of an eye. "With pleasure," Andrea said.

"Where the hell do you get off throwing me out, you bitch?" Sonia shouted as the bodyguard grabbed her and hauled her to her feet.

Elynn stepped up to her. Sonia was a good six inches taller than her, but she didn't flinch or back down. "You're a terrible actress. No wonder you didn't win that Oscar," she said as Andrea started to pull the woman to the door.

Male laughter took both women by surprise. Elynn whirled around. Alex was standing in the doorway still holding his briefcase. His chief of security was behind him, shooting daggers at the junior man he'd left in charge. Someone was going to get hell later for letting Sonia into the house.

Alex didn't even look at the actress. He continued to ignore her as he went to take Elynn in his arms. His eyes searched hers rapidly before he kissed her softly. Despite his laughter, she knew he was anxious underneath the façade. She could see the tension in his posture. And he should be anxious. His womanizing past was catching up with him with a vengeance.

He turned back to Sonia, his face growing cold. "Baby, go upstairs to our room and wait for me," he said in a tone of controlled anger as he focused on the actress.

Very sensibly, Sonia kept quiet, and for all of two seconds, Elynn thought about moving.

"No," she said quietly. Alex turned back to her, surprised. But Elynn was fine. She had this. "I think you should go upstairs," she said firmly. Alex started to protest, but she cut him off. "I want to handle this," she said, touching her hand to his chest. "It's my right. Don't worry. I know what I'm doing. Why don't you take a shower? I'll be right up."

ALEX STARED at Elynn's face. She seemed so calm. He didn't know what to do. He wanted to throw that bitch Sonia out. The sooner she was gone, the sooner he could apologize for ever having looked at the woman. There was no way Elynn was as calm as she was acting.

If she wants to do this, maybe you better let her.

He would probably do whatever she wanted right now. Even leaving her alone to deal with one of his biggest mistakes.

But he wouldn't go far. If Sonia lashed out or did anything to upset Elynn further, he would be nearby to throw her out on her ass. Reluctantly, he nodded slowly and left the room, enjoying Sonia's slack-jawed amazement. She had always thought of him as a control freak and a misogynist because he never indulged any of her whims. Not that that had mattered to her. Only his money mattered, and the press they got when they were together.

He went upstairs, but came back down the second the women's backs were turned. He ducked into the dining room next to the salon, keeping the door open so he could hear everything. If Sonia so much as looked at Elynn funny, he would swoop in to take care of matters himself. As it was, his security team was at her side, eager to protect her from the shallow actress who had treated them like dirt.

There were a few minutes of quiet conversation. Elynn stood very close to Sonia, and he couldn't hear what she was whispering into the older woman's ear. He shook his head in agonized frustration. His sweetheart wouldn't stand a chance once Sonia started in on her. The actress was a snake-tongued tart, and he regretted every second he'd ever spent with her.

Sonia started to interrupt whatever she was saying, but Elynn silenced her with a swift motion of her hand. She hissed something in her ear and Alex was stunned when Sonia burst into tears.

Elynn continued whispering and eventually Sonia nodded. After that Elynn's expression softened and she actually put her hands on Sonia's shoulders in a comforting fashion. She murmured something else and led the crying woman to the door.

"Good luck," she said generously as she shut the door.

Bewildered, Alex stepped out of the dining room. The security staff melted away when Elynn returned. He met her at the stairs, trying to decide if he should apologize first or demand to be told what she'd told Sonia to make her cry.

But she didn't give him a chance. She just rolled her eyes at him and went straight up the stairs.

"Elynn?" he called after her. When she didn't respond, he started after her. She beat him to the bedroom, and he followed her in, holding his hands up in surrender. "Baby, I know you're upset. It's only natural. I don't know what that woman told you, but she lied. She—" he stopped short when he realized she was undressing.

She was down to her bra and panties, and he lost his train of thought. He made an inarticulate noise as Elynn turned to the bathroom, her back to him as she removed her bra. She tossed it behind her, and the blood rushed completely out of his head.

The torture continued as she turned on the shower and shimmied out of her panties with a provocative look over her shoulder. Her adorable heart shaped derriere had a pink flush over it. His muscles locked tight.

She should be trying to twist off one of his testicles right about now, not getting naked.

ELYNN WANTED TO LAUGH. Alex looked so confused. When he still didn't move, she decided he needed a little more incentive to join her. She stepped under the water and reached for the soap. With slow deliberate movements she lathered the soap in her hands and ran it over her body, paying special attention to her breasts.

She shot him another heated look, and he cracked. With quick jerky movements, Alex grabbed at his clothes, tearing off his shirt instead of trying to open it properly. Buttons flew everywhere. The pants and boxers followed, and he rushed toward her.

"Alex your socks." She laughed.

"Oh, right," he said, bending down to yank them off.

He was on her in seconds, lifting her up and wrapping her legs around him. His lips came down on her, and he plunged his tongue inside her mouth—kissing her long and hard before pulling away.

He breathed into her mouth. "I'm sorry about all that downstairs."

"Shut up," she whispered back before she kissed him again, pulling him closer by tugging on his hair.

ALEX RAN ecstatic hands over Elynn's body, enjoying the silky feel of her skin under the warm water. Her tongue stroked his, and he growled low in his throat as the hunger rose higher. He shifted her in his arms and prayed she was ready for him as he pinned her to the wall of the shower.

"I'm sorry I can't stop. I can't wait. Kiss me harder," he ground out between kisses as he worked himself inside of her.

Blood pumping in his ears, he stroked into her again and again. He couldn't seem to stop himself. Luckily for him, she was right there with him, tightening around him and crying out in climax. He tried to make it last, but the way she was clamping down on him was too intense. He came hard, groaning as he poured himself into her.

It was the longest, hottest climax he had ever experienced, even compared to the others he'd shared with her. They stood under the water for a long moment before she pushed at his hands, and he let her slide down off him. He leaned back against the wall with his eyes closed, resisting the urge to collapse down on the floor until he regained his strength. His eyes flew open when he felt Elynn's hands over him. She was smiling up at him as she soaped his body, washing him gently until he was hot again. He grabbed her roaming hands to pull her roughly to him. He didn't let go for a long time—not until they were both ready to collapse.

Afterwards, he took great pleasure in drying Elynn with a big towel. He even brushed her hair, taking his time to work out the slight tangles so he wouldn't pull on it too hard.

"Are you sure you don't want me to do it?" she asked, prompting him to put the brush down.

"No, I love combing your hair. We should do this all the time," he said before he pulled her into bed, wrapping himself around her. "I missed you. I hate going anywhere without you. I would refuse leaving town without you from now on, but I know that's not possible. You have your own career to build, and the best I can do is make home wherever you are."

"I missed you, too," Elynn whispered back, cuddling closer to him. "And I want our home to be so filled with warmth and happiness that you'll have no choice but to hurry back whenever you have to leave it."

He smiled in the darkness, but she couldn't see it. After a moment, he circled back to the apology he'd wanted to make since he'd arrived to see Sonia there in their home.

"I'm sorry that woman showed up here. She or anyone like her will never bother you again here in our home. I promise you that."

She shifted to face him. "Well, I'm feeling especially generous right now, so I'm going to overlook the home invasion. Don't get me wrong —you're still in trouble. And I want to say that, in the past you have exhibited a rather appalling taste in women, present company excluded. But since you've obviously rectified that situation, I'm prepared to be forgiving. This time," she added with a poke to his chest.

Elynn was so amazing. "I love you and only you. I wish to God you had been a little older when we met," he grumbled as he tugged her closer, not satisfied until she was pressed against him. He could feel her cheek moving against his chest when she smiled. "Are you going to tell me what you told Sonia?"

"Never," she said emphatically. "All I'm going to say is that I think I must be a better actress than the movie star."

CHAPTER 21

"Oh," Mary breathed with tears in her eyes. "It's so beautiful, sweetheart."

She was holding one of Elynn's wedding gowns in her hand. Elynn was going to wear two, a formal one with a train for the service and another shorter cocktail length one for the reception afterwards.

Alex had finally finished renovating everything at the Oxford estate in preparation for the ceremony. The helipad was finished, and a special arbor had been constructed for the exchange of their vows. In two days, a group of well-paid caterers and florists would descend to transform the rose garden for the ceremony.

Until then, Elynn was enjoying the time alone with her mother—except for the conversation her mother broached after viewing the dress. The one about how to handle intimacy in her marriage.

"Oh, Mom, you know Alex wasn't actually noble enough to wait for our wedding night, right? He's a good man, but he's not a saint," Elynn muttered uncomfortably.

Mary cleared her throat. "I realize you've already been intimate. And I'm glad that you've found happiness with Alex. I was worried that you wouldn't be comfortable enough for that for a long time. But it takes work for a marriage to succeed, and you might still have some issues. I hope you continue to see your therapist for the foreseeable future. I think it would be a good thing to have an impartial third party to talk to, especially in the early days of your marriage. And not just because of what happened back home in the states. I think all newlyweds could probably use that kind of help. And if Alex is anything like Costas, and I know he is, then you're going to have your hands full.

"He's very aggressive," Mary continued, with a commiserating pat of her hand. "Much more so than his father. If I wasn't aware of how much he loved you, I would be trying to talk you out of marrying him right now. But I know he'll take good care of you. I just think getting some advice on how to handle him when he gets all...all Alex-y…is a good thing."

Elynn laughed. She had let Alex get away with a lot, but not anything she hadn't been willing to give him. Even marrying him so soon. She wanted everyone to know that he was hers and she was his.

"I'm not about to let him walk all over me," she assured her mother. "Believe me, that is not ever going to happen. And I honestly hadn't even thought about stopping counseling. Even when I was so busy the last year, I checked in once a month at least. Seeing a therapist is so ingrained now that I don't know that I'll just completely stop. Not anytime soon anyway."

She shrugged, and luckily her mother had been satisfied enough to change the subject to wedding preparations.

THE NEXT DAY, Alex was late getting home. Her mother was somewhere downstairs directing the decorators. There was more staff on hand than there would be guests at her wedding.

Alex hadn't wanted to go into his London office for the last minute meeting. His staff had done everything possible to reschedule, but a new business partner had made a huge fuss, and the meeting had been unavoidable in the end. But that was okay with her. Elynn was using the time alone productively, exploring the wilderness around them to her heart's content. It would be fertile mushroom hunting ground when the wet season returned.

That morning, she investigated the bottom of a ravine that she had discovered from the top of a ridge the day before. There was a little stream at the bottom that kept the whole area damp enough for mushrooms, even in the heat of summer. There were some decaying ones on the hillside right now.

High in the trees above her was an innocuous black box. It was one of many. Alex had had the electronic surveillance devices placed throughout the woods in the last few weeks. He'd insisted, saying that if she was going to be out there on her own, he would have the security monitor her in case she turned an ankle while mushroom hunting. Since it actually made sense, she'd accepted the devices with little argument.

Well...only a small fight anyway.

Pleased with the location, she looked around, trying to commit the area to memory. From the bottom of the ravine she could see a deep recess underneath the overhanging lip of the ridge high to her left that hadn't been visible from the top the day before. Some long tree roots spilled over the edge of the ridge to hang over the recess. It reminded her of a hobbit hole straight out of Tolkien. Smiling at her own whimsy, she decided it was time to head back to the house for lunch.

After a light meal, Elynn went upstairs for a shower. Humming softly to herself, she entered the master bedroom. She stopped short in the doorway when she saw the blonde man in front of the closet, studying her wedding dress. He turned to her, and her heart dropped to her feet.

"Come inside Elynn," Stephen Wainwright said, motioning her inside with the gun he was pointing at her.

CHAPTER 22

Elynn couldn't move. It was a scene copied straight from her worst nightmares. Stephen was here, in the flesh. He had finally found her. For years, she had looked around every corner and jumped at every sudden noise because she had believed he was coming after her. It had taken her years to stop. And now he was here.

She had never been safe from him, not really.

"Come inside and close the door," Stephen ordered.

With her heart drumming in her ears, she stepped into the room and closed the door behind her. For a moment, they simply stared at one another.

Stephen had changed, grown taller and broader. He wasn't as tall as Alex, but his body was still athletic, and his face had those boyish good looks that had charmed all of her girlfriends. His appearance and charm had captivated everyone but her. Then he had started terrorizing her—but not all of Windsor's residents had believed that. His popularity and money had acted like a shield when the accusations were first made.

He probably still turns heads wherever he goes, she thought disgustedly.

Stephen kept the gun trained on her while he lifted the skirt of her wedding gown, the longer formal one she had planned to wear during the ceremony. He ran his hands over the silk and lace almost reverently.

Suddenly, his features contorted, and he made a fist in the lace, yanking hard until it tore. In a rage, he grabbed the gown off the hanger and shredded the dress to pieces.

Elynn inhaled reflexively, her head drawing back. Stephen threw the dress to the floor and turned to her, out of breath. Then he smiled slowly, making her blood run cold.

Oh God, please help me, she prayed silently, her heart pounding.

"Come here," Stephen coaxed, his voice soft and pleading as he held out his free hand.

His other hand kept the gun trained on her. Trembling, she could barely walk straight as she slowly made her way toward him. Her vision was darkening at the edges, and she was suddenly more terrified of passing out than of him.

If she fainted, she'd be at his mercy.

Impatient, Stephen closed the distance between them and hugged her to him tightly. Elynn broke out into a sweat as she felt the gun pressing against her back. Trying to calm down, she held still while he rubbed against her, his cock growing hard with the friction.

Eventually, he stood back enough to look down at her pale face. He kissed her lips softly, the way a lover would.

"I've missed you so much, Elynn," he whispered. "I know you missed me, too. I tried to come for you before when we were first separated, but your new family kept getting in the way. I did call you. You knew it was me right? Even when I didn't say anything?"

Numbly, Elynn nodded. She had known it was him in the beginning. As the years passed and the silent phone calls became less frequent, she'd convinced herself it was someone else, wrong numbers. She had thought Stephen had forgotten her, that he'd moved on. But here he was, standing in front of her. With a gun.

"Did you get my flowers?"

Confused, Elynn looked up at him. "What?"

Stephan scowled. "My roses. I was letting you know I was thinking of you, that you were still on my mind."

The red roses. Oh God. She hadn't realized.

His expression became thunderous. "You thought they were from *him,* didn't you?" When she stayed quiet, Stephen shook his head, making a visible effort to control his temper. "Your new family surrounded you with bodyguards, so I had to go away. I tried to forget you," he continued, stroking her cheek. "I'm sorry about that now. But I didn't know about your stepbrother. I should have realized sooner what was happening. I would have rescued you long ago," he said before kissing her again.

"Rescued me?"

She could barely get the words out. He thought he was rescuing her? From Alex? She felt sick, and there was a real danger of throwing up all over him. She suddenly thought that was a great idea, but his next words distracted her.

"I didn't know that he wanted you for himself. Not until I saw the tabloids. If I had known, I would have come back sooner and taken you far away, where he wouldn't be able to touch you. But it's not too late. I'm here now. Just in time," he said, gesturing to the torn gown on the floor before he pulled her to the door.

Breath fracturing, Elynn tried to pull away from him, but Stephen raised the gun and pushed it against her temple. He drew her closer with his free arm and lowered his lips to her forehead, pressing them right next to the barrel of the gun.

"I know you didn't mean to betray me with him," he said. His hot breath filled her face. It was minty, and she recognized the smell of her own mouthwash. "Your stepbrother is a powerful man. You didn't stand a chance. I know he forced you into his bed, and now he's forcing you to marry him. I don't blame you for not being strong enough to resist him," he said pressing his lips harder into her temple.

Elynn swallowed hard. "Thank you for understanding," she whispered.

Stephen rewarded her with a brilliant smile. "None of this was your fault. First your mother forced you away from me. Then your stepfather made sure we stayed apart. And now Alexandros wants to keep us apart by marrying you. But it's okay now. In a few hours, we'll be on a plane to someplace far away. I promise you, he will never find us. But first you're going to lead me out of here. If any of the bodyguards Hanas has watching you get in our way, I'll take care of them," he said, gesturing with the gun.

Elynn's heart was threatening to give out in her chest. She had to get them away without running into anyone. Sweat dripping down her spine, she led Stephen downstairs and out of the house through the library, away from the bustle of people preparing for the wedding ceremony.

She prayed that they wouldn't run into her mother. Stephen blamed her for taking Elynn away. There was no telling what he would do to Mary if he saw her now.

"We should go out through the woods. It's the only area not patrolled by the bodyguards," Elynn lied.

Stephen was pleased by her ready assistance. Formulating a desperate plan, she led him deep into the woods.

ALEX COULDN'T WAIT to see Elynn. He had gotten all the way to town before being informed that the rep from the Rand group had cancelled the meeting.

Furious, he immediately ordered his staff to cut all ties with them. Their deal had promised to be a good opportunity to get a foothold in the southeast part of China, but after dragging him to London the day before his wedding and then canceling, there was no way he was going to do business with them.

After using some of the time in his office to make a few calls, he had the chopper fly him back to the Oxford estate. Running eagerly up the stairs, he made his way to their bedroom. A maid had seen Elynn heading upstairs to their room to wash, and she hadn't come back down.

The thought of surprising her in the shower put a big smile on his face, and he quickly forgot his annoyance over the cancelled meeting.

Alex entered the room, calling her name. She wasn't in sight, and he couldn't hear the shower. Assuming she might be in the tub, he walked past the bed toward the bathroom doors.

There, on the floor on the other side of the bed, was Elynn's wedding gown. Blood freezing in his veins, he pulled it from the floor. It was in pieces.

What the hell was going on? Did Elynn do this?

Oh God. Was she leaving him? He reached for the dresser surface for support as he doubled over in pain.

"No!" he said aloud, forcing himself to get a grip with several deep breaths.

No, this wasn't happening. Elynn loved him and she was too smart to doubt his feelings for her. She had seen right through Sonia and her lies. If something had happened to upset her—if someone tried to sabotage their marriage with some lie—she would be here trying to twist off one of his testicles right now.

And there was no way she had done this to her dress. Somebody had torn it apart with their hands. Someone strong. A terrible suspicion filled his mind.

He started yelling her name.

CHAPTER 23

Alex paced in front of the monitor display in the security control room. Most of the bodyguards were scouring the grounds for signs of Elynn and all were checking in with his security chief. They were going over the estate's camera footage with a technician.

A shout drew his attention. He turned to the display and felt his lungs crumple in his chest. On the screen was a still of Elynn being forced out of the library window with a gun to her back. The technician rolled the footage forward until they had a clear shot of the assailant's face.

"It's him. It's Stephen Wainwright," he said tightly. His security chief nodded before he swore under his breath. "How the hell did we not know he was in the fucking country?"

"He must have bought a fake passport and ditched his tails," the chief muttered before shouting orders through his walkie-talkie to the bodyguards fanned out over the grounds.

"Sir, some of the sensors in the woods have been tripped," the technician said.

Alex looked at his chief of security. "Let's go."

They both ran.

Please, God, let her be all right. Please let me be in time, Alex prayed as they pounded up the hill to the entrance of the woods.

ELYNN WAS ALMOST to the ridge when Stephen grabbed her.

"Where are we going? This is not the way out," he said as he pulled her to him with hard bruising hands.

"It is. We just need to go over the ridge and then there's a road. We can flag down a car or take one from a neighbor."

"I still think we should take my car," he argued.

"I'm sure they've found it by now. Alex keeps really close tabs on me. His security team watches my every move," she said. "I still don't know how you made it past them," she added in a tone of fake admiration.

"It wasn't easy," he said, taking the bait, detailing how he had fooled Alex into leaving for an emergency meeting while he snuck onto the grounds with the florists.

"That was brilliant," she said softly as she spotted a thick branch on the ground a few feet in front of her.

She gasped when he stopped her with an arm, pulling her in for another kiss. When he tried to slip his tongue into her mouth, she froze and tried to pull away. He grabbed her by the arms and looked down at her face.

She couldn't hide her disgust at the taste of him, and his face filled with rage. With a roar, he threw her to the ground.

"You bitch! I knew you were lying to me! I knew it!" he screamed as he came down on top of her.

Terrified, she put her hands up when he started tearing at her clothes.

Stephen lowered his head to speak directly into her ear. "Once I'm done with you, he's not going to want you back."

He sneered as he pulled her hair, yanking her head toward him for another brutal kiss.

Desperately afraid, Elynn shoved up against him, using the force to move herself away from his grasping hands. She slammed her elbow into his head as hard as she could. It caught him in the ear with a resounding thud. Screaming obscenities at her, he put both hands onto his head as she scrambled away.

She had only cleared a few steps when Stephen recovered. He grabbed her from behind. Heart pounding, she used her body as a counterweight the way Andrea had taught her long ago. With a grunt, she flipped him over her shoulder before running flat out toward the fallen branch.

Holding it firmly behind her like a baseball bat, she forced herself to stay still until he was within striking distance.

Wait.

She could feel her hands shaking, her whole body tensing as Stephen charged at her, determined to knock her off her feet. When he was a few feet away, she swung the branch, the muscles in her arms screaming as she struck him in the head.

Her aim was a little off. The branch made contact, glancing off his head. He'd moved so the blow didn't land with all her force, but it was still enough to make him stagger to his knees.

Elynn swung again and he fell to the side. Not stopping to see if he would get back up, she turned and ran to the edge of the ridge, using a boulder to screen her from view.

Praying that he was still down, she scrambled over the edge, using the overhanging roots she had seen from the ravine as ropes.

Crawling into the space under the overhang, she pulled herself into a small ball. If she was right, Stephen wouldn't be able to see her unless he climbed to the bottom of the ravine, and there was too much foliage at the bottom for him to be sure her body wasn't down there from the ridge.

She clung to the thickest roots in the space around her, desperately hoping Stephen was too hurt to move...but she wasn't that lucky.

He had started shouting again. She could barely make out the words over the rush of blood in her ears. The only thing she could hear clearly was her name. He was screaming it over and over. Loose dirt and stones fell from the top of the overhang.

Please let him think I'm dead.

"Elynn!" Stephen roared from just above her.

He sounded like a wounded animal. When he burst into loud sobs, she realized her plan had worked. He thought she had jumped or had fallen off the cliff.

Squeezing her eyes tightly shut, she tried to press herself tighter against the back wall of the opening.

Hurry, Alex, she begged silently as another one of Stephen's roars filled the air.

CHAPTER 24

Alex was running with at least six security personnel at his side. The technician was relaying the location where sensors had been tripped to guide them.

Fuck, Fuck, Fuck. Heart pounding, he realized Elynn must be leading Wainwright to the bluff near the edge of the estate property.

Please let me be in time. Please let her be okay, Alex thought as he ran up the hill as fast as he could. His heart nearly stopped when he heard Wainwright roar in the distance.

He was screaming Elynn's name.

They burst up the hill in a group. Wainwright was on his hands and knees at the top of the bluff. His screams filled the air.

"Elynn!"

Her name was distorted as Wainwright sobbed. The sound was heartrending, but it didn't compare to the blackness seeping into Alex's head as the situation became clear.

Elynn must have fallen off the edge of the bluff in her attempt to get away from him. There was no way she had survived the fall. The distance was too great, he thought as the bottom of his world dropped out.

Not caring if Wainwright had a gun, he leaped on the smaller man with a strangled cry. Pulling him from the edge, he flipped Wainwright over so he could punch him over and over.

Blind to anything else, he drove his fists into his face until the other man was swollen and unrecognizable. He would have kept going, but the asshole had collapsed to the ground, and Alex's security men pulled him off.

"Stop now or you're going to kill him," Andrea said, getting in his face.

He blinked as he stared up into the hard planes of her face. He hadn't even realized she was there.

"Then he dies. Let go of me," he said in a low harsh voice, struggling against the restraining arms of at least three of his men.

"Elynn wouldn't want you to spend your honeymoon in jail," Andrea said gently. "Get him out of here," she said, pointing to the unconscious man.

"Elynn's gone," Alex said in a broken whisper, still on his knees on the ground. "There's no way she could have survived the fall."

"Oh, ye of little faith. You forget I trained that girl myself," Andrea returned. Her voice was confident, but Alex could detect the underlying anxiety in it. "Elynn?" she called out in a louder voice.

"I'm here!" Elynn's voice came from the ridge.

"Holy fuck," he groaned, relief coursing through him. Alex ran to the edge of the bluff where his men had gathered. Stunned, he looked down to see Elynn peeking up at him from underneath the lip of the edge. "Oh, thank God. Give me your hand," he ordered as he lay down to reach over the edge.

Holding on to a thick root, Elynn extended her upper body to reach out for his extended hand. There must be a ledge underneath her, one he couldn't see. Her small hand took his with a wet, slippery grip. Behind him, Andrea and someone else grabbed hold of his waist and leg to brace him securely.

"Wait," Elynn said, letting go of his hand and nearly stopping his heart.

She wiped her free hand on her shirt and tried again. Wrapping both of his hands around hers, he hauled her up to him, pulling her into his arms. Shaking from head to foot, he picked her up, carrying her away from the edge.

He didn't get far before he collapsed onto the ground, holding her tight in his arms. For a long moment, everyone else just stood there.

"Take him away," Andrea said, snapping to attention and pointing to Wainwright's prone body. "We'll call the authorities," she told Alex before signaling to the assembled group.

They melted away into the forest. Alone with her, he pressed Elynn to his chest as if he was trying to meld their two bodies together.

"Alex you're hurting me," she said, poking him in the ribs.

When he just squeezed her tighter, she put her arms around him and stroked his back until he finally relaxed his hold.

"Don't ever do that again," he whispered into her hair.

"I won't, I promise," she whispered back, despite his request making no sense.

Grateful that she knew well enough to humor him, she stayed quiet in his arms for a long time. Eventually, however, she pushed until he let her up enough so that she could look him in the face.

"I'm okay," she said, putting her hands on either side of his face. "I knew about the overhang. I saw it earlier from the bottom of the ravine. I also knew you would come," she said. When he didn't respond, she pressed her forehead to his. "Hey, do you think we could take turns?"

"What?" he asked, confused.

He felt numb, a million miles away.

"I said I think we should take turns. I want you to console me now," Elynn said, staring into his eyes with a steady expression.

It worked. He gave a choked laugh that he quickly cut off before he grabbed her and kissed her softly.

"I don't know what I would do if anything happened to you," he told her, his voice cracking. "You mean more to me than my own life. I love you, and I'll never let you down again."

"What do you mean? You've never let me down," she said, getting up and tugging him up after her.

"I should have guessed that Wainwright might travel with fake documents. We monitor his movements. If he had used his own passport, we would have known he was here. I don't know what set him off after all this time, but I let my guard down, and you paid the price," he said, the agony in his voice clear.

Elynn shook her head. "He must monitor the UK tabloids from home. He mentioned seeing them. But you can't anticipate the actions of a crazy person. And Stephen *is* insane. There was no way to know that he would do this. You didn't let me down. And you never will. I won't let you," she said forcefully.

Alex stopped walking and pulled her into his arms. "You're still marrying me. You may not want to go through with the ceremony so soon, but I need this. I know it won't solve anything, but I don't think I'll be able to sleep until my ring is on your finger."

He could feel her smile against his chest. "We are getting married in two days. There is no chance I'm going to back out just because of an uninvited guest," she said.

He stopped short. "An uninvited guest? That is how you're characterizing that psycho?" he said in disbelief, too much testosterone and adrenaline pumping in his veins.

Suddenly, he couldn't seem to calm down.

"I'm not going to let him win, Alex," Elynn said quietly as they made it to the house.

Alex passed a hand over his face and looked up at the windows before they went inside. "I'm going to fire everyone on that security team."

She frowned. "No, you're not. It wasn't their fault."

"Elynn, someone has to pay."

"Then let it be Stephen. I don't want you to fire anyone just before our wedding day," she said.

He kept arguing with her for a good hour after that, and she let him, saying that he needed to get it out of his system. Once he had tired himself out, Elynn ordered dinner sent to their room and told everyone to leave them alone.

In their bedroom, she calmly picked up the shredded wedding

gown and shoved it into the trash bin. Then she led him into the shower and goaded him into making love—was insistent on it, in fact. He couldn't help but suspect that she wanted his touch so she could forget that Wainwright had laid hands on her.

If she did feel that way, she knew better than to tell him that.

CHAPTER 25

Their wedding day was fun and festive. Elynn didn't let anything spoil it, choosing to let the events of the previous days roll by her. Stephen was in the past—and in jail—and Alex was her future.

Their friends had been kept in the dark about the attempted kidnapping, although their parents had been informed. Mary had nervously agreed on the need to keep their plans on schedule, while Costas had shouted at all of the security staff for the breach that had allowed Wainwright access to his beloved stepdaughter.

Stephen was locked away somewhere. She didn't want to know where. It didn't matter as long as it was far away.

Alex wasn't so sanguine. He was happy, but still a little shaken. As she requested, he didn't fire anyone, but he didn't leave her side the entire day, not even before the ceremony.

"I don't care if it is bad luck," he had argued when she complained that he was breaking tradition. "I'm not letting you out of my sight now or in the near future. Maybe the whole of next year."

Elynn stopped arguing, choosing to concede the battle in favor of winning the war. And honestly, she didn't care. She didn't want to leave his side, either.

Eric and Fred shouted with delight when they realized they were attending their wedding. Alex had also managed to keep his university friends in the dark about the real purpose of the event until they arrived. There was a lot of back-slapping from the rowdy bunch of bachelors, none of which she had ever met.

"No wonder you didn't want to introduce any of them," Elynn teased when Alex pointed out his friends as they arrived. "You were afraid of the competition," she said.

His friends were gorgeous, almost as handsome as Alex.

He growled. "None of those ugly bastards compares to me, and you know it," he said, reaching to hug her from behind as he finally introduced her to Sergei, Calen, and Gio.

The men were pleased to meet her—a little too pleased if she could judge by the tightness of Alex's grip on her waist.

She smiled at them. They smiled back, their forceful personalities pressing in on her like a wall of testosterone. All that masculinity should have intimidated her, but she felt secure at Alex's side.

Sergei, who turned out to be a tall, dark-haired Russian with the same kind of build as her husband, gave her a long searing appraisal.

"No wonder Alex never let any of us near you. He was obviously determined to keep you all to himself," he said in a slightly slurred voice, waving a glass of vodka in her direction.

"As well he should have," Calen added, giving her a suggestive wink.

Their Italian friend, Gio, laughed aloud at the look on Alex's face, causing her new husband to shoot all of his dear friends a dirty look.

"Okay, that's enough," Alex said with a scowl as he led her away with a possessive hand on her back.

The men's loud booming laughter followed them as they mixed and mingled with their other guests.

Elynn danced in Alex's arms under fairy lights hidden in the shrubbery and the trees above them, content in the knowledge that she was his wife. They ate the savory appetizers Mary had requested and drank fine wine, occasionally trying to remember that they had guests long enough to stop to talk to them. Their friends and parents excused their self-involvement with indulgent smiles and whispers.

No one blamed them for only having eyes for each other.

EPILOGUE

Elynn was decorating a raspberry and almond cake with sweet cream in the kitchen. It was Alex's favorite, and she wanted to surprise him with it on their first wedding anniversary.

The kitchen of the Oxford estate was her favorite, mostly because it was empty on the weekends. Unless they specifically requested otherwise, their chef only worked during the week because Elynn enjoyed cooking meals herself on the weekends unless she had to work in the lab. She finished decorating the cake and had started to clean up when she heard cooing.

Smiling, she grabbed the baby monitor and went upstairs to play with her son before Alex got home.

Alexandros Hanas Jr. was flailing his adorably chubby baby arms in the air when she entered the nursery. She hadn't planned on getting pregnant before she finished her doctorate, but a particularly adventurous sex-filled honeymoon on Alex's yacht and her own absent-mindedness had led to their joyful little accident.

Elynn soon discovered from her female mentors that having young children during her graduate studies was, in the opinion of some, actually more manageable than at a later point in her career. She didn't know if she agreed, but her husband had a plan for everything, and she didn't have a lot of misgivings about it once she told him she was expecting. It might take her longer to get her degree, but she would get it. Elynn was determined.

Alex had been so happy about her pregnancy he had run out and started buying baby clothes and toys the same day. And he had promised to hire whatever help they needed. He even managed to convince her that hiring multiple nannies was perfectly acceptable. A wonderful matronly woman watched baby Alex during the week and a night nurse took care of him on weeknights when Elynn had to work early the next day.

But she loved the weekends best because she had her two men all to herself. Her husband had cut back on his heavy travel schedule as much as possible. He had finally learned to delegate now that their son had been born, but occasionally a deal still required his personal attention. This time he had been away for two days.

Even when he was forced away on business, Alex kept a close eye on his new family. Stephen Wainwright was in prison. After his arrest, a number of other women had come forward to add their own charges of stalking and assault.

Alex had never intended to tell her that all the women had had black hair and green eyes, but Elynn found out that disturbing detail from the news. The idea that Stephen had sought out other women who reminded him of her—had hurt them when he'd been unable to get his hands on her—made her feel responsible in a twisted way.

When she'd confessed that to him, Alex had reminded her of what she'd once told him. Stephen was crazy, and trying to take responsibility for what he had done was pointless.

And he told her to stop reading the Internet, because there were things she was better off not knowing. Deciding this was a better philosophy, she agreed and moved on.

ALEX RAN up the stairs to the nursery, taking the stairs two at a time. The helicopter had just landed. Its blades were still spinning, but he was already upstairs looking for Elynn.

He could usually find her in the nursery when he came home on the weekends. Struggling to loosen his tie as he went, he burst into the nursery, a miniature tornado of impatient energy.

His beautiful wife was sitting on the carpet playing with their son, but the instant she saw him, she leapt up to kiss him hello. He gathered Elynn into his arms for a rib-squeezing hug.

"God, I missed you. I hate going out of town. I wish I could take you guys with me," he said as he swung her in his arms a safe distance from where the baby was lying and kicking his feet.

Elynn hugged him back. "I hate it, too, but I'm glad that you were able to make it home for our anniversary."

Already starting to get aroused, Alex hugged her tighter. He had no intention of letting go—until the baby started fussing for their attention. Smiling, he set his wife down on the couch before scooping up his son so he could sit next to her while holding him.

"This right here, this is my favorite place in the world," he said as he put an arm out to include her in his embrace. Elynn nestled against him, and the baby chortled. It sounded like he was laughing. Alex sighed. "He's such a perfect little miracle. I hope you know how blessed I feel that I have the two of you," he whispered, nuzzling his wife's neck.

"I'm glad you feel that way. Because our blessings are about to multiply. I'm pregnant again."

The End

ABOUT THE AUTHOR

A 7-time Readers' Favorite Medal Winner. USA Today Bestselling Author. Mom to a half-feral princess. WOC. Former scientist. Recovering geek.

Lucy Leroux is the steamy pen name for author L.B. Gilbert. Ten years ago Lucy moved to France for a one-year research contract. Six months later she was living with a handsome Frenchman and is now married with an adorable half-french 5yo who won't go to bed on time

When her last contract ended Lucy turned to writing. Frustrated by a particularly bad romance novel she decided to write her own. Her family lives in Southern California.

Lucy loves all genres of romance and intends to write as many of them as possible. To date, she has published twenty novels and novellas. These include paranormal, urban fantasy, gothic regency, and contemporary romances with more on the way.

Subscribe to the Lucy Leroux Newsletter for a free full-length book!
www.authorlucyleroux.com/newsletter

facebook.com/lucythenovelist
x.com/lucythenovelist
instagram.com/lucythenovelist
tiktok.com/@lucythenovelist
bookbub.com/authors/lucy-leroux

Printed in Great Britain
by Amazon

38330061R00126